Canaryville Bridge

An Urban Mystery

by Paul Terrazino

ISBN: 978-1-7363246-4-6

For those who have since departed:
A.M., E.S., G.K., K.M., S.C. and T.B.

Contents

Introduction

"We arrived at the hospice center about 7:30am. Kathleen was keeping vigil. He was lying on his right side, his breathing short and labored, but we could sense he could hear us. Kathleen started weeping. My wife, Col hugged her. I started to choke up a little too and had to turn away and face a wall for a moment.

Col announced to him that we were in the room. We both thanked him for being so kind to us. Col sat down on one side of the bed, and I stood at the other. She held his left hand for a bit and I touched the other as I thanked him one last time. We said goodbye to Kathleen, who was reaching for more tissues as we left."

When I began this adventure in 2013, I had no idea that among its many twists and turns would be the passing of someone who I had only met once, yet felt as if I'd known even longer than my wife.

I first met Colleen "Col" Garrity, in 1978. We dated briefly, back when dating was brief. She was nineteen, I twenty-three. We met through my sister, Maria. They were roommates and coworkers at a McDonald's in Col's neighborhood, Canaryville, on Chicago's South Side. The Terrazinos were from the next neighborhood to the north, Bridgeport.

We tested those always-flowing carnal waters a bit and then went our separate ways. Col went on to marry. I continued floundering in the single pool until 1994, when we crossed paths again. By then she was a divorced mother of two. Thomas James was thirteen, Mary Therese ten. The second time around, Col and I chose the opposite of brief. We wed three years later.

When I first dated her in 1978, as the "disco" music scene was—thankfully—dying, I couldn't help noticing how obvious it was Col had been through surgeries. She had no vision in one eye. She was born with a cataract and the nerves for her left eye

1

were rendered useless. Doctors had to perform two surgeries so she could control and maintain the vision in the remaining good one. But it was what I saw when Col was unclothed that indicated some serious work under the hood:

One scar, about the width of a child's thumb, starts at the top of her chest and runs better than halfway to her navel. Another starts beneath one breast, outlining it as it heads around back, tracing her shoulder blade. There are a couple of other permanent mementos of knife work here and there. I assumed they were from catheterizations and other forms of scalpel-ing.

It would be when we dated permanently that I would learn those scars were from two life-saving surgeries she had endured before reaching four years of age:

When a newborn lets out that first cry in the delivery room, it's not just because it is so happy—or not, to be done and out of the oven. There is a physiological reason as well. As it is no longer needed, the artery that had been supplying blood to the fetus during gestation closes with that first vocal outburst. In Col's case, doctors claimed it had, but that it re-opened in the days following her birth. This is known as "patent ductus arteriosis".

Once she was old enough to withstand the trauma of a surgery, that had to be closed before they could perform the next procedure, to repair a "ventral septal defect". A hole in her heart. Without those surgeries, it was estimated she would not have survived much more than a few years. The first surgery was considered "closed heart". In the early 1960s there was no arthroscopy as we now know it, so an incision wrapping halfway around a toddler's body was considered "closed".

The wide scar down the center of her chest is the result of the second procedure, "open heart" surgery to repair the hole in one ventricle. She was split open like a Thanksgiving turkey. Then, like an inner tube on a kid's bike, they patched her tiny heart with a chunk of teflon and humpty-dumptied her chest plate back together with metal staples.

More than half a century later, all of this hardware still resides in her. Airport security always gives up and lets Col through when she sets off the metal detectors.

In 1994 I also learned that she was born an orphan, adopted by Tom and Mary Garrity when she was an infant.

Col had always told me that, even though she loved her adoptive parents and they gave her a fine upbringing, it was one of her life wishes to meet her natural mother. Because of the physical issues she had at birth, she wanted to share her medical information and to know the medical history of her natural family. There was an emotional component as well. She said she'd always had a gut-level, heartfelt need to know who her natural parents were.

The reason many adoptees give for setting out to locate their natural family is that they feel as if there's a hole in their heart that requires healing in order for them to be complete. I found it fitting that Col was not only born with a physical hole in hers, but that a key lifeline, the artery that connected her to the mother she had been torn away from at birth, probably never to see again, had become literally open-ended. Professionals repaired those holes. A half-century later, this amateur sleuth decided to try and help her suture the emotional gaps.

The following is based on a true story.

Chapter 1
Needle in a Needlestack

Gotta' Start Somewhere

Some "Background History"—you'll soon learn why it's "capped and wrapped", is in order:

In her professional, adult working life, Col has had five employers. After McDonald's, she worked as a waitress at a local Poppin' Fresh restaurant. Prior to her first marriage to Michael Schmidt in 1980, she completed some nursing training at a local hospital.

Child rearing took up too much time for her to complete nursing school, but she applied for and then worked at Mercy Hospital in Chicago, first as a receptionist and then on the hospital Quality Control team, for a total of twenty years. She then went to an accounting firm, again as a receptionist and again on to administration in that field, and she has worked in that capacity for only one other firm since 2004.

I'm the opposite: Factory worker, furniture mover, truck driver, taxi driver, taxi dispatcher, school bus driver, courier, bartender, construction worker, roofer, electrician, carpenter, painter, handyman, stagehand, theater technical consultant, salesman for various industries, actor, writer, clown (yes, a real one).

There've been so many employers within all of those "vocations" that I can't even remember them all, and I've only listed the legal endeavors. So, let's just say there were a lot, and let's just say I consider myself not a "jack of all trades", but a run o' the mill ne'er do well who took a few years longer than most to recover from youth-related dementia, whose most redeeming quality is never being afraid to jump into anything head first and who also, thanks to a loving and stable spouse, has miraculously managed to stay alive and kickin' for six decades.

Col and I are ordinary folk, just trying to dance through life without crunching toes beyond our own.

The Canaryville and Bridgeport neighborhoods that we hail from are well known for producing many an Irish politician, including past Chicago mayors Richard J. Daley and his son, Richard the Younger. In our youth, both neighborhoods were primarily composed of working to middle class families. They were home to an abundance of police and firemen, streets and sanitation and other municipal workers.

Both of our respective sets of parents were born in America. My dad, Vito "Bill" Terrazino, whose parents were Italian immigrants, fought in WWII after landing at Normandy. My mom, Mary Jane Landon Terrazino, was a mixed breed that covered Denmark and northern Germany through the U.K., Ireland and France.

Col's adoptive parents' roots were Irish, as far back as anyone could tell, going back centuries. Thomas Garrity, the son of immigrants from Westport, County Mayo, was born in the Detroit area. He served in the U.S. Army, in both the African and Italian Campaigns in "The Good War". It was while on leave in Chicago that he met first generation Chicagoan Mary Agnes Walters, whose parents were from County Cork. They married in 1948, and the newly formed Garrity family settled in the Canaryville neighborhood of Chicago.

A good number of the neighborhood kids our age were first generation. It was their parents who came over, who were "off the boat". Many of our friends' moms and dads had brogues or other accents. There were Italians scattered throughout Bridgeport, but Irish was the dominant lineage. We were all part of the melting pot, and our religious pedigree was Roman Catholic.

The strictest interpretation of the Vatican rules regarding birth control meant employing the near-roulette wheel of the "rhythm method"—timing intercourse to avoid days of ovulation—was all that was permitted. I have three siblings of each gender. Col has two brothers and three sisters.

But unlike my siblings, who essentially resemble variations of our parents or grandparents or other close relatives:

"You look so much like your uncle Guiseppe, God rest his soul..."

None of the Garrity kids are blood-related. Col is not the only adoptee. They all are. Between 1950 and 1960, Tom and Mary Garrity adopted all six through the Catholic Home Bureau of Chicago, a division of the Archdiocese.

As far as appearances go, Col's brothers and sisters don't look like siblings. I never had the opportunity to notice these physical differences between Col and her siblings until we were dating, round two, when I got around to meeting them.

The Garrity kids are a watercolor pastiche of the American melting pot. Patrick looks like many a French-Canadian National Hockey League star. Kevin could be in a Scottish bagpipe troupe, Maureen belongs in a turtle neck and Capri pants, scarf flowing in the breeze, shifting a whiny Vespa through the streets of Rome, Kathleen casting a sieve net for lutefisk-destined cod along the fjords of Sweden, and to me, Eileen's look has always seemed French.

And in Gaelic, "colleen" means simply, "girl". Her name could not be more fitting. From 1978 to this day, I've envisioned Colleen in a simple, homemade muslin dress, skipping barefoot over the soft, green, mossy hills of Eire, warbling an ages-old Celtic folk melody, all the while balancing two wooden pails of milk, or Guinness, on a strong stick spanning her shoulders. She is that Irish lookin'.

Col said that while growing up, when the common, "Mommy, where do babies come from?" question was posed by curious young minds still too young for the graphic truth, the Garritys needed no stork scapegoat and offered up the truth to those inquiring, sponge-like brains:

"Babies? They come from the orphanage."

To top it off, the Garritys also took in temporary infants from time to time, providing them with a home when the orphanage was full! Their stays would usually be brief. Often it was while they were in orphan limbo: not yet placed in an adoptive home. I learned later that one infant, Jimmy, wound up staying with the Garritys for a couple of years, because that was how long his natural mother had refused to relinquish him officially, on paper. It was distressing to Maureen, the oldest, when Jimmy's natural mom finally signed him over and he was taken from the Garritys to his permanent adoptive home. Maureen had grown attached to him.

When the older Garrity kids had grown of age and flown the coop, Tom and Mary filled the gap with Irish Setters, raising them as show dogs and transporting them, along with Col and the remaining siblings, to shows as far away as Duluth, Minnesota, almost five hundred miles northwest.

Not that it really mattered, but no one in Col's family knew precisely why the Garritys could not physically bear children. Maybe Mom was unable. One rumor was that Dad became sterile when he contracted malaria while serving overseas.

I have often regretted never getting to meet Thomas and Mary Agnes Garrity. I was told they were great parents. People like them, who took in six children to raise and provided a loving, caring, temporary hotel for many others, deserve a special place. Somewhere.

Pre-Techno Gatekeepers

In 1979, Col had been my sister Maria's roommate for a year. They shared an apartment on Parnell Avenue, near 35th Street in Bridgeport. She had always wanted to learn more about her natural parents, but she knew that it would upset her adoptive parents, Tom and Mary Garrity, if they learned she was snooping around and asking questions of the Catholic Home Bureau. But, as a legal adult with her own mailing address, she requested, for a fifty dollar fee, any information that could be provided.

She received a response from Ms. Frances Cashman, who was familiar to the Garritys. She was the caseworker for the adoptions of all six of Tom and Mary's children. When they were kids, the Garritys would go every year to an annual holiday event at the orphanage. They knew "Miss Frances" and even a couple of the nuns by name.

Miss Frances shared that in 1958, Col's natural mother was a single woman of nineteen, born in Ireland, had been in the U.S. for two years, and that she had a married brother living in the States as well. She said Col's natural father was thirty years old in 1958, also single, and worked in law enforcement. Col's natural mother claimed they had been dating but had not planned on marriage. Ms. Cashman also said that by the end of 1958, just six weeks after Col was born, her natural mother returned to Ireland.

In early 1980, Col's adoptive father Tom Garrity passed away. Adoptive mother Mary Agnes Garrity followed, almost three years to the day in 1983. By then, Col and her husband Michael Schmidt were living in Canaryville, raising their son Thomas, a toddler at the time. Col found the certificate below after Mary Agnes' death. It was among her belongings, along with some handwritten medical notes that appeared to be created by orphanage personnel. Items in parenthesis are my additions:

Certificate of Baptism
The following baptism is found Recorded on the Register of the:
Holy Name Cathedral
730 North Wabash Avenue
Chicago 11, Illinois

Name: Colleen Mary Garrity
Born: October 28,1958
Baptized: November 26, 1958
Father: Thomas P. Garrity
Mother: Mary Agnes Garrity
God Father: Casimir J. Bielanski
God Mother: Virginia E. Bielanski
Officiating Priest: Roger J. Coughlin
(signed) Reverend James P. Roache
August 9, 1963 (the date Reverend Roache pulled the
original to create this copy)

And so in Col's case, it appeared Holy Name Cathedral was her default church. St. Vincent's Orphanage is less than a quarter mile away, at 731 North LaSalle Street, Chicago.

"Holy Name" is the flagship church of the Archdiocese of Chicago. It is the church of the Archbishop, or Cardinal if he has risen to the rank of the red-hats. Unless it has been repaired, the stone doorway of the church still has bullet "dings" from a gangland drive-by shooting during the 1920s. The Capone Era.

Unlike most adoptees who are placed not long after birth and then baptized in the adoptive family's church under their new, adoptive name, it appeared Col was baptized when she was not even a month old, possibly due to the physical mess she was at birth. It was up in the air if she was going to survive. The decision was probably made to baptize her, so that she'd have her express ticket to Roman Catholic heaven if she perished before she was ever placed with a family, in her case the Garritys.

However, when Col was less than a month old, I don't think the Garritys or Bielanskis, who would become Col's godparents, even knew who she was. Why were their names on this 1958 Baptismal Certificate? Something just didn't jive.

The other item of significance that Col found in Mary Agnes' files was a copy of the Adoption Decree. That document was the legal proof from the Circuit Court of Cook County that the adoption was finalized. Col's contains no information that even acknowledges the existence of her natural parents. It only makes mention of the Catholic Home Bureau and a "guardian ad litem", someone to act in the best interest of the adoptee, appointed by the State of Illinois. The decree gave Col, the adoptee, the birth name Mary Eileen O'Brien.

If Col's name on the Adoption Decree was Mary Eileen O'Brien, was her birth mother an O'Brien or was the name fabricated? O'Brien is one of the most common surnames in Ireland. If her mom was an O'Brien, how could Col, when she first attempted in 1979, have found a woman with that surname who, according to the Catholic Home Bureau, returned to Ireland not long after Col was born?

Back then, that was as far as Col got. If her natural mother was an O'Brien, her first and middle names might as well have been the equally common Mary Margaret.

What separated Col's Adoption Decree from most others is that Col remembers when it was handed down. She was in the courtroom. It was June 2, 1963, and she'd been living with the Garritys as their child, Colleen, since March of 1959, when she was four months old. She always enjoys telling the following, from her four-year-old point of view:

"I remember standing in front of a man in a long, black dress. He looked me in the eye (appropriate, as she has only one working one) and said, 'Your name is now Colleen Garrity' ".

Even with the street smarts she'd picked up from her older siblings, that proclamation by the "basic black" cross-dresser in the courtroom had her young mind stymied. As far as she knew, her name had always been Colleen Garrity!

Col had seen the Adoption Decrees of three of her adoptive siblings. Theirs had "Baby" as their birth names on the decrees: Eileen was Baby Girl Zygot, Kevin was Baby Boy Haddon and

Maureen was Baby Girl Roache. If a 1963 copy of the Baptismal Certificate said she was baptized Colleen Mary Garrity in 1958, why did the Adoption Decree give her name as Mary Eileen O'Brien in June of 1963?

It may have been because legally, Colleen Garrity was not her name until the decree was handed down in the courtroom that summer, not long before she was scheduled to start kindergarten.

Now Col understood fully why, when she was a kid, her older siblings loved to tease her about it, "Oh, Mary Eileen, would you please pass the salt?". Maybe they were a little jealous. Before getting their "real" names, they were "Baby Girl" this and "Baby Boy" that:

"Mommy, how come Colleen gets to have a real first and middle orphan name! No fair!"

By that summer of '63, Col had undergone several operations, all performed by some of the best surgeons available at the time, that were necessary to give her a reasonable chance at surviving to adulthood and to continue with a somewhat normal quality of life.

She remembers tiring very easily prior to the completion of those operations. Most three-year-olds are tough to put down for a nap. Due to her defective heart, Col would often tire so much from insufficient blood oxygenation that she'd say, "I go sleep now" and stop and nap right on the spot: in the yard, out on the sidewalk in front of the Garrity home, where and whenever rejuvenation was needed.

Col also recalls her adoptive parents arguing on the phone with representatives from the Catholic Home Bureau. She learned later that the disagreements were probably insurance-related, and that at one point in those arguments, Tom Garrity even offered to pay for the surgeries completely "out of pocket".

We felt he and Mary Agnes just wanted Col to be a full-fledged member of the Garrity family, instead of a visually impaired fledgling with scars on her and parts in her, living beneath their roof, but under a name that was not even officially and legally hers.

The Catholic Home Bureau probably did not want to finalize the adoption until it was reasonably safe to say Col would survive. Therefore, her name could not officially be Colleen Garrity until the adoption was finalized, and it could not be finalized until she was healthy enough to be adoptable. She had been living in legal limbo with the Garritys since she was placed with them in early 1959.

Intriguing Paranormals

Col often said that as a child she confided to her siblings that she felt as if she belonged "over there". In Ireland. Later, a linguist who was a client of the firm she was working for, a man who'd never met Col and had only spoken to her by phone, asked her how young she was when she emigrated to the U.S.. He was surprised when she said she was born in Chicago. He said his years of training told him she was born in Ireland.

Yet Col has no trace of a brogue—to a lay person anyway, and her adoptive parents, who raised her from the time she was four months old, were first generation American.

As her birth certificate claimed she was born in Chicago, I found that experience of hers to be mysterious, but others that she shared with me I found ethereal, even spiritual. I felt that the following added those elements to this, and I simply had to get to the bottom of it. For all my adult years, I'd labeled myself a "non-denominational believer". Learning the identities of all involved could further validate my belief in the often hidden, yet powerful potential of our collective, connected souls:

The first incident was when she was ten years old, standing alone in the basement of the Garrity home. She sensed she was being watched. A vision of a young woman in a plain dress and a man with a "pack of smokes" rolled up in one sleeve appeared in one of the ground level basement windows. She ran upstairs, shaking, to her older brother Kevin.

"I think I just saw my real parents!"

A child's imagination? Not according to Col. She said it was a visceral, gut-level feeling that it was her natural parents. She wasn't distraught at the time over anything. Or exhausted. Or feverishly recovering from flu, measles, or any other physical or emotional childhood rite of passage.

Even though it had no obvious direct connection to Col's search, the next event is still worth mentioning. Her son Thomas was born in 1981. In the two years that followed, two pregnancies, both of twins, ended in miscarriage. In the second one, Col literally died on the table. She heard the doctor say, "We're losing her." Then her consciousness shifted, and she was floating above the operating table, looking down on the chaos. She heard her recently deceased mother Mary Agnes' voice tell her she could not leave yet, that her work was not complete and that she could not leave yet because of her children. What Col found interesting about that experience was that at that time, she only had one child.

In 1984, Col and her husband Michael and two year old son Thomas were living back in her childhood neighborhood on 46th Place near Union Street, in Canaryville. Michael was working in security and Col worked at nearby Mercy Hospital. In the fall of that year, after those two—one momentarily fatal for her— miscarriages, she was about five months into what was becoming yet another difficult pregnancy. One day, she ordered a cab from their apartment to take her and Thomas first to the daycare center where she would drop him off, and to then proceed to her job at the hospital. A short and quick two-stop trip most of the time. Her recollection began with the cabbie:

"Where to?"

"I need to drop off my son at the daycare on 43rd and Halsted, and then I have to go to Mercy. Thanks."

After a few moments of driving, he inquired:

"Have you lived in this area your whole life?"

"Yes"

"You were born in late October and you are twenty-six years old."

Col said she had never seen this man before. She was so shocked that she started shaking and, in the midst of what was becoming yet another difficult pregnancy, sick as a dog and with a toddler in tow to boot, all she could manage to blurt out was:

"How long have you been driving a cab?"

"Oh, I just started recently. I had to leave my regular field due to an on the job injury."

She said she was still shaking when she arrived at the hospital and described the scenario to her coworker, Pamela:

"Dat was probably your father! What's a matta' wit' you? You couldn't look on the dashboard to get his name off o' the chauffeur's license?"

"It was that scary."

"What did he look like?"

"He was a big guy. Maybe in his mid-fifties. He was in the front. I was in the back. It was a cab. What was I supposed to see?"

"I'll call their office right now as you and tell 'em I didn't leave him enough of a tip and ask that they contact him and ask him to please come back so I can pay him properly."

Pamela, much bolder and daring at this sort of thing, tried that ploy. No dice. They said that if she'd like she could mail the tip (a strictly cash business in those days) to them and they'd be happy to forward the money to the driver for her.

Yeah, right.

Mary Therese was born in early 1985, quite premature, weighing little more than two pounds. She spent the first three months of her life in an incubator at the University of Chicago Hospital. Col's doctors strongly suggested she not attempt to bear any more children. As one put it, "Get your tubes double-knot tied, burned and cauterized. You have a defect. A heart-shaped uterus."

For a few years after that 1984 incident, there were four or five times when Col was walking down Halsted Street, or Pershing Road, and that cabbie would double-toot his horn at her, wave and keep right on driving.

Also, for those same few years, her phone would ring right around her birthday and the caller would hang up.

Communication technology was a bit simpler back then. Col was able to get the phone number that was used to place those calls. It was an unassigned extension within a nursing home in nearby Oak Lawn, a suburb bordering the Southwest Side of Chicago. She dialed that number. No one answered, but she never got a call from that number again.

Whoever the cabbie was, why did he not tell Col who he thought she was during that brief ride? Why did he not, instead of honking his horn whenever he saw her in the neighborhood for a few years afterward, pull over and ask to speak to her and then explain how he knew exactly when she was born?

In all likelihood it was because when he recognized Col that day, he didn't know what her situation was. For all he knew, the Garritys may have never told Col she was an adoptee.

Some parents who adopt don't disclose it to their children. He probably didn't know the Garritys and that they skipped the stork excuse and were up front about that fact with their melting pot of adopted children.

Did Col bear a strong resemblance to her natural mother, and was that why the cabbie recognized her? Was the cabbie Col's natural father? Was he her natural mother's older brother who was, supposedly, her only sibling living in the U.S. when Col was born in 1958? Did those annual birthday hang-up calls from the nursing home mean anything, or were they flukes?

In 1984, Col had no idea. She only knew she wanted an inkling. But life always seems to get in the way of what you set out to do. It was no longer the "Ozzie and Harriett" days of the 1950s and 60s. Col had priorities: one child, another on the way and a job to hold down.

Fast forward to 1992. Col and Michael Schmidt's marriage ends, leaving her a single parent of two children. Thomas is eleven and Mary Therese seven years old. Col now has much less time on her hands to try and solve these mysteries.

There wasn't much spare time after we rekindled our relationship in 1994 and then double-knot tied our vows in 1997. I had never raised children of my own and was looking forward to being stepfather to a boy and girl whom I had grown to love as my own. However, that role comes with an assortment of complications. And even though every book out there—Freudianly clinical, "New Age" or anything in between—spouts the details of those challenges and just how to handle every situation, it's no less time consuming. Col's natural family mystery was relegated to a burner so far back it was in the pantry.

For three more years. In 2000, we were renting half of a "two-flat" in Hyde Park, a diverse neighborhood southeast of Canaryville that includes the University of Chicago. One day, Col and Mary Therese, then sixteen years old, were at the local Border's Book Store. Here is her description of what happened:

"Mary T was upstairs thumbing through the CDs (remember those?) and I was sitting on a bench on the ground level, browsing through a magazine. I heard a page on the intercom."

"Will a customer named Colleen please come to the Customer Service Desk."

"I thought maybe something had happened to Mary T. I headed for the service desk. At the same moment she came bolting down the escalator."

"Mom, what's wrong?"

"As soon as Mary T hit the bottom of the escalator and I realized she was fine I ran to the desk and asked the attendant why he was looking for me, let alone how he knew my name."

"A woman asked me to page you and to ask you to come here."

"What woman? Where is she?"

"I don't know who she is, but there she is."

"All I could see, at the other end of the store, was the back of a woman about my height, in a raincoat, wearing the type of scarves that were fashionable with older women: sheer and pastel. She was halfway through the revolving door exit. By the time we got past other customers and outside, she had vanished."

Col said it was her gut feeling that this woman was in some way connected to her natural parents. I labeled these two mystery players "The Cabbie" and "The Bookworm".

I was starting to fully gain an appreciation for why Col wanted to trace her true roots. At birth she was not expected to live. As an adult, bearing children became unbearable—even life threatening. Any health conditions that might be considered genetic would be important information for her birth mother, her birth mother's kids if she had birthed any more and, should she desire to bear children one day, her daughter Mary T.

Rattling Chains

Bitten by the bug of The Bookworm incident, Col wrote to the Catholic Home Bureau again, asking if they could share any further Non-Identifying Background History. Shortly afterward, she received a reply in the mail, from a social worker with the Post Adoption Department.

That response only outlined the costs for various services that they provided: Non-Identifying Background History had gone up 50% since 1979, to $75. Counseling, $50 per hour. Search and Intermediary: A social worker with the Catholic Home Bureau would act as a confidential "go between" and try to initiate contact with a birth parent, $300.

I suggested to Col that we pay the three hundred bucks:

"The Catholic Home Bureau has the sealed adoption records that you aren't allowed to see that contains the information most needed to find your birth parents. Why not let them conduct the search and hopefully, the reunion and be done with it? Why try to find them on your own?"

Col said it was because she considered it a private, personal matter. She wanted to be able to personally reach out, especially to her birth mother, and approach her as her daughter. Among other things, she wanted to personally thank her for giving her life. I don't think Col wanted to be represented by an intermediary employed by the same agency that had gone to lengths to hide her from her birth mother in the first place.

I agreed fully with those feelings. Also, if we went the Catholic Home Bureau route, and they found Col's birth mother and she wasn't interested in having contact with Col, that might just be the end of it. Her biological mom might be rattled at being found and we still would not learn her identity without her permission. She might shut down and disappear. By law, the Catholic Home Bureau could not reveal her identity, and the birth mother would then hold all the cards and could choose to remain anonymous forever.

But if we found her on our own, we would know who she was, and she'd know who Col was. That would be the difference. So, she ponied up the seventy-five bucks for a fresh, 2001 version of Non-Identifying Background History and received the following by mail, about a month later:

"July 30, 2001
Dear Colleen,
We have received your request for background

information and I am happy to be able to help you. We fully understand and appreciate an adopted person's very natural need to know something about their biological heritage and the circumstances of his/her adoption.

The Illinois Adoption Law requires mutual consent. We must have the written permission of both the adoptee and the birth parent before identifying information of any kind can be legally shared. We do not have this permission from your birth mother.

Should your birth mother ever inquire in the future, we would inform her of your interest and we would inform her of your inquiry. For now, we are happy to share the following:

Your birth mother, whom we shall call "Mary", approached our agency for assistance in June 1958. She requested medical care and adoptive planning for her expected child. Mary entered one of our Mutual Services Homes where she lived with a private family, helping with child-care and light housework in exchange for room and board and a small stipend. She made a good adjustment here and remained until after delivery.

Mary was a 20-year-old single Catholic girl of Irish descent. She had been born and raised in Ireland and emigrated to the United States in 1956. Mary had completed three years of high school in Ireland, had several months in finishing school and then was trained as a domestic. Since her arrival in the U.S., Mary had done general office work. The record reads:

"Mary is 5' 2 1/2" tall and normally weighs 127 pounds. She has rather broad features and is very well-groomed. She is a reserved type of person but related the necessary information freely. She feels her only alternative is to place the child for adoption."

Mary impressed as a nice young woman, cooperative in counseling and most anxious to make the best plan for you.

She chose not to inform her family, back in Ireland, of

her situation. Confidentiality was very important to her and she chose to use an alias, to protect her privacy. This was a common and perfectly legal practice used by many girls in those days. Her only sibling in this country, an older brother, was aware of her pregnancy, while the rest of the family remained unaware. Mary's mother, age 57, was a housewife, and her father, age 64, was a businessman. The record refers to another brother and sister, both age 75, but does not specify that they were twins. No other family is mentioned in the file. Mary's father had fallen ill (illness not specified) and Mary had been asked to return home to help. She returned to Ireland in mid-December, after being assured that you would be placed in a good adoptive home.

Mary described your birth father as a 30-year-old single Catholic man of Irish descent. He was 6'1" tall, 200 pounds, with dark brown hair, blue eyes, and a fair complexion. He was employed in law enforcement. There is no further information on file on your birth father and there is nothing at all on his extended family.

Apparently your birth parents had dated a while but they were not planning a future together and your birth father was not involved in the planning for you.

Under the circumstances, Mary felt that adoptive placement would be best for all concerned, especially for you and Mary wanted you to have a stable two-parent home with a normal family life. She wanted you to have advantages that she was unable to offer at that time. The decision to relinquish one's child is never easy, of course, but we have learned from experience that adoption is often the mature choice of a caring and realistic parent made in the best interest of her child.

You were born on 10/29/58 in St. Francis Hospital in Evanston. A heart murmur was noted, as well as cataracts in the right eye. On 11/2/58 you were transferred to St. Vincent's

Infant and Maternity Home (now closed) where you remained until placement with your family. While at St.Vincent's, you had two medical evaluations, one at St. Joseph's Hospital from November 3rd through November 10th and one at Mercy Hospital, from December 9th to December 17th. The recommendation was that you be placed with a family who was accepting of your medical needs and agreeable to the necessary future surgeries and special care.

On 2/28/59 you were placed with your family. You had been eagerly anticipated and were joyfully received. You appeared to make a fine adjustment into this home and we trust you enjoyed many good years with your family. It was nice to read your positive comments on your adoptive experience.

We hope this brief history has answered some of your questions about your early beginnings and the circumstances of your adoption. You can be sure there was much love and careful planning that went into your placement, from your birth mother and your adoptive parents as well as from our agency.

With kind personal regards, I am,
Sincerely Yours
Marjorie Dooley
Caseworker/Post Adoption"

This 2001 response certainly had discrepancies compared to Frances Cashman's 1979 letter! According to Marjorie Dooley, "Mary" was 20 years old instead of 19. It also stated Col was born October 29, 1958, not October 28, the date on her Adoptive Birth Certificate and the Certificate of Baptism that was on file at Holy Name Cathedral. We decided that the age difference may have been the result of one caseworker or the other seeing a birth date in the file for the mother and incorrectly adding things up in her head, and that the latter was probably nothing more than a typo.

But the discrepancy that shocked us was that the record refers to "a brother and sister, aged 75, but does not specify that they were twins." How does a twenty-year-old woman have two seventy-five year old siblings, when her parents are only sixty-four and fifty-seven years old? Were they actually only twenty-five years old and was this another typo? Looking at the average keyboard or, in this case a typewriter (remember those?), that seemed unlikely.

Perhaps Marjorie Dooley was working from handwritten notes taken when "Mary" first approached the agency in June 1958 and she saw a "7" instead of a "2". Twenty-five year old twin siblings made a lot more sense, as it would create a family of four with "Mary" the youngest, just as the 1979 letter stated, preceded by twins about five years older, with the oldest the brother she probably lived with here in the States.

As for whether they were twins, they didn't have to be. They could have been what is often called "Irish Twins", born within a year of each other. That was the best almost-uneducated guess I could come up with.

I also found the tone and language used by Ms. Dooley disturbing, especially considering she was writing to Col at the dawn of the 21st century. Col's birth mother used an alias because a lot of "girls" back then did. She was a legal adult when she gave birth to Col—not a girl! And she said Mary was described as "well-groomed". Even if Ms. Dooley was only echoing words used by Fran Cashman, the original caseworker in 1958, what was Col's birth mother, the Irish Setter entry in a dog show?

On the bright side, the 2001 letter did contain a few clues that I thought might help us, even though many seekers, after learning the truth, have coined their letters from agencies "Non-Identifying Background Bullshit".

It was interesting that Ms. Dooley said Col's birth mother provided the physical description of her birth father. That implied no one from the Catholic Home Bureau ever met the birth father and that, with her older brother's help I'm sure, Col's birth mother handled all of this on her own.

What concerned us the most, though, was that this 2001 letter said Col's birth mother used an alias. What Ms. Dooley did not specify was just when and where Mary used this alias.

To get a clue about her mother's real name, Col wrote again. This time, she asked about her name, Mary Eileen O'Brien, prior to the Adoption Decree of 1963, and if that meant her mother was also an O'Brien:

"November 13, 2001
Dear Colleen,

In response to your letter of 8-23-01. Requesting further information, we have reviewed our records.

Regarding the question of your origin surname, the name that appears in the Adoption Decree is the alias that your birth mother used. We do not know if the first name, Mary Eileen, was chosen for you by your birth mother or our Agency. If the birth mother did express a name preference, it was always honored.

It was not uncommon for the adoption of a child placed with a medical diagnosis to be delayed until the medical questions were resolved. It was necessary to know if the adoption would be a standard finalization, with the adoptive parents assuming full responsibility, or subsidized, with on-going funds provided for a chronic medical condition

In your case, after an extended period of observation and evaluation, a standard adoption was finalized.

We hope the above explanation answers your questions...
With kind personal regards, I am,
Sincerely,
Marjorie Dooley
Caseworker
Maternity-Adoption Department"

That letter created more questions. The Adoption Decree found in Mary Agnes Garrity's paperwork did not contain any name other than that of the child: Mary Eileen O'Brien. Was there something else that we were not being allowed to see?

Col then sent yet another letter to Holy Name Cathedral requesting a copy of her Certificate of Baptism. This time as if her real name was Mary Eileen O'Brien, without mentioning her adoptive name, Colleen Mary Garrity. She was hoping that someone would slip up or even be sympathetic and release a copy of a certificate that had her birth mother's real name on it.

No dice again. Holy Name Cathedral issued a copy of the same Colleen Mary Garrity certificate she had seen before. In her adoptive name with Garrity parents. The only difference was a fresh signature and date was given by the priest who pulled the file this time around. Now I get it.

Then, in late 2001, Col contacted retired Chicago policeman Jack Abernathy, who was willing to help. Jack had connections, including a "sympathetic clerk" who, for a fee, was able to get a look at Col's Original Birth Certificate, also known as the "OBC". This is a legal document that is supposed to have the real name of the birth mother. So, she coughed up a few hundred bucks to him. Following is what the clerk relayed to Jack, which he then shared with Col in an email:

Name of Newborn: Mary Eillen O'Brien (not Ellen or Eileen, E-I-L-L-E-N)
Born: St. Francis Hospital, Evanston, Illinois
Date of birth: 10-28-1958
Time: 6:15 AM
Mother's name: Mary Margaret O'Brien

Crap!

Chapter 2
Rogers Park Mary
Urbanese 101

For almost a decade our lives got in life's way again. On occasion we would discuss what we might be able to do with our only clues: "Non-Identifying Background History" that, for all we knew, was horse dung-based, and some extremely common Irish names: Mary Margaret O'Brien as birth mother, and Mary with the middle name of either Eileen or Ellen or who knows, maybe not a typo and intentionally created as "Eillen", as Col's middle birth name.

I Googled around and it did not appear that "Eillen" was a Gaelic name or version of a more common name. But it was an ancient Greek name. Fascinating information, but I didn't think "Eillen" held some secret clue for us, even though we had been told that sometimes, if the birth mother requested a certain name be given to the child she was giving up, she would request a name that could be an intended clue for a searching adoptee. My hunch was "Eillen" was a typo.

Because Mary Margaret O'Brien is laughably stereotypical, we also considered that the birth mother's name may have been fabricated. I tended to disagree because it was my impression the Original Birth Certificate is a legal document that can only contain true information. And if it was her real name, with one that common, why bother making one up?

By 2011, Col's kids Thomas and Mary T had both flown the coop. Thomas moved to Upper Michigan, where he and his wife Erica began raising their family. He secured work in the food industry. Mary T married, she and her husband Kevin had their first child that year. She followed in Col's footsteps when she landed a position at Mercy Hospital.

Also in 2011, Illinois State Representative Sara Feigenholtz spearheaded passage of legislation that would give adoptees fifty-three years or older something they were never allowed to have before: A non-certified copy of their OBC!

Until then, adoptees only had an amended birth certificate that had the correct birth date, but listed the adoptive parents, in Col's case Tom and Mary Garrity, as father and mother. But the OBC is what is created at the time of birth. Finally, Illinois adoptees could see their birth mother's name and signature, the handwriting of one of the people responsible for their existence.

Col would have to wait a few months to be old enough, but her older brother Kevin had turned fifty-three several months before, and it took him very little time to find his birth mother. The copy of the Adoption Decree he already possessed gave him the name "Baby Boy Haddon" prior to finalization. The OBC he received in 2011 gave the birth mother's name as Gertrude Haddon.

Kevin found a Gertrude Haddon Sampson that seemed to fit the bill. Apparently, she'd kept her maiden name within her full name all those years. He pulled up her phone number from the internet and called. Living in Florida. Alive and well. "Trudy" said she'd been waiting for that phone call for fifty-four years.

She said that after giving birth, she refused to sign the relinquishment papers until she had a chance to see Kevin once. The nuns allowed it, and she did notice one of his eyes looked as if it had a problem. She asked Kevin how his eye worked out. As Kevin did wind up needing some heavy-duty corrective lenses from an early age, this helped confirm he had the right birth mother.

Trudy said she had always hoped the child she gave up would one day locate her but, fearing possible rejection, she'd been reluctant to seek him out. At the earliest opportunity, Kevin traveled to Florida, where he met her and his half-siblings, her three children from a later marriage.

After seeing the photos of Kevin and Trudy standing together, the resemblance is so striking that the "eye test" was unnecessary. The two are in constant communication now. Nothing like a happy ending to usher in a new beginning.

But such is not always the case and that was something Col thought long and hard about. She'd read stories of the not-so-rosy skeletons that were unearthed by other adoptees upon learning the circumstances behind their conception. Was Col the product of an extramarital affair? Worse yet, a rape? An incestuous rape? Or any combination of the above?

What if she found her birth mother and father and both wanted nothing to do with her? She'd heard that one, too. That would probably hurt more than anything. She ultimately decided she could handle whatever cards she was dealt.

Col felt, regardless of the consequences, this was something she had to do, and her reasons were not just to fill an emotionally-perforated heart. Frances Cashman, in her 1979 letter, had stated that "there was no indication heredity was involved" in her diagnosis when she was born.

Of course she would say that. When Col was an infant, DNA science was in its infancy. Just as the surgeries that left her looking like a Bradburian "Illustrated Woman" have come a long way since 1963, genetic science has enjoyed great strides as well.

Maybe one or more of the issues Col was born with is hereditary in nature. If we succeeded in finding her birth parents, for their benefit and the sake of future generations, we would try to get both to agree to an exchange of medical information.

Col had heard theories that perhaps she was born a "rubella baby". Also known as German measles, the Mayo Clinic in Rochester, Minnesota website states that up to ninety percent of infants born to a mother who had the rubella virus in their system during the first trimester (eleven weeks) of gestation are born with one or more of the following: growth retardation: Col was very small as a child, deafness: no, cataracts: her dead eye, congenital heart defects: two in her case, defects in other organs: her heart-shaped uterus, and mental retardation: according to her tongue-in-cheek siblings, debatable.

Through the 1950s and 60s, parents vaccinated their children the old-fashioned way against measles, mumps and chicken pox: by contracting it. One kid would get infected and, for efficiency's sake, all the siblings in the home would then, hopefully, get it, the theory being that the whole family, immunities now bolstered, would then be done and over with the diseases for life.

I remembered that row of Terrazino kids when we had the mumps. Like chipmunks, lined up on the long, blue naugahyde family couch—thankfully sans those noisy, sweat-collecting clear slipcovers.

If Col's birth mother had rubella when she was pregnant, she could have picked it up anywhere, perhaps while living in the Mutual Services Home. It was not unusual for the family that an unwed mother lived with before bearing a child, to have children of their own. The expectant mom would help care for the children of her host, learning a little about childrearing while the one that she was scheduled to give up for adoption grew within her.

I wondered what effect this might have had on a young pregnant woman. She was getting to witness and take part in what she would shortly be missing out on. This was probably one reason it wasn't unusual for a woman to marry and have children within the first few years after relinquishing their firstborn to adoption. I've often wondered too if the incidence of "post-partum depression" is greater among mothers who "give up" their firstborn child.

Many researchers feel the health of a fetus can be affected by emotional stress of the mother. If being an unwed mother, barely two years in a country, feeling no choice but to give up what was probably her firstborn in Irish Catholic Chicago is not cause enough for stress, I don't know what is.

The Real McCoy

Col turned fifty-three in October 2011. Now eligible, she requested a copy of her OBC from the State of Illinois. The cost was minimal: fifteen dollars. She received it by mail about six weeks later. It matched what retired policeman Jack Abernathy's sympathetic clerk had seen on the OBC:

Name of Newborn: Mary Eillen O'Brien
Born: St. Francis Hospital, 355 Ridge, Evanston, Illinois
Date of birth: 10-28-1958
Time: 6:15 AM
Mother's name: Mary Margaret O'Brien
Mother's Home Address: 731 N. LaSalle Street, Chicago, Illinois (the Orphanage)
Mother's length of residency in Illinois: 2 years
Mother's Birthplace: Ireland
Mother's Age: 21
All information regarding the father: Legally Omitted
Attending Physician: Dr. Carl P. Mattioda

Even though it only contained a few more bits of information, having this document was a psychological plus for us. We actually had something in hand. Something with a signature.

Once again, our lives got in the way. But in late 2013, we decided to step up the search effort. No one involved in this was getting any younger. According to the Catholic Home Bureau and the OBC, Col's birth mother was, if living, now between seventy-four and seventy-six years old. Her birth father would be about eighty-five. I started thinking of ways to find the right needle in this tarnished stack.

In January 2014, I contacted an old friend of mine, Kirk Schwarz. We attended Tilden High School together, where we were pals from our sophomore year and then for over ten years until the mid-1980s. We lost track of each other until more recently, when I learned that he and his wife Hilary both worked for the Archdiocese of Chicago. Maybe they would be our inside connection or knew a sympathetic clerk at the agency.

Col and I drove to their home in West Suburban Riverside one Sunday afternoon. I brought with what little evidence we had at that point. A few days later, Kirk replied by email:

"Hi Paul,

My scenario is this: Mary Margaret O'Brien was not an alias. I believe this was her given name, and immigration records should so reflect. Her entry into this country in 1955 or 1956 was by invitation of her brother.

She most likely approached a priest at her parish and asked for help. The priest referred her to Catholic Charities. Catholic Charities had her sign the adoption papers in advance, and in return she was promised housing, employment and prenatal care. Additionally, The Catholic Home Bureau agreed to have the child baptized soon after birth, explaining Fr. Coughlin's involvement...If the mother genuinely believed the child would die, she may have asked for this to happen sooner than later.

The papers you sent are not reproductions of the certificate. They are merely office forms that are filled out when requests are made of the Baptismal records. The original certificate went to Mary or to the Garritys when they adopted her. When inquiry was made about the baptism, a priest (in 1963 it was Fr. Roache) looked up the record in the ledger and filled out the form according to the information he found in the book. I am a bit surprised that Holy Name Cathedral did not find a copy of the certificate. Colleen may want to look into that. I am quite sure that Holy Name has boxes of records stashed somewhere that would contain certificate copies. You may need to ask around and pull some strings, but the certificate copy should be available somewhere.

As to the God Parents, there is too little information about them. Are they perhaps the people who housed Mary in return for light housework during her pregnancy? Were they sworn to secrecy? Or were they part of a pool of God Parents that Fr. Coughlin kept on hand for orphans who were scheduled for Baptism and had no one else?

In reference to your mention of the cab driver and the page for Colleen at the bookstore, it seems very plausible to me that a former policeman had the resources to find Colleen. All he needed to do was call his buddies at the CPD (Chicago Police Department) and ask them to look.

Best Wishes,
Kirk"

When Col saw Kirk's remarks regarding her godparents, the Bielanskis, she mentioned to me that she thought they were related to the Garritys, her adoptive family.

Cyber-Digs

From the website Legacy.com, you can find more recent—especially over the last fifteen years—obituaries from all over the U.S.. I found notices for Casey and Virginia Bielanski. Hers gave her maiden name: Walters. The same as Col's adoptive mother Mary Agnes. We still had no idea if the Bielanskis knew who Col's birth parents were, but I didn't think so. I found no ready information regarding the current whereabouts of any of the three Bielanski children mentioned in Virginia's obituary. But I felt they probably did not know anything.

It was possible that the Garritys knew of Col's existence and medical issues when she was only a month old and they planned on adopting her anyway, making it further possible that the Garritys requested Col—actually still Mary Eillen O'Brien, be baptized in case she didn't survive. But it seemed to me her baptism would have to have been in her legal name in 1958: Mary Eillen O'Brien.

Was it changed on the Baptismal Certificate to Colleen Mary Garrity at a later date, perhaps in 1963, when that did become her legal name?

I was starting to learn a little about "digging" for people. Websites like U.S. Search, Whitepages Premium and others tease you with things like approximate ages, known relatives and previous addresses. Then, for a monthly fee of course, you can see more details. But I didn't care if any of these folks had a criminal history. I didn't care, at this point anyway, in having anyone's current email address or phone number. I cared about connecting dots.

I did a little more digging and was surprised to find that Dr. Carl P. Mattioda, who delivered Col in 1958, was still practicing obstetrics/gynecology from his own clinic about a hundred miles away, in Downstate Illinois. With Col's permission, I posed as her and wrote a letter to him.

"Colleen" thanked him for delivering her, mentioned that she'd been born with serious health issues and was seeking her birth mother, and as some maternity doctors keep personal records of every child they deliver, asked if he happened to have anything he could share.

Col never received a reply. I was a little surprised that he hadn't, even if he could not or did not want to help. I would learn later that my timing on that letter was not so grand. "Colleen" had written to Dr. Mattioda barely a month after Alice, his wife of fifty-seven years, passed away on February 2, 2014.

Kirk Schwarz suggested that, because they hold records that might be useful and the staff can be very helpful, we start by going to the nearest Church of Latter-day Saints Reading Room.

There are two in the Chicago area. I found the nearest and visited it one weekday morning, when I figured it would be quiet. They do have lots of records. But everything I saw was way too old to help me. The material in their reading room was mostly related to 19th and early 20th century immigrants, not post World War II arrivals.

But they do have a website, familysearch.org, that offers a free subscription and access to online databases. We also decided to purchase, for $110, a six-month International subscription to Ancestry.com, which has an even larger database and would give us access to birth, death and marriage records, ship manifests and U.S. naturalization indexes, obituaries and other useful information.

Armed with these spiffy digging tools, the first task was to see, just for grins and giggles, how many Mary O'Briens were registered as being born in Ireland between 1936 and 1938 by the General Registry Offices in Ireland, known as the GRO.

The number born in Ireland during those three years with that name was comically long. Without a means to narrow the list it would be fruitless. So I started looking through travel records for Mary O'Briens who emigrated, or as it's commonly referred to, "came over", from Ireland between 1955 and 1957. I only found two that specifically stated they were headed to Chicago in 1956:

A Mary M. O'Brien arrived by boat from Cobh, County Cork. She disembarked in New York City on April 20, 1956. She appeared to be traveling alone and gave as an ultimate destination 6623 North Greenview Street in Rogers Park, a neighborhood on Chicago's Far North Side, not far from St. Francis Hospital in neighboring North Suburban Evanston, where Col was born.

Before moving to Bridgeport in 1954, we'd lived in Rogers Park. It was my Italian grandparents' neighborhood as well. I still had a few cousins living in and around the area. The address this Mary gave was in St. Ignatius parish. My older brother Bill was baptized in the next parish north, St. Jerome's. Both these Rogers Park parishes held large Irish populations through at least the mid-1970s.

The other Mary O'Brien, no middle initial, flew in from

Shannon, County Clare, Ireland on October 24, 1956. She was on a manifest of "Passengers destined for Chicago" and was listed as an immigrant when she was checked in at U.S. Customs in Detroit, Michigan.

Until 1959, a passenger flight from Shannon to Chicago typically stopped in Gander, Newfoundland, possibly to refuel, and then it was on to Detroit, Michigan. As Chicago did not have an international airport, all passengers were then admitted to the U.S. through the Customs Office at the Detroit-Wayne Major Airport. Those destined for Chicago then flew on to Chicago's Midway Airport.

All the manifest said for this Mary O'Brien was that she was "Immigrant #2630". No ultimate destination address given. The only other immigrant listed on the leg of the flight to Chicago was a Mary G. O'Shea: #2649. I'd no idea if she was traveling with this Mary O'Brien, whom I also could not assume was on her way to live in Chicago. I had no way of knowing if either or both got on another flight, train, bus or relative's car and headed elsewhere. I decided to name this O'Brien "Pan Am Mary", honoring her choice of airline.

There were four others in 1956. None indicated any connection to Chicago:

On June 10, a Mary M. O'Brien stepped off a plane from Shannon at New York City's Idlewild Airport. On August 8, a Mary O'Brien arrived by boat in New York City. Another immigrant, Mary E. O'Brien, arrived at those same set of docks on October 10, headed for Brooklyn. Finally, there was a Mary O'Brien who disembarked on December 21 in New York City, headed to an address in Boston, Massachusetts.

Even though he thought some of the Non-Identifying Background History was bullshit, Kirk Schwarz and others we'd spoken to about our search gave the following advice: Treat what the OBC says and what the Catholic Home Bureau told you in those letters as truth until it can be proven otherwise.

We were also advised to always approach any person representing any institution, religious-based or non, as if we were nothing more than amateur genealogists interested in our family history and not admit that the true reason was adoptee-related. One might not receive the desired level of cooperation if the secretary or clerk on the other side of the desk, or phone, or in an email exchange, feels adoptees should "leave well enough alone" and not be out trying to locate their birth parents.

I understood the advice, but felt I needed to follow it with one caveat: If I had the gut feeling that whoever I was trying to gain information from would be sympathetic to our cause, I would divulge the true reason for the search. I was about to test those waters.

Although Col's experience with The Cabbie and The Bookworm indicated she was conceived in Chicago, that didn't mean we could ignore the immigrants headed for New York City and Boston. But I felt my best bet was to look at those specifically headed to Chicago first.

Pavement Pounding

I decided to start out with the Mary M. O'Brien who gave an address in the Far North Side neighborhood of Rogers Park as her ultimate destination when she arrived by boat in New York City. I called my cousin Tom Bernardi, who still lives there. I asked him if he knew any O'Briens in that neighborhood who had been around long enough to perhaps remember a Mary O'Brien of that age range:

"I sure do, Paulie (he's the only relative allowed to use the nickname). Stop in at the A&T Restaurant on Clark and Greenleaf almost any weekday during breakfast or lunch. Ask for Angie O'Brien. She's been waitressing there forever. She and her husband Jimmy are both Irish, in their seventies and know everybody. Between the two of them you might be able to get something."

At the next opportunity I drove to the A&T Restaurant. The A&T, shorthand for "Abundant and Tasty", is a popular spot, known for football-sized omelettes, ham on-the-bone and great Lunch Specials. It's in St. Jerome's Parish. Close enough to St. Ignatius. Parishioners of both frequented the A&T.

And though it was such a common name, I'd be talking to an O'Brien. Who knows, maybe we'd get lucky and she would know who I was asking about and perhaps luckier yet, "Rogers Park Mary" would turn about to be Col's birth mom. Let's be positive and optimistic.

Yeah, right. Nothing wrong with dreaming.

This was my first try at playing this sort of role. I was confident I could pull it off without coming across as a mush-mouthed fool. Nonetheless, I had a good case of butterflies going and my mouth was talcum dry when I arrived, midmorning on a winter weekday, when I figured Angie O'Brien would be the least busy during her shift.

I grabbed a booth and singled out which "waitron"—a genderless, non-sexist term I first heard tending bar in the mid-1980's—she was. There was only one candidate who was even close: the woman who appeared to be the right age with a full head of curly Irish tresses. So far, I'd only been served a sorely-needed glass of Chicago "tap" water—obvious tap because it's chlorinated to damn-near swimming pool levels, along with a menu by a passing busboy. I waited until Angie's rounds brought her near:

"Excuse me, are you Angie. Angie O'Brien?"

"Yes!"

"I'm Tom Bernardi's cousin Paul."

"Oh, Tommy! I haven't seen him in a long time. How's he

doin'?"

"Great. He told me to say hello. I've had breakfast. I think I'll just grab a snack. That carrot cake looks pretty good. Let's have a slice and a cup of decaf."

Certainly, no caffeine needed and maybe the cake would settle my stomach.

"Right away, sweetie."

This was a good sign. Butterflies, prepare for landing.

In typical A&T fashion, Angie was back in no time and, barely breaking her stride, she flipped over a standard issue six-ounce white ceramic coffee cup and swirled in the perfect amount of steaming industrial-grade restaurant supply house brew without spilling a drop from the green-necked unleaded decaf urn.

A real pro.

"Here ya' go. I'll be right back with that carrot cake."

She scribbled some server hieroglyphic onto a small Guest Check pad and, quicker than a gunslinger, holstered it in her apron as she pivoted on one of her orthopedic-clad feet and disappeared. About one minute later, like a good bartender who pours a double and charges for one shot, she returned with an at least thousand-calorie wheel chock of a chunk of the "snack" I had ordered.

Another good sign. After I'd wolfed it down and she was reloading my cup:

"I wonder if you might be able to help me."

"Sure, honey."

She sat down in the booth, across from me. Good signs times two.

"I'm trying to find a long-lost relative of my wife...."

Without letting on that it was Col's birth mother I was seeking, I gave her the particulars that I had. That in 1956 she had emigrated from Ireland, possibly to St. Ignatius parish. That this long-lost relative's name was Mary O'Brien, that she had an older brother here and she may have returned to Ireland by 1959.

"None of that rings a bell with me but give me your phone number and when I get home, I'll ask my husband. As long as you're in the neighborhood, why not stop by the rectory at St. Ignatius? Maybe they can help."

I sensed that she had a notion what was up. So much for not letting the cat out of the bag. My gut said take the plunge.

"My wife is an adoptee and she wants to find her birth mom. None of us is getting any younger and I'm trying to help her."

"Oh, sweetie, that is so sad. There are a lot of people out there in her shoes. Such a shame. I hope you find her."

I gambled right that time. A sympathetic waitress... sorry, waitron.

My tab for the bottomless cup of decaf, and "snack" that negated the need for lunch, was three-fifty. I thanked Angie and bid her farewell. After tucking a "fin and a single" under my used cup I headed for St. Ignatius Church, one mile southeast of the A&T.

The church rectory sits just north of the main entrance to the church. It's not unusual to find a woman, usually a layperson, manning... sorry, person-ing, a church office during most weekdays.

This would be the first time I was going to approach someone with the only intent being to locate a possible or former parishioner. This wasn't a public place of business with carrot cake and other props to hide behind. The butterflies and cottonmouth returned.

By now, it was almost noon:

Did I want to arrive at the church rectory when the church secretary, the usual "gatekeeper", was hungry and getting ready for lunch? On the other hand, if she had something planned for after lunch, would my timing be even worse?

I felt I'd be better off if I had to deal with a layperson. But I had no choice on that one. What if the only one in the office today was the pastor? Or, having been educated nine years by them, heaven forbid a nun? I could feel my sweat glands kicking in. The slight rise in my pulse.

I opted to stop thinking and just do it.

Walking up the street to the rectory door, I popped a mint straight from its individual wrapper under my tongue so I could talk and activate my salivary glands simultaneously, and pressed the yellowed, cracked ceramic button next to the door. I was buzzed into a vestibule that led to a small shelf-lined office, where a woman in her seventies sat behind the desk:

"Can I help you?"

She looked Irish so I used the husband of your countryman... countryperson approach:

"I just happened to be in the neighborhood, and I thought I'd stop in and see if you can help. I'm trying to find a relative of my wife. She's a Garrity, but the woman she's looking for is Mary O'Brien and I think she may be related to the O'Briens who lived on Greenview. The 6600 block."

"How long ago did she live here?"

"Oh, in the late 1950s."

Not surprisingly, she chuckled.

"I don't personally know of any O'Briens who are parishioners. But that doesn't mean there aren't any. This parish has changed over the years. There's a few still around, but a lot of the people from that time are long gone now."

True that. I had a feeling in 1958 they didn't offer that second Sunday Mass in Spanish I'd seen advertised on the internet.

"Tell me, are there any old-timers who go back that far in the parish who I might be able to contact?"

Her silence told me she sensed this was not a casual visit. My gut said go for it:

"My wife is an adoptee and she's trying to locate her birth mother."

"Oh, that is so sad. Why is she looking now, after all these years?"

Uh oh. Questioning why is not what I would call "sympathetic". Had my sugar-laden gut lied to me? I put a little bit of a plea into my answer.

"There are medical reasons. She has been looking for a very long time and I'm trying to help her."

"If you stop in at Bruno's after Sunday morning Mass, you'll usually see a few from that generation."

I assumed she was referring to the English version of Mass and that Bruno's was a tavern. She'd opened a door for me to play the fellow Catholic card. I had to phrase it just so. I hadn't been to church in forty-five years. I did not want to lie and be struck by lightning right there in the rectory.

"Thanks. Maybe I'll bring Colleen to Mass sometime and we'll go by there afterwards for a pint."

A small fib. Col dislikes beer immensely but loves Jameson and Diet Coke. Stop laughing; it's not bad. Think Irish "Jack n' Coke". I was just trying to keep it simple, Lord Almighty.

No lightning. Thanks.

"It's always a wonderful service and I'm sure you'll both enjoy it. If you do make it for Mass, there is one old Irishman who is there every week. I'm almost positive he was around back then. I forget his name, but everybody knows him. Just ask around when Mass is over."

"We will. Speaking of names, what's yours? Mine's Paul Terrazino."

"Bernadine. Bernadine Dolan."

We shook hands. I'd decided it was best to not carry around an official-looking binder or the like. I jotted down the particulars and my contact information on a piece of the 4 x 3 note pad I had in my jacket pocket.

"Here's my number and email. Thanks very much Bernadine. If you think of anything else, please let me know."

Then, in true Peter Falk/Columbo afterthought fashion, I

turned back as I left, reaching for the brass ring:

"Say, does the church have any parish registers with birth, marriage, or even lists of the congregation members that might help me?"

"Well, yes. But I don't know that we are allowed to let that information out. You know, for privacy reasons."

Bernadine Dolan seemed like a nice person, but smart money said she wouldn't be my first sympathetic clerk. I clumsily blubbered some response that indicated I understood her position, thanked her again and, wiping away a salty tsunami of brow sweat with my jacket sleeve, left.

Despite not really getting anywhere with Bernadine, I felt good, like an actor once opening night is under his belt. And playing "Columbo" was a lot of fun, butterflies and all. But this approach alone didn't seem very efficient. It was likely it would always be a crap-shoot to drop by rectories in the hopes of prying information out of people who probably were not around over half a century ago.

I wanted to know more about the address that Roger Park Mary was headed to. I called Bill Finch, a friend of mine who I'd known since grammar school at St. Mary of Perpetual Help in Bridgeport. Bill put himself through law school and then practiced real estate law for many years. He's a very generous man, always willing to help an old friend. I got him on his cell phone, explaining my plight. He queried:

"Do you have the pinumber?"

Spoken like a true Chicagoan. We slide things together into one word: "pinumber". "Jeet jet?" is "Did you eat yet?". "No, jew?" is "No, did you?". No room here to get into how much, in our native, nasal, urban tones we butcher street names like Goethe, Honore and Devon.

We chatted for a moment, just catching up, and he said he'd get back to me. He dug up what he was referring to: the Cook

County, Illinois Property Index Number, commonly known as the PIN, and called me back.

For 6623 North Greenview, Chicago, Bill was able to see any transactions regarding the property for the preceding thirty years. It was a single-family dwelling, or "stand-alone" home, and had changed hands in the 1990s. But that transaction involved no one named O'Brien. A Mrs. Ellen Kerry bought the home, and it was tough to determine just who she bought it from. It was in some sort of "Trust" at that time.

If Rogers Park Mary was the O'Brien we were seeking and her married brother lived there and she joined him in 1956, he may have been renting. Or, if her brother did own the home, he may have sold it to someone else prior to Mrs. Kerry. According to internet phone listings, Mrs. Kerry was about ten years too old to be Col's birth mother.

"Pan Am Mary" was the only other immigrant Mary O'Brien offering up Chicago as her possible destination. Like many others, her one-piece paper trail ended, in her case, the day she headed off to Chicago's Midway Airport after being checked in at Customs in Detroit on October 24, 1956.

The problem I had with her was that it was just a name and the number "2630". That number was probably an internal one for Pan Am Airlines and there was nothing I could do with it. No way to connect a name as common as Mary O'Brien to that number and frankly, for all I knew, this Mary O'Brien was seventy years old in 1956.

I put Rogers Park and Pan Am Mary aside to have a look at the other four Mary O'Briens who provided addresses other than Chicago on their respective travel manifests:

All four might as well have vanished into thin air after getting off the boat or plane that brought them here. I decided to look at things from the back end of the immigration angle.

One could not, under almost all circumstances, apply for

citizenship for at least five years after the date of immigration. Serving a minimum two years in the U.S. Military was one exception.

If odds were that she had married within a couple of years of giving Col up for adoption and, if she stayed in the U.S. as Kirk Schwarz had suggested, the birth mother probably would have applied for citizenship as early as late 1961 or early 1962 under her quite possibly by then married name—a name that could be anything.

I emailed, as myself and not Col, the "info@" email address of each United States National Archive Regional Office that would be likely to have a naturalization record for any of my Mary O'Briens. Chicago, Boston, and New York City.

All three offices responded. Nothing. None of the Mary O'Briens they had were even close in age or had a naturalization date that fit. The man who replied my email from the New York City office was a Timothy McHugh. I could tell he was really going the extra mile in looking for any naturalization record.

Time to pull out the "cute little Irish wife card". I wanted to see if I could get him to release anything based on the immigration numbers that the three Mary O'Briens who arrived in New York City in 1956 had been assigned. I schmoozed him about poor little Colleen Garrity Terrazino's long-lost relative.

I wondered if he had gotten these type of requests before, and if he'd wondered what I meant by "long-lost relative". I had a hunch he knew, but his reply indicated he could be of no help:

> "Hi Paul,
> You may have to make a Freedom of Information Act request to access Mary O'Brien's Immigration and Visa information."

That was slightly encouraging. It would be golden If I could see the Immigration and Visa information for my Mary O'Briens.

His reply contained a link to the governmental agency that oversees Freedom of Information Act (FOIA) requests:

The U.S. Department of Homeland Security! That department (Javol, mein Fuhrer) was created after the 911 terror attacks on The World Trade Center and U.S. Pentagon in 2001. Thirteen years later, it was still wound up tighter than an organ grinder's tail.

I opened the link and went through the paces to see what it would take to make a FOIA request. There was no way in hell I could even fill out the form without falsifying it. You must be a close relative, or someone with the Power of Attorney of a living relative, to get Immigration and Visa information out of that department.

The risk of being struck by lightning for lying to religious institution personnel was tolerable, but I didn't want to mess with "the Feds". Given my luck, I'd get busted pretending to be an O'Brien and shipped off to "Gitmo", the gulag at Guantanamo Bay, Cuba.

I then decided to revisit the ship and flight manifests where I'd found these six Mary O'Briens. I wanted to make sure that there wasn't a relative of one on the next page of manifests who had provided an address, or next of kin, or anything else that might be useful.

No new clues. The six possible birth mothers had vanished into the Irish American landscape. But in revisiting those manifests, I did learn a valuable lesson. At the top of the manifest page that contained "Rogers Park Mary" O'Brien, headed for St. Ignatius parish, was the criteria for all those on that page, including her:

"List of U.S. Citizens and Nationals disembarking in New York City."

That meant Rogers Park Mary was already a U.S. Citizen in the summer of 1956. If Col's birth mother emigrated here in 1956, this could not be her. I guess I still hadn't put into practice what I'd been reminded of my whole life by teachers, employers and on occasion Col:

Go through the danged instructions! In this case, that means don't just zero in on the manifest entries for names and possible ages and addresses. Read the whole blasted thing.

I had to find a way to up the game.

Chapter 3
A Bigger Shovel
Reaching Across the Pond

At this early stage, the few people I'd discussed the search with had suggested this was probably going to take more than what could be accomplished by clicking around in cyberspace. I agreed.

In cities the size of New York or Boston, ultimate destination points provided by four of my six Mary O'Briens, there would be no need for a woman who had "gotten into trouble" to shamefully slink halfway across the country to Chicago to bear a child. All she'd have to do is shift to a different neighborhood, preferably on the other side of either city, during those final physically noticeable months of pregnancy.

That made it more likely that Col was conceived in the Chicago area. The possibility did remain that her older brother may have lived on the East Coast when she arrived and they, or maybe she alone, moved to Chicago at any point after 1956 and before Col was born in 1958. And so, the Mary O'Briens who gave addresses in New York City and Boston on arrival to the U.S. in 1956 would not be forever trash-canned.

They were only going to be set aside. I wanted to first play the possibilities with the shortest odds, and only return to the East Coast contenders if the Chicago tack caught no favorable wind.

In a "town" the size of Chicago—a term a lot of us natives prefer because Sinatra was right, the odds also favored Col's birth mother being placed with a Mutual Services Home for the second half of pregnancy in a different neighborhood and if possible on the other side of town, to help lessen the chance of her rounding a corner and running expectant-belly-first into someone who was not supposed to be aware of her predicament.

Col was born at St. Francis Hospital in Evanston, the first suburb north of Chicago proper, along the Lake Michigan lakefront. Col's 1984 experience with The Cabbie, followed by The Bookworm in 2000, happened in or not far from her adoptive South Side home neighborhood in Canaryville, lending credence to the theory that she was conceived on the South Side, possibly even in Canaryville or adjacent Bridgeport.

Perhaps the birth parents lived in, or close to, Col's adoptive Garrity parents and the Catholic Home Bureau placed her with the Garritys because they were willing and the only choice. Col was born as damaged goods. A "dud". There probably weren't many couples willing to adopt her.

When the full extent of Col's physical maladies and prognosis were explained to them, the Garritys probably could have opted to cut bait and run, pulling the plug on the deal. But they were willing to take little "Mary Eillen O'Brien" into their home anyway, birth defects, future surgeries, misspelled middle name and all.

I couldn't completely leave Chicago's suburbs out of the picture. But I felt, again, that I needed to go with what provided the greatest odds. Chicago then was not Chicago now. There were suburbs in 1958, but nowhere near todays far-reaching sprawl.

Now, national newscasters refer to cities like Joliet, Aurora, and Elgin as "Suburban Chicago" because now they really are. In 1958 a mix of farmland, floodplain and a few remaining strips of forest straddling rivers and creeks separated Chicago and its bordering suburbs—Evanston, Oak Park, Park Ridge and others, from these smaller cities that, even as late as the mid-70s, we city kids considered "out in the sticks".

I felt a slight advantage. The 1950s version of Chicago was a smaller pond to fish in than the goliath it has since grown to be, even if I would be dragging my lure through half-century old muck.

Advantages of a Cultural Capitol

Fortunately, if Col was conceived in Chicago, "The Windy City"—a nickname originally coined by a journalist over a hundred years ago that referred not to the weather but its windbag politicians, has two free resources that could hold helpful clues: The Newberry Library and the Chicago Public Library. My best bet was to start at The Newberry Library, simply called "The Newberry", even by their own website:

"The Newberry has actively collected research and reference materials since its foundation in 1887. From the mid-1890s on, its collecting activities have focused on the humanities, with an emphasis on original sources for the study of European and Western Hemisphere history, literature, and culture since the late medieval period. The Newberry has also continued to build its collection of secondary books – including reference works, monographs, periodicals, and other serials – and more recently digitized reproductions to support the use of its original sources."

Sounds like pretty highbrow stuff. But that was not the purpose of my first trip in mid-February 2014. Maybe someday I'd have the time to peruse their exotic older holdings. Eisenhower Era Chicago was more anemic.

I picked a Tuesday in January. Midmorning. Even by Chicago standards, it was a cold day. Teardrops turned solid before they hit the ground cold, with a northerly wind barreling down Lake Michigan so violently—so much for hot-aired politicians—that it wrapped itself around every building and billboard, creating a whirling cacophony that, no matter what direction I faced in hopes of temporary relief, still struck me flat in the face.

No matter. I was on a mission. In more clement weather I would walk the couple of miles from our Hyde Park condo to the

CTA Red Line Train Station, but this time I opted for the Garfield Avenue CTA bus that would take me to it. From there, it's about nine miles—thirty minutes or so if things go well, to the Division Street stop along Chicago's upscale Near North Side. That left a short walk of a few blocks to The Newberry.

The library inhabits a large, early 20th century, five-story, fortress-like brown stone building. There's a locker room on the first floor where a quarter is required to open your locker of choice. You even get your "two bits" back when you leave. Next to it, there's a small vendetteria with several formica-topped tables, plastic and chrome chairs, along with snack, coffee, pop machines, and a microwave oven.

I had to apply for a free "Reader's Card". It took very little time to take care of that paperwork, procure a locker for my coat and the laptop case with a seemingly bottomless number of pockets containing any notes I had, a legal pad, pens and pencils, and what was equally important:

Lunch. The delicious yin/yang combo of a peanut butter and sliced dill pickle sandwich on toasted potato bread (uncurl your noses, it's not bad) paired with locally made, "gmo free" tortilla chips, a carrot and apple—both organic—for dessert. I left everything in my locker but the legal pad that contained my notes on the search. Much easier to waltz through security.

Years earlier, I'd used The Newberry when in research for a barely mediocre screenplay I wrote that nearly breaks every rule a first-time screenwriter should follow, about the early days of movie-making in Chicago. Then, I was trying to learn more about people whose identities are well known: Charlie Chaplin, Gloria Swanson, Wallace Beery...

The 2014 birth family search was more involved. Were there a lot of O'Briens living in one section of a neighborhood or parish? Often, they would be relatives—"cousins" from the old country. That might be good. It might mean nothing. But I needed to go through this tedium to get a feel for the pockets of Irish American Chicago during the 1950s and 60s. Maybe in the process I'd stumble across something. The Newberry had what I now needed for the 2014 birth mother search:

Chicago Phone Directories. Loads of them. And for this project, all the years I needed: 1945, as it was likely our birth mother's brother emigrated post WWII, through 1960 and, because I didn't know where the trail would lead after she supposedly returned to Ireland in late 1958, beyond.

The Newberry is in the process of creating digital versions of these directories. Almost all of them were the original Residential "White" or Business "Yellow" Pages. These phone books—the lucky ones are kept in binders, the not-so-lucky have homemade cardboard reinforcement fronts and backs added by Newberry staff—are housed on the second floor.

They also have the 1953 and 1955 "Criss Cross" books for Chicago. A Criss Cross book lists addresses alphabetically, street by street, providing the names of adult residents of each address the year of publication. Although Criss Cross books only seem to reveal adult names and do not provide the wealth of information available on a census record, such as ages, state or country of birth, head of household, occupation, years living in this country—all things I would love to have for 1950 through 1960, they still held potential value to this search.

U.S. Census reports—images of the actual form the census takers fill out when going door-to-door every ten years, are only available for viewing by the public after seventy years have passed. In 2014 I only had access to the 1940 U.S. Census on Ancestry. com or any of the other sites that have census data. Therefore, a Criss Cross book might come in handy.

According to Newberry staff, these two Criss Cross editions, '53 and '55, are the only two in existence for Chicago from the 1950s and 60s. I would have given "my eye teeth" for the Criss

Cross books for 1956 through '60. If any copies exist, there might be a set tucked away in the attic of a real estate or surveyors office or a retired lawyer's garage. It wasn't yet time to start soliciting for those via Craigslist or a similar platform. Hopefully, it would not come to that.

I filled out the request cards for what I wanted: Chicago residential White Pages from 1954 through '58 and both the 1953 and '55 Criss Cross books. You then hand your requests to the librarian covering the counter that day. Everyone is always knowledgeable, polite and very helpful, and you're assigned a desk that has its own green-shaded "bankers lamp".

Have a seat and the requested material is personally delivered— due to the enormity of my request on a metal mail cart. Because some of the books I requested get a real workout and they're trying to keep them in one piece, I was also given two short blocks of two-by-four wood, covered in upholstery cloth, to support the bindings when spreading them open for viewing.

Rogers Park Mary was a U.S. citizen in 1956 and therefore a less likely candidate for birth mother. But this was the only Chicago address I had. Even though she was not considered a good fit, it would be wise to consider that perhaps the ship manifest was incorrect, or that to present herself as a naive bumpkin from Ireland, she lied to Frances Cashman at the Catholic Home Bureau and had been in the U.S. for more than two years. That made her—if nothing else just to get my feet wet at this—worth checking out. My primary order of business for this first of what would be many visits to The Newberry, was to see if any O'Briens lived at the address she provided on arrival in NYC in 1956: 6623 North Greenview, Chicago.

Both Criss Cross books, 1953 and '55, showed a Thomas F. O'Brien as being the resident of 6623 Greenview. He was in the phone books also, same address, from 1955 through '58. Not at all surprising was that in the 1950s in Chicago, there were pages of

O'Briens in the phone book.

I made note of the other O'Briens in or near Rogers Park and recalled the technical level of phone communication from my boyhood. Most residential systems were on a "party line". You shared the phone line with others. The families in my neighborhood usually had only one "rotary dial" phone—extensions were "verboten"—in a common area with a cord that parents preferred be short. Especially if they had daughters.

It was unlikely a young, single woman, especially a recent immigrant to mid-1950s Chicago, would have had her own phone listing. Yet, I still took note of the half-dozen Mary O'Briens scattered throughout Chicago that were listed in the White Pages between 1954 and '59.

Maybe she came from a well-to-do family in Ireland and had her own flat with a phone. Possible, but it was more likely that she lived with her brother. That was usually the way it worked. Without a first name for the birth mother's brother, where was I to even begin? The brother was another needle in a separate stack.

And with all those pockets in my laptop bag, I hadn't thought to include a magnifying glass. Most of what I was viewing was faded, in eye-squintingly tiny fonts and, if on microfilm, through machines that had seen better days.

I made any notes I could on what would be the first of several yellow legal pads on that first visit to The Newberry. I only spent about ninety minutes researching the Chicago Criss Cross and Phone Directories before my nearly sixty-year old eyes were ready for a break.

I left the pile of books I'd requested at my desk and let staff know that I was going to take a lunch break and would return in thirty minutes or so.

"Thank you for letting us know. You can leave the books at your desk and we won't touch them."

I love this place.

It was that day in mid-February, downstairs in the tiny Newberry vendetteria, while looking over notes and adding "to do's" to a growing list between bites of bizarre-sounding yet tasty sandwich, that the realization of just how daunting this search might be really started sinking into my thick skull.

I wanted to take some of the O'Brien names I'd made note of thus far and try to connect them to any that I might be able to find via Ancestry.com, familysearch.org and any other available genealogy website. Even though the library has internet-ready computers available for use, I preferred the comfort of home.

The apple dessert wasn't enough to scrub the odiferous memento of the peanut butter/pickle combo. I jettisoned a mint out of its wrapper, very nearly chipping a tooth as it ricocheted its way to the source, and headed back up to the reading room to make a final "idiot check" as insurance that I'd not missed anything.

Making sure no one was looking, I scooped into my pocket the few tiny crumbs of half-disintegrated White Pages that had eroded off the corners, hid the evidence in my pocket, bade the librarian du jour good day, allowed security to perform a cursory glance through my notes to make sure I hadn't slipped any priceless medieval holdings between the pages and, braving the elements once more, was on the next southbound Red Line.

I felt that first field trip to The Newberry was not a complete waste. But I also felt I could stagger around forever if I only followed this prescription of throwing darts to connect dots. I had not read any articles or books or even consulted "Professor Google" for any helpful tips on conducting this type of dig. I was just machete-ing my way along, albeit with what I had always considered to be reasonably good common sense, based on the dearth of clues I had.

Alma Mater

Ensconced comfortably, cold brew in hand, in our twelve-by-twelve foot office/den/futon-equipped guest suite, I started poking around on the internet for any records that might match some of the male O'Briens listed in those old phone books, attempting to link one of them to one of my immigrant Mary O'Briens. We were only told that "Mary" had an older, married brother who was the oldest of four and lived in the U.S.. I began by trying to figure out who Thomas F. O'Brien of 6623 North Greenview, Rogers Park, Chicago is. Or was. I wanted to see how likely a candidate he was to be the brother.

I had to wrap my head around a pretty wide age range for the birth mother's supposed brother, but based on the average number of years a woman, in this case their mother, devotes to childbearing, and that "Mary" was the youngest and born in about 1937, I felt it a safe bet he was born between 1924 and 1935. I needed another good laugh, so I took a quick look at the number of Thomas O'Briens born in Ireland during that period.

The length of that list was hilariously longer than three years worth of Mary O'Briens. I searched any available records for the same O'Brien immigrating to the U.S. between 1946 and 1955. There were several, but not one gave an address in Chicago as an "ultimate destination".

This did not mean that, among the many, I wasn't looking right at the Thomas F. O'Brien who eventually wound up at 6623 North Greenview. It meant there was nothing in the information I could see that had him dancing off the page waving an old wooden shillelagh at me.

I did find a 1993 obituary in online newspaper archives for a Thomas F. O'Brien. He was the former principal of a Chicago Public High School in Albany Park, a Northwest Side neighborhood of Chicago. The wake and funeral mass did not take place in Rogers Park. Not at St. Ignatius, St. Jerome's, or any other of the parishes in or near that neighborhood. It was in the suburb of Park Ridge. If he and Thomas F. from Greenview Street were one and the same, he may have retired there. That's where that trail stopped.

My gut told me to set Thomas F. O'Brien the educator aside for now. I needed to follow the initial credo:

Treat what you've been told as truth.

If I did that, it was less likely that in 1958 a young woman who became pregnant by a police officer had a brother who eventually became a high school principal. It was more likely that the birth mother's brother was a friend of Col's natural father and was also a municipal worker.

There was a sizable spike in immigration numbers into the U.S. after World War II. I imagined many who came over from the U.K., Ireland, and other European countries developed an interest in emigrating after meeting Americans who were serving, or preparing for D-Day and other operations, as my Dad had in 1944 in the English countryside.

Also, transatlantic travel, almost exclusively by water then, was greatly limited from 1941 through most of 1945. Many who had planned to emigrate earlier were handed a delay that lasted until after the war was over. I felt the brother was probably in that Post WWII wave that roiled over the Atlantic. And more than likely headed right to Chicago.

In those days, Chicago's largely Irish American Democratic party political machine was well-oiled and firing on all its gas-guzzling Motown-made V-8 cylinders. Prime jobs were available for many Irish immigrants to Chicago, and the best way to land those jobs—after gaining U.S. citizenship when required—was through the local alderman or precinct captain, or someone closely connected. "City Jobs": Police. Fire. Streets and Sanitation, also known as "Streets n' San".

Many of these positions were "patronage jobs". You got your foot in the door by helping your local—in Chicago, Democratic Party—politicians at election time. Knocking on doors to get out the vote, encouraging your neighbors and friends to vote for your "chinaman", or sponsor, or whoever he supported. You were expected to volunteer for the ward in which you resided. It was a "given".

One hand washes the other, or in this case, feeds it votes. That was the political culture in Irish American Chicago, especially during the reign of Richard J. Daley, "Richard the First", from 1955 through '76, when he died while still in office and physically in an office, his doctor's, when his ticker stopped firing during a routine visit.

It was suggested I try asking around with the two largest Irish American community organizations in the Chicago area: The Irish American Heritage Center on the Northwest Side of the city, and Gaelic Park in Southwest Suburban Oak Forest. A quick look at the Gaelic Park website told me that it was more a deluxe rental facility, complete with restaurant and ballroom, suitable for weddings and the like.

I was familiar with the more cozy, rustic Irish American Heritage Center. Usually referred to as "The Heritage Center", it occupies a full city block of the Mayfair neighborhood on Chicago's Northwest Side. Built in about 1910, it's a large, three-storied, dark brown bricked building with ornate, white carved terra cotta exterior accents.

Originally settled by many Scandinavians, my Danish grandmother Alma lived in Mayfair when she was a child. In 1975, I took an apartment in the neighborhood. At that time The Heritage Center building housed Mayfair Junior College, an outpost of the City Colleges of Chicago. I attended college there.

When my "Granny Alma" came to see me in the first of several theatrical plays I was in during my two-year tour of duty, she informed me it was her grammar school. I did the quick math in my head and she would have been a student there during World War I.

The college moved out in 1976 and the building eventually became the non-profit center devoted to all things Irish that it is today. Every summer they sponsor the highly-attended Irish Folk Festival. There's music on temporary stages in the parking lot, theatrical and poetry performances, booth after booth of Irish-related products in the old hallways and classrooms, and food and beverages, adult and non, to be enjoyed by the throngs that attend from all over Chicagoland and beyond.

On the third Sunday of every month, the Heritage Center Genealogy Club meets in their library. Free for all members. We went online and joined for a year. Forty dollars.

We arrived for the February 2014 meeting and, as we were running almost late, skipped the elevator—which had been updated since I was a college student there—and took the stairs to the library on the third floor.

I felt I was contributing to the provenance of the grand old building as I frictioned off a few more molecules from the child and later all-ages depressions in the center of each stair, and rubbed a few more off the ornamental wood bannisters with my still-gloved hand.

Having driven crosstown after a few cups of tea, I also felt in need of a restroom. As Col headed for the library, I headed for the commode still marked "Boys" in the center of the third floor footprint. It was right across a short vestibule from "Girls". Over the years, none of the school buildings renters had removed the original designations.

Nor had they replaced the original grammar school urinals. They were set at a height for little tykes! I then remembered those holdover porcelain relics from my days attending college there, and from the annual festivals in years since, when by midafternoon the floor surrounding the flushable pisspots would become sticky-slick from the misdirected streams of Irishmen and Irish "wanabees" who'd been enjoying the Guinness, Harp and Smithwick's that for three days flows like water.

Sober and 5' 7" tall, it was fairly easy for me to contribute to the urinal's history without christening the linoleum.

This is a non-profit organization, keeping afloat from any available grants, contributions, renting the center for events to the general public, that sort of thing. Perhaps the expense outweighs the need, but I hoped someday they'd collect enough funds to "scootch" those urinals up a foot or so.

The monthly Genealogy Club meeting is a casual event. So casual that the moderator, a red-haired, mustached middle-aged man named Brian, did not even ask if we were members. We could've saved the forty bucks.

Col and I were probably the youngest in a group of eight or so—six of them women, who attended the Genealogy Club meeting that month. They all seemed to know each other. It appeared Brian's standard procedure was to go around the room to each, who would then report on any new findings and/or ask for help from others in the group.

These folks were working on their own, or a friend's or relative's, family tree. As newcomers, we felt it best to go last. That way we could also get a feel for what others were doing and sources they were using in their research. It quickly became apparent that this group might not be of much help. They were talking about Irish "Land Plats" and early 19th century church baptismal records. We weren't looking for Irish ancestors who'd come over during "The Diaspora" or who had never left Ireland at all.

The history we were seeking was recent by genealogical standards. This was much the same problem as I'd experienced at the Church of Latter-day Saints. We were trying to dig up people from at the most two generations ago. That's not genealogical study. It's detective work. But I wanted to learn from people who knew how to "dig".

When it became our turn, we explained the nature of our search and a little about what we had so far in our box of clues. Although everyone's ears collectively perked up when we first described our reason for attendance, any resources they suggested were already in our arsenal.

Brian said he didn't know of any records they had that might help us find a Chicago policeman about the right age. We were sure there were probably many "coppers" of Irish descent of that approximate age.

He did mention they had a set of books devoted to historical rosters of Chicago firemen. He also said that the Irish Consulate of Chicago has an extensive collection that includes records of immigrants who, over the years, have approached them for assistance with immigration details, connecting with others, finding work—anything that might help strangers in a strange land. He said the records were currently being stored in an off-site location.

That's not a good thing. There's no way they were going to let strangers rifle through their records and getting someone to dig through "bankers boxes" stuffed with files is time consuming; no one really has the time. We made note of both resources. I intended to contact the Irish Consulate to see what, if anything, they might have to offer and kept knowledge of the Chicago Firemen archive at the Heritage Center in my hip pocket for possible future use.

We told the group that when we concluded our search we'd return and update them. Optimistically hoping that our second visit would be within a few months, we thanked everyone for their support and advice and, after Col stopped at the "Girl's" room, we left.

Back in the car I couldn't resist asking. Col informed me that the girl's toilets were, though not of the taller seat height type, definitely not designed for ages "K through 8". When she mentioned that women never have any aim issues, I one-upped her with a reminder that they can't write their names in the snow.

So there.

Back at the ranch, I took a gander at the website for the Irish Consulate of Chicago and emailed their general info box with a very polite inquiry regarding my efforts to locate a long-lost relative of my wife and my hopes that they could be of some assistance.

The reply was not encouraging. It came from a person who did not even want to identify him/herself:

"I have sent your query to the Chicago Immigrant Support group.

They may be able to help, they will contact you.

The Irish Consulate Chicago"

I decided that this anonymous respondent was, as succinctly as possible, passing the potato along. I was the cyberworld equivalent of an unwanted telemarketer.

A quick look at the Chicago Immigrant Support website told me they probably did not have fifty-year old information in their coffers. Their function centers on helping immigrants now—in the 21st century. I thought it highly unlikely that, as the mystery man behind the mouse at the Irish Consulate put it, "...they will contact you."

I would probably have to chase them down, and I wasn't even being given a name there to start with. Like the Irish Consulate, the Chicago Immigrant Support Group went into my hip pocket for now. It was getting crowded in there. I never did hear from them. "Down the road" I noticed they had added me to their email spam list.

Thanks.

The Free Press

Then, we decided to let the magic of modern science help our search. Ancestry.com was running a "Special" on their version of a DNA test. Only eighty bucks. This was definitely worth a try.

We read a bit about the success stories. One guy who has been on at least one television talk show got extremely lucky with his birth mother search. She had already submitted her DNA to the same database. So when he submitted his, bells rang and flags waved. Mother found. End of search. A fairy-tale ending.

Without holding our breath we hoped we might be just as fortunate. When you stop to think about those odds, they are akin to winning the lotto. But, "you can't win unless you buy a ticket."

The way we saw it, even if we didn't hit the jackpot, we would at least be able to confirm Col's heritage and, who knows? Maybe a close-enough blood relative of either one of her parents had also taken a DNA test through Ancestry.com. We would then have something solid to work with.

We forked over the money and Col was sent a vial with markers indicating the minimum amount of saliva needed to fully analyze her DNA. Always the lady, she appeared a little embarrassed— even in front of her husband of what was now over fifteen years— at the task at hand, so I looked the other way as she released a good-sized goober into the tiny vessel.

She sealed it up in the pre-paid postage return carton and dropped it in the mail. The website claimed that the test results would be sent via email and to the internal message system associated with our Ancestry.com account within four to six weeks.

A few more weeks passed. I pondered where to go next. I didn't feel as if I'd hit a brick wall. I did feel I needed to broaden the effort but wasn't sure what avenues might glean a result. Any result.

Then, in mid-March, I was visiting long-time friends Connel

and Felicia "Pinky" McDermott. Pinky, whose nickname since childhood is due to her coral-toned complexion, is a journalist, with a weekly column in a free local paper available in Downtown Chicago and three neighborhoods: Bridgeport, Rogers Park and Lakeview.

She said she might be able to get approval from her editor to devote a few words or more about the search in her column and, if approved, Pinky would interview Col.

A long-overdue lightbulb illuminated my very balding pate:

It pays to advertise. Stop trying to only play "Columbo" and openly solicit what you are after.

Connel mentioned he'd seen people look for their birth mothers and other lost family members via Facebook. That sounded like a great idea. I had a Facebook page that I rarely paid any attention to. So did Col.

Our first task on Facebook was to create a public post. The post had a recent photo of Col with the text in the comment section. The text contained a plea from her: "Please help me find my birth mom" along with the particulars of her adoption. Her name, month and year of birth, her mother's name and age as given on the OBC, and the fact—or maybe fiction—that her mom returned to Ireland shortly after Col was born.

The post made no mention of Col's dire physical condition at birth. If we were lucky enough that the birth mother saw the post, we had to withhold some information to verify we had the right person, and we felt fairly certain that she knew there were medical problems when Col was born. We did not think the Catholic Home Bureau would make up that Col's birth mom was concerned for Col's welfare and was assured she would be placed with a family "willing to take on someone who would need surgeries and ongoing care".

Connel saw the post and his response was immediate:

"Paul, people have short attention spans, especially when it comes to the internet. Everything has to be in as few words as possible, and it has to be in the pic you post, not below it in the description or in the comment section. You have to do it in black marker on a poster board that Col is holding in front of her. Anything more complicated than that people are not going to bother reading."

We retooled our post to reflect exactly what Connel was suggesting.

Pinky got the approval from her editor. She interviewed Col by phone and the result was much more than a mention in her weekly column. It was a stand-alone article of about six hundred words. It included a "head and shoulders" pic of Col, in the hopes someone would recognize her as resembling a relative.

The article offered what little clues we'd started with, the OBC and the gist of what the Catholic Home Bureau had shared in their Non-Identifying Background History. The article quoted Col about the emotional and medical reasons for her desire to find her birth family.

Again, we were careful to not mention the exact date or any specific birth defects. Caseworker Marjorie Dooley's letter implied that the birth mother knew Col was born with a laundry list of issues. We had to keep those specifics in our vest pocket if we ever found or were approached by a possible birth mother. For all we knew, there may have been a few babies delivered by unwed mothers at St. Francis in October 1958.

We wanted to get the right birth mother. There was also the risk of a lonely septuagenarian reading the article and deciding to be Col's birth mom to fill a void in her own life.

It was a very well-written piece. Pinky included her email address for any readers who might have information to share.

Outside of a couple of people who emailed her mentioning investigative resources that we were already aware of, the article yielded nothing immediate. Zip, naught, diddley squat.

Or, did someone know exactly who Col was, and was unwilling to speak up?

In a way, it didn't matter. Between Pinky McDermott's article, our Facebook posts and the Ancestry.com DNA test results we were anxiously awaiting, I could smell we were entering a new phase of the search.

Someone out there, beyond her birth mother, whomever she tangoed with to create Col and her older brother, may very well remember something about what was considered a shameful event in 1958 in Irish Catholic Chicago.

And if the event was so shameful that Col's birth mother felt the need to use a false name on the OBC as well as the Adoption Decree and create a back story of "Non-Identifying Background Manure" for Caseworker Fran Cashman, we had to keep getting that Mary Margaret O'Brien name and fairy-tale out there so that maybe, just maybe, someone would recognize it as being a friend's, relative's, neighbor's... or maybe even their own, line of bullshit.

Chapter 4
worldwide.spittoon.com
Twenty-First Century Sherlocks

March, 2014. The DNA results were in.

Following are three of the responses received from an inquiry I created as Col and sent out, via the Ancestry.com internal messaging platform, to each of the three dozen DNA matches out of more than three hundred that showed up as being her closest relatives, possible 3rd–4th cousins:

"Hi Colleen,

This is Tim Sullivan and it is my family tree that I manage. You are related to me and my mother Nora (Connelly) Sullivan. My mom is from County Galway, specifically the Connemara region. So, you are related to us from County Galway 100%. My mother's ancestors have been there since people settled Ireland.

I see you write about Chicago and that your natural father could possibly have been a Chicago policeman. I am corresponding with an Ancestry.com user name MadDawgBobby (Robert Lynch), a retired policeman whose Lynch ancestors were all Chicago policemen. Some Lynches are from the area where my mother grew up so it is a distinct possibility you come from Lynches in Connemara. This Robert Lynch's people came from a village/area of Connemara called Lettermore.

If you look up the Griffiths Land Valuation records and the 1901/1911 Ireland Census online you will see Lynches in this area. Check to see how many people you are related through that have ancestors in Galway. Let me know if you have any more questions. My aunts, uncles and many cousins still live in Galway so I can help you if you need anything there as well! - Tim"

"Hello Colleen,

I checked our Family Trees and we do not have any individuals named O'Brien in our families. Of course we do not have the names of all the people in our families yet. Our relatives came from the west of Ireland around the Galway area. Good Luck with your search. - Heidi"

"Colleen,

I reviewed the close match yesterday and noticed that the names in your tree are all new to me and don't seem to match other matches that I have. You are related to me on my mother's side, as you matched her too, as opposed to my dad's tree.

My mother's Irish line came from Galway and maybe Mayo, specifically, Loughrea area and Inishbofin. The families immigrated from Ireland to USA in mid-1800s.

The Tierneys, Kings, Fords, O'Malleys, Connors, Nee, Lynch, Kelly, Crosby. Other DNA matches indicate Murphy, Walsh, and Pendergast. - Tina"

All remaining matches were shown as 4th–6th cousin or beyond. "Distant". I plugged in Colleen Mary Garrity Terrazino as the spittoon contributor. You can also include an email address for others to reach you, so I set up a Yahoo email account under Col's birth name from the adoption decree: Mary Eileen O'Brien.

Under her other possible birth name, Mary Ellen O'Brien, I set up a Facebook account. I did not hesitate to tell those I reached out to the reason behind the search. My gut said we'd now be better off, in bald-faced defiance of the policy I'd never followed anyway, that more people would want to help searching adoptee Colleen Terrazino/Mary Eileen O'Brien than not.

It was slightly reassuring to know that in 1958, Col's birth mother told Caseworker Fran Cashman the truth regarding herself and the birth father's heritage. The test showed Col as being ninety-six percent Irish and four percent "other U.K.". It would be ridiculously far-fetched that, by chance, all three hundred plus matches were from Col's maternal side. We were seeing genetic matches from both sides. We were new at this and had no idea if there were ways to determine what side these DNA cousins were from.

Fran had stated Col's birth mother was born and raised in Ireland, but we still did not know for certain that her birth father was born in Ireland. She wrote that the birth father was "of Irish descent" which, depending on how one interprets it, could mean he was born there, or he could have been born anywhere and had Irish ancestors.

At this point, we didn't care that much. We were seeking both. As Tim Sullivan's response was the most informative, I posed as Col and replied to him via the Ancestry messaging system. This time, I gave him a little more information about what we knew from the caseworkers.

We never heard back from him. Had "Col's" reply unraveled something for him, making him now quite aware of who she was seeking, maternal, paternal or both, and he didn't want to be the one to roll over and give either up? I felt I gambled and lost. I sent a message to "MadDawgBobby" Lynch—the Chicago police family connection Tim Sullivan had mentioned but received no response.

The Ancestry DNA responses that were most specific all mentioned counties in the west of Ireland: Galway, Mayo and Clare. Even among the distant relatives, more respondents mentioned Galway than any other. Still, that didn't mean Col's parents—or even her grandparents—were born in Galway. But for the moment we opted to keep it simple and hope we'd get lucky and that they were both immigrants from County Galway to the U.S., and that upon arriving they headed straight to Chicago.

Usually, someone who'd already "come over" and gotten him or herself established would become the conduit and way station, inviting siblings and others to join them until they got set up and the pattern would continue. You moved in with that relative/sponsor until you could have a place of your own.

This was a large component of how ethnic neighborhoods were formed. Yes, of course both presumably Irish birth parents could have been living in an Italian, Polish, German or any other neighborhood in Chicago. But I had to go with the odds and "play the favorites".

My astute knowledge of the Chicago area—now I saw the value of all those crappy driving jobs I'd held over the years, the 1940 Census, and what I'd seen thus far in the Criss Cross books, made it clear where these Irish neighborhoods in Chicago were when Col was born. I had some surnames to work with and was beginning to see the same ones repeated in connection with the areas of Ireland being mentioned.

It seemed odd at first that we weren't seeing the O'Brien name mentioned much. But all it takes is one marriage and surname change to bury the O'Brien name. How many 3rd–5th cousins have the same surname? When you stop to think about it, very few. I have cousins that carry the surname Terrazino, but they are first cousins. We felt we had a long way to go, but that we were getting somewhere.

Spreading Our Wings

In early spring 2014, Facebook "Mary Ellen O'Brien" joined several Facebook groups that are dedicated to adoption: The Adoption Rights Alliance, Adoption Truth and Transparency Worldwide Network, Adoptees In Search of Their Birth Family, Adopted Kids Looking For Their Birth Parents and Parents Looking For..., Birth Parents Looking For Birth Child, Family

Footprints, Adoptions-Adoptees and Birth Families Search & Reunion, and the Adoption Search Registry.

I was sure that if I kept digging, I could find even more groups for her to join. Some seemed to get more traffic than others. They all had rules about posting, usually regarding how often one could post or re-post that—once again read the instructions Bozo—I broke immediately. Any reprimands by those group administrators were kind. So long as "Mary Ellen O'Brien" didn't do it again.

Some groups do not allow professionals to advertise their services. The pages of others contained offers from "pros" who, for a price will find your birth family. On average, fees ranged from $1,500 to $3,000.

A lot of these professionals appear to be "skip tracers". Skip tracers usually work for insurance companies, debt collectors and the like. Their job requires they have access to information not readily available to the public.

They might be great at finding birth parents in America, but I had a hunch it would be more difficult and cost more for one of these search mercenaries to find someone overseas. We could've dug into our mothy, lint-filled pockets and paid for this, but we just didn't like the "Dog the Bounty Hunter" feel of it.

There are also many adoption "search angels" out there. This is someone, often a fellow adoptee who is adept at digging up information and offers to help a searching adoptee or, less often a natural parent, find their birth relatives. They do this out of the kindness of their hearts and the internet is chock-full of them. We would learn in the coming months how truly angelic they are.

Seven of the nine Facebook groups Mary Ellen O'Brien joined have their fiber optical roots in the U.S.. The other two, the Adoption Rights Alliance and Adoption Truth and Transparency, are Ireland-based.

The Adoption Rights Alliance is a "closed" group, limited to adoptees in Ireland or those directly connected to them. Col's was a slightly unusual case, in that she was born in the U.S. and there was a possibility her birth mom had almost immediately returned to Ireland, so "Mary Ellen O'Brien" was allowed to join. The members of both these groups are knowledgeable and politically active in Ireland.

When Col joined there was a great deal of activity in Ireland regarding the Mother and Baby Homes, what we in the States call an "orphanage". New revelations beyond the horrors that had been exposed in films and books like "The Magdalene Sisters" and "Philomena" were a regular occurrence. Town names like Roscommon, Bessboro, Tuam and others that since the late 19th century had contained these homes were on the lips of people well outside of Ireland.

If the caseworkers were telling the truth regarding Col's birth mother, Mom had it a lot better than the young women who got shipped off to these birthing prisons scattered across Ireland. Matter of fact, an unwanted pregnancy wasn't even an admission requirement. "Old School" Irish Catholic parents, intent on limiting the possibility of the sin and shame of their most attractive daughter ending up "with child" before marriage, would place her in one of these god-forsaken gulags just for being pretty, perhaps even to be eventually transformed into a nun.

What an odd blend of faith, social engineering and profiteering it was to have these girls working off the debt for their sensual sins by performing labor in the homes. Some were still in operation as recently as the early 1990s.

It seemed the general culture of Ireland was now 21st century in many ways but mired somewhere in the early 20th in others. And religious. Deeply, Vatican-ly, Roman Catholic religious.

Maiden Voyage

We'd only been to Ireland once. Col had often told me she wanted to go, and I'd never been either. Following brunch on Christmas Day 2006, I stowed two round trip tickets onboard a paper airplane and winged it across our living room to her.

The following May, we overnight jetted to Dublin, checked our bags at a hotel next to the airport, and took a bus to Dublin City Centre. We spent the day exploring the city: O'Donnell Street, St. Stephen's Green, the Ha' Penny Bridge, a casual cricket game on the Trinity College playing field. The next morning, we checked out and grabbed a rental car at the airport.

A virgin at Irish road rules, I wanted to avoid the added task of shifting left-handed, so I picked a car with automatic transmission. We drove west across the island's midsection on what felt like the wrong side of the road. That day, our ultimate destination was the city of Westport, County Mayo, on the Atlantic coast. We were to meet May Corcoran, a cousin of Col's adoptive father, Tom Garrity.

Not long after the Old World urbanity of the Dublin area vanished from our rearview mirror, the landscape quickly transformed to a sedate roller coaster of verdant hills. It was pretty much what I'd expected Ireland to be. Green. Lots of cows and sheep grazing in the fields, and the farmland is often separated by roughly four-foot high walls, built from home grown, no two alike stones or made of evergreen hedges that at the time held huge clusters of beautiful, yellow flowers. I would learn later that this plant is called "gorse" and is quite common throughout Europe.

What a friendly way of delineating your property from your neighbor's. High enough to discourage cows and sheep from attempting to scale or jump it, yet low enough for the average farmer to hop over to retrieve any strays, or chat across over morning tea.

The things that stick in one's head... Right around mid-trip we stopped at a small roadside pub for lunch. Whenever possible, when we stop to eat while traveling, we prefer to sit at the bar or lunch counter. It increases the odds of talking to others.

It was quiet, only a couple of "locals" at one end of a short bar. We took the other end and, not being too hungry, ordered only soup and appetizers to keep us both sated until Westport.

A small, elderly woman, probably in her early eighties, slowly strolled in. She wore the precipice of too much makeup and a perfectly tailored, Kelly green skirt and jacket adorned with a multi-colored, jewel-encrusted broach and stylishly fashionable hat, shoes, and a clutch—all green of course.

She had a peaceful, almost politely understated smile that didn't shift an iota as she acknowledged us with a head nod sweeter than a blushing ballerina's curtsey and pulled up a stool mid-bar. The tender had already readied her libation: a glass of Guinness. Not a manly, Euro-style half-litre that would have taken both her porcelain white hands to lift, but a ladylike 330ml "tulip" type to go with the rest of her impeccable outfit and matching demeanor.

I decided her husband had passed, their kids had their own by now, and this was part of her daily routine, her happiness germinating the soothing smile she now shared with us. Her well-soled heels probably landed in the same exact spots on each visit.

Usually when in a new country, bellied up to the bar with an obvious native only a few feet away, the first thing I want to do is strike up a conversation. Instead I preferred melding in her silent serenity.

As we left, I felt obligated to return her anonymous graciousness with my own macho Yankee masculine version of the head curtsey. I think she liked it. Even though we weren't actively searching at the time, I wondered if Col's birth mother was anything like this stately lady.

We drove on. The further west we headed, the still-dominant

hue of green was a little less saturated than the lands outside Dublin, and the terrain got a little rougher, hills and valleys less rounded, more defined. It was late afternoon when we rolled into Westport.

We knew that May's husband, Peter "Petie Joe" Corcoran, had passed away some years ago. Originally Petie was a farmer, but at some point, I think in the 1970s, he and May opened a Bed and Breakfast, a "B&B", in Westport. May now owned the Castlecourt Hotel. Col had booked online in advance and I had only given their website a cursory glance, not paying much attention to the specifics of the hotel or its amenities.

We pulled into the parking lot where, still not used to wheeling a car from the right side, I rubbed off the left rear hubcap on a curb. It was easy enough to pop back on, and I finished parking and checked in.

Apparently, the lodging biz has been good to the Corcorans! The Castlecourt is the centerpiece hotel in town with 240 rooms, 5 bars, 4 restaurants, a conference center, ballroom, swimming pool, spa, you name it.

We met May's daughter, Ann. I could not hazard a guess as to her age, but I'm sure Ann's older than she looks. Fairly small, slender, with close-cropped blonde hair and blue eyes, she reminds me of many an actress who's played "Peter Pan" on stage and screen. She's bubblingly energetic, always on the go, amiable and engaging. In conversation she always looks you right in the eye. En route to our room we met her brother Joe. It was obvious he was in the midst of a task of sorts, so it was quick hellos and handshakes.

It seemed Ann and Joe ran the day-to-day hotel operations. We sat in the dining room, quiet as it was midday, and had tea with her. She only had time for a quick chit-chat before heading off to her next task. She informed us that May was at afternoon Mass, and that afterwards she would be off babysitting for a friend in the area and would not be back until early evening.

Figuring we were on our own for dinner, we strolled around the center of town a bit to build our appetites and found a pub/ restaurant a short walk from the hotel. It was there that I learned a cheeseburger in Ireland usually includes a slice of what we in the States call Canadian bacon as a garnish—to them it's just "bacon" and our bacon is considered "streaked". And there's no need to order "chips"—their version of French fries—on the side because you get an ice cream scoop of nicely-seasoned mashed potatoes "gratis" next to your burger anyway.

After dinner, figuring we still had time to kill, we stopped in at Matt Molloy's. Molloy is flautist for the multiple Grammy-winning, traditional Irish band The Chieftains. They weren't playing in his tavern that night, but the place was crowded and a quartet was a pickin' and a fiddlin' away in a corner.

We found two seats at the bar. It was there that I learned the correct, physiologically safe, Irish way to drink Jameson whiskey from a man seated next to us, a talkative local of about thirty-five named Andrew, with his friend John, who barely spoke a word. Probably because with Andrew it would be tough to squeeze a word in edgewise:

As Andrew explained it, drinking any strong distilled spirits undiluted is a toxic shock to the human system. This is not a healthy or enjoyable experience and the reason downing a shot can often make one shiver.

In Ireland, whiskeys are served "straight up", often in a miniature pitcher similar to the crucibles used by a Catholic priest when performing Mass, and you're provided two approximately eight-ounce glasses, one of water and one empty in which to create the final product.

And something Andrew didn't need to include in his tutorial: Never ask for ice. I don't care if you know there's some behind the bar. It's as sacrilegious as squirting ketchup on your hot dog in Chicago.

Just don't do it.

You then mix booze and water in the empty glass to taste and to arrive at the correct ratio, which should be at 15% ABV (alcohol by volume) or less, slightly more than most wines. I assumed arriving at the correct percentage is a learned skill and figured I could eyeball the right maximum percentage. It did go down nice and smooth.

Every time. After a while, many sizzling brain cells began whimpering "uncle" in their pleas for mercy, and the remaining still clicking ones wisely realized I'd conducted this newly learned imbibing experiment enough times for one evening. We decided it was time to see if May had returned from babysitting.

Bidding Andrew and Silent John farewell and promising to look them up the next time we "came over", Col and I wobbled our way to the Castlecourt.

Boy, was Ann glad to see us. May had returned some time earlier and had already retired for the evening, but when she'd returned earlier from babysitting and couldn't locate us, she had sent out a search party.

They were so concerned that they called Chicago and talked to Col's daughter, Mary T in the hopes she would be able to reach us by cell phone. We had no international component to our phone service. Over an ocean away and now equally concerned for us, Mary T could be of no help. Next time that happens, they'll know where to look. Start with Molloy's and take it from there.

The next morning, we joined May and Ann for breakfast in the hotel restaurant. May, a very congenial woman in her early eighties, seemed thrilled that her cousin Tom Garrity's daughter was visiting "from the States".

Breakfast was buffet style, but an abundance of servers let nothing go unattended for a moment, and it was obvious the level of service was not just because we were dining with the owner. Everyone received the same stellar treatment.

There were eggs, "bangers" (sausage), brown bread, all manner of cereal, fresh fruit and yogurt. And something new to me called "black and white pudding".

Nothing like the sweet, gelatinous dessert, usually chocolate or vanilla, that I've always enjoyed stateside, it's a meat item. Miniature hockey pucks of seasoned minced pork, usually served in pairs, one black, one white. The black variety gets its color because it includes pork blood. It's not bad as a breakfast food. Hearty.

It appeared when it came to her family tree May had a sharp memory. Col had told me that she thought May was aware that her American cousin Tom and his wife Mary Agnes had adopted all six of the children they raised in Chicago. It probably slipped her mind because at one point she looked at Col and whispered to Ann, "I see the family resemblance."

After breakfast, Ann had to get to work. May wanted to take us sightseeing, and I offered to drive. Our first stop was Croagh Patrick, the famous perfectly peaked, stand-alone mountain that appears to be made of nothing but small to medium-sized rocks. With a statue of St. Patrick at its base overlooking Clew Bay, the croagh can be seen from much of Westport. I'd heard the truly religious follow the annual soul-cleansing pilgrimage of walking barefoot to the top.

Why do so many paths to self-realization have to be bumpy?

Anyway, following May's navigation, we headed out of town. At one point, I had to make a left turn from one two-lane, un-shouldered, hedge-strangled country road to the next. I was having such a good time that after completing the turn I forgot to drive on the left side. An approaching truck driver's blaring horn reminded me, and in the nick of time I was back to driving Ireland style. May's reaction was understandable:

"My God, you'll kill us all!"

I promised her that would not happen again. We arrived at

Croagh Patrick, and May stayed in the car while we took a walk to the base of the mountain to look around. The view of Clew Bay and surrounding area was spectacular. I took a picture of a woman and her probably pre-adolescent daughter, walking sticks in hand, beginning their ascent up the well-worn path to the summit. Both had on proper footwear to brave the stones. Hrrumph... Cafeteria Catholics.

When we returned to the car, May was in the back seat, slightly bent over and praying, her hands clutching a rosary. Apparently, my promise to drive on the correct side wasn't convincing enough and she was seeking supplemental divine insurance.

That night, May wanted us to join her at Petie Joe's, the "disco" named after her late husband. It's attached to the hotel, and the place was jumping. Flashing lights, mirror balls, and everybody was up and dancing to music I normally don't care much for. But I loved disco that night.

May looked happy and proud to have relatives from the States over for a visit. Suffering from what she described as a "bit of a sore throat", she said she was only going to have tea that night. I noticed that she was slipping bits of whiskey into it from one of those cute little crucibles. She'd probably trained Andrew at Molloy's.

The next day we met May's brother, Tommy. Little more than five feet tall, in a woolen tweed jacket and vest and a "tam" cap perched above a perpetually smiling face, he offered to drive us to the village of Killicroy, where the Garritys are from, just northwest of Westport. A couple of other cousins lived there.

Tommy had a unique driving style. He owns a small, "stick shift" sedan, perfect for the winding hilliness of the area.

But he doesn't like wearing a seat belt, so his solution was to drive with his left thumb pressed in on the belt buckle sensor to keep the alarm from chiming and interrupting the never-ending conversation. He only releases the buckle when he needs that hand to shift gears—and often he doesn't bother, or forgets to.

So this little car was rounding the switchbacked hills, often doing 60km an hour in second gear, its motor screaming like a banshee at 4,500 rpm. Tommy didn't seem to care. He never stopped smiling and talking, so I decided I didn't care either. At least he knew what side of the road to drive on.

We pulled up to an old home with a thatched roof. It had been modernized some over the years, but I guessed it was built in the late 19th century. We weren't there long, and I don't recall their first names, but they were a lovely older couple, and they were Garritys.

This was the first time I was in a home heated by turf, the byproduct of which I would soon learn is a sooty grime left on everything, even the glass of water I requested, which gave it a slightly peaty taste. Now I felt properly indoctrinated into the Irish culture.

I liked it.

We stayed one more night in Westport, relaxing and enjoying this quaint town on Clew Bay. On our third morning there, we bid Col's adoptive relatives farewell. They were fabulous folks and we hated to leave.

Our plan was to drive along the west coast of Ireland and spend a couple of nights at a Bed & Breakfast: A B&B I'd picked randomly online for price and location, the Bay Mist in Clifden, County Galway.

As we left Westport and headed south along the coast, leaving County Mayo behind for Galway, we felt like we were entering a different land than the postcard greenishness of shrubs and shamrocks most people associate with Ireland.

Even though we were driving along the Atlantic Ocean in May, the land was dry and rocky. It reminded me of parts of the western United States. We wound our way around numerous bays nestled in steep mountains peppered with off-white splotches that, until getting closer, we couldn't discern if they were sheep or more rocks. Oftentimes they wound up being a combination of the two.

Motoring closer, we sometimes had to wait for them to cross the road and realized the sheep were "branded". Not American style with a red-hot iron, but a splotch of spray paint on the hindquarters of their authentic woolen coats. Red and blue seemed to be the most common colors. I guessed they alternate through the countryside. If the farm next door has one color, you take the next. Keep it simple.

We drove on through these dry hills, dotted with "famine houses", one-room stone homes with a window or two, a fireplace and nothing else, that are no longer occupied, but remain as monuments to the population-decimating "potato famine", the Diaspora of the mid-19th century.

Later, I would learn we were in the region of Connemara. The land appeared much less arable than other parts of the country, making the challenges of scratching out a living greater. A prevailing ocean wind seemed to be constant. I bestowed a sort of underdog status upon this area, feeling a visceral beauty that eclipsed postcard perfection. If you could make it as a Connemaran, you could make it anywhere.

Our three-day stay in Clifden was probably the most relaxing part of our journey. We had no timetable. We checked in at the Bay Mist, and each day we would just walk around the area, breathing it all in. After dinner, we'd find a tavern with live music and spend a little time there before walking back to the peace of the B&B.

As we were in the general area, we drove south one day to County Clare and visited the famed Cliffs of Moher and O'Brien Castle, just in time to observe TV crews covering the fatal fall of someone who had ignored the warning signs and gone off the edge.

Sunday morning we drove southeast to the airport at Shannon to drop off the car and fly home. Somewhere in our travels since leaving Westport, that same danged hubcap had fallen off again.

When I noticed the remaining three had been secured with strong nylon "cable-ties" to their respective rims, I presumed this aftermarket solution was due to a common issue on that make and model and figured they wouldn't charge me for it.

To the tune of fifty euro, I'd figured wrong.

We had the good fortune to visit when the Irish economy was in pretty good shape. It would not be long after our return that things would collapse globally, starting in 2008.

From everything we heard later, Ireland suffered just as much as the rest of us in 2008 and beyond, perhaps even more. But the Irish seemed to have a cavalier attitude about 2008. They enjoyed the boom that started in the late 1980s, but many felt that if things went bust, they would not be much worse off than they were prior to the upswing. They were always prepared for the worst and grateful for the present.

I guess being invaded many times over oh... several centuries, topped off with a crushing diaspora would tend to make one appreciate whatever one is handed.

Irish Turnkeys

Back to 2014 Chicago. We were plugged into Ireland through the internet, especially through the Adoption Rights Alliance, the "ARA", and there were a lot of people offering help.

It was from these ARA "angels" that I'd learn how to procure a copy of an Irish Birth Certificate, a "birth cert", through the General Registry Office, the "GRO". It could be done online, for about fifteen euro. But for a few euro a copy could be requested by someone physically visiting one of their offices.

One who would prove to be a true angel in that regard was Kathy Finn. An active member of the ARA, Kathy lives in the Dublin area and makes periodic trips to the GRO and will pull a birth certificate or two for seekers like Col and me. In the coming months, she would be an invaluable help, not just for pulling birth certs, but in explaining the culture:

If Col's "birth mum", or "bmum", or simply "bm" as ARA members call them, had returned to Ireland after giving up Col and lived there since, we were getting an idea from Kathy of the mindset of who our bm likely was: an "old school", Irish Catholic woman. To someone like her, there was likely overwhelming guilt and shame over getting pregnant out of wedlock. Then there was the guilt of not raising that child and the strain of keeping the event buried deep for decades.

If that's how she felt. Yes, that was how an Irish Catholic woman of that generation would usually feel. But we didn't know Col's bm from Eve or Adam, what kind of person she was or if this had any lasting psychological effect on her. Might have turned a good girl bad, or a bad girl good, any shade in between or none of the above.

While sitting in eternally snarled Chicago traffic or parked in front of the TV after dinner, we'd create various possible scenarios of who or what type of person Col's birth mum was and where her life had gone. I kept hoping that our imaginations would steer us towards some angle we had not yet considered. Long shot? Sure, but at this point what wasn't?

Using Ancestry.com and familysearch.org, I started looking for Mary O'Briens of the appropriate age born in the areas of County Galway mentioned by Tim Sullivan and the other respondents. I was a little surprised that, even with that common a name, there were only about thirty in total. But, how could I possibly connect the dots between one of these Mary O'Briens and Chicago of the late 1950s?

At this point, I had no idea. But I knew I had to do what I was doing. Go with what you're given and see what roly-polies wriggle up after lifting those chunks of turf. I was hoping that one of the Mary O'Briens was one I'd found on a travel manifest as having emigrated in the second half of 1956, the approximate time frame that the caseworkers had said our bm came over. If I could connect that dot, I planned to then try to figure out if she still lived in the same area.

There was a chance she was still on the same property, even if she had married. It may have been part of her dowry.

Land in Ireland is extremely valuable. For some families, it's the only thing of real value they have, and it stays in the same families for multiple generations. They've had to fend for themselves for so long on this small island. It's their source for so much. It supports crops, dairy cows, sheep for food and textile, turf for fuel and grain for Guinness and Jameson.

If our bm did go right back in late 1958 and later married there, online Irish Marriage Certificate databases are not nearly as available as in the States, making it tough to figure out her married name, especially since I had absolutely no idea what it might be. But the land belonging to her family that probably carried her maiden name, supposedly O'Brien, might be a little easier.

Until distant cousin match Tim Sullivan mentioned them both, I had no idea what the Griffiths Land Valuation was and that the Irish Census' from 1901 and 1911 were available online.

I checked them both out. The Griffith Land Valuation is exactly what it says it is. It's a plot by plot listing of land in Ireland and its estimated value, in rural areas based mostly on soil quality, and often having to do with its value from "turf". At this point I wasn't sure if this would be of any use to the search.

But the 1901 and 1911 Irish Census records, especially if the ages provided of the bm's birth parents, Colleen's maternal grandparents, was correct, could be helpful once I had a solid lead or more to work with. Especially the 1911 Census, when Col's bm's father, sixty-four years old in 1958, would have been about sixteen years old, and her bm's mother about ten. They would both be in that census. Somewhere.

I started scratching around a little in the 1911 Census to see how it works, and in comparing what I saw with the birth and marriage records online with GRO it was apparent that, especially in the farming communities back then, the potential spouse pickins' could be slim. It appeared it was not uncommon for brothers to marry sisters from the next family down the road and vice versa and that could continue for more than one generation.

Making the search even more confusing was the common practice when naming one's children. It wasn't unusual for a firstborn male to be given the name of a parent or grandparent. There were preferred first names, often of other ancestors, given to subsequent offspring.

Here's an extremely exponential hypothetical example of just how mind-twisting this would become down the road of our search:

If John Murphy had three boys and four girls and his neighbor Patrick Duffy had three girls and four boys, and all fourteen of their collective offspring had been given first names according to these time honored traditions, and the Murphy men married the Duffy women and vice versa and everyone followed the same general formula when naming the next generation of Duffy/Murphys, you might wind up with a lot of folks with the same first and last names in the same area.

This was not limited to Ireland. I saw the same patterns when, just out of curiosity, I tried to piece together the history of my maternal ancestors in rural New York and Pennsylvania during the American Civil War.

But this search was for anything but the heck of it. Whether or not she returned to Ireland, our bm probably wound up marrying and raising a family. Statistically, the majority of those who give up their firstborn child, regardless of nationality or religion, bear another child within five years.

Perhaps she was right up front about it and told her husband

and children. Given her age and upbringing, my hunch was she may have told her husband about the event before they wed, but they probably kept it secret from their children.

That limited the number of people with any knowledge of Col's birth who might still be around. The supposed brother would be at least eighty. The birth father would be closer to ninety than eighty. And her bm would be closer to eighty than seventy. If she was alive and we found her, did we really want to blindside her at this stage of her life?

Something inside both of us felt it was worth rolling those dice.

Chapter 5
The Leader of the Pack
A Shoe That Fits...Almost

By late April 2014, distant DNA cousins were still responding and mentioning surnames and it looked as if both Col's parents had roots in Western Ireland. But none of the genetic matches had ever heard of a relative named Mary Margaret O'Brien. Or another possibility: no one wanted to admit it.

Then, Col received a Facebook message from a retired Chicago school teacher living in Florida, Gwen Burke Brennan. She's the mother of a friend of Col's niece, Chloe. Col's Facebook post seeking her birth mother caught Gwen's eye. She had been piecing together her own family tree and ran across a March 2012 obituary for a Chicago man named Anthony Burke.

Gwen believed Anthony was a cousin of her grandfather. Born in County Monahan, Ireland, which I immediately noted is not in the West, Anthony's obituary said he was survived by among others, his wife Mary (nee O'Brien) Burke.

I did some digging and determined that Anthony Burke was born about 1928 and Mary O'Brien Burke about 1938, correct approximate ages for both Col's birth parents. A significant age gap was not uncommon for Irish-born, or Irish American couples of that era. The men often married when they were established and could provide. Many were at least thirty years old when they "settled down", usually marrying younger women with plenty of childbearing years.

It was not unusual for an unmarried couple to give up the child they had not intended to conceive, only to wind up marrying each other later. It was also possible that this was the right Mary O'Brien, but that Anthony Burke was not Col's birth father.

The obituary listed the Burkes as having four children, oldest to youngest: Mary, James, Kathleen and Michael, and internet phone listing searches indicated her daughter Mary was about five years younger than Col.

We decided to take a somewhat-in-the-dark shot and send Mary O'Brien Burke a letter of inquiry. If we lucked out and it was her and she responded favorably, great. We had nothing to lose.

It appeared she was living with her daughter Kathleen in Bridgman, a town in Southwestern Michigan. Col's letter would not be at all accusatory. It would simply ask her if she was her bm. Plain and simple:

"Dear Mary,

My maiden name is Colleen Garrity. I was born in late October, 1958 and given up for adoption to The Catholic Home Bureau of Chicago. I was told my birth mother's name is Mary O'Brien. If you are my birth mother I want you to know that my adoptive parents were wonderful in bringing me up and that I bear no ill will towards you for the decision you made, and I would like to have contact with you.

Thank you for your time,

Colleen (Garrity) Terrazino"

She received an immediate response:

"Dear Colleen,

I'm sorry I'm not your mom. I emigrated here in 1956. I hope you find her.

Sincerely,

Mary Burke"

Up until that point, we had no idea if Mary O'Brien Burke was an immigrant or born in the U.S.. Yet here she was denying being Col's bm, and in the same breath telling us that she came over the same year as the woman we were seeking. And when I held her note next to Col's OBC, which was supposedly signed by the bm in 1958, the handwriting was similar.

Suddenly, I wanted to learn as much as I could about Mary O'Brien Burke. Phone records revealed an address of 11503 South Talman Avenue on Chicago's Southwest Side as being where the Burkes had lived for decades. It made sense. After her husband passed, she probably sold the home and moved in with her daughter Kathleen, in Bridgman.

I asked Col to write another letter, thanking her for her time and, in case this was her bm, to pull on her heart strings a bit with photos of her and her children. I also made certain that Col mention we had a few friends in Dublin helping us out. If she was Col's bm, she would now know that we would eventually get to the bottom of this mystery, so if it was her, she might as well "fess up" now.

I also wanted to find out where she was from in Ireland. Along those same lines was one simple request:

"There are so many Mary O'Briens that we have been looking at. If you don't mind, please let me know what town you are from, so we can cross you off our list."

Once again, the reply was immediate.

"Dear Colleen,
My name is Mary O'Brien, no middle name. I am from Galway. I have four brothers and one sister. I met my husband in 1957 and we married in 1961. You do resemble a girl I used to see Celi dancing at The Irish American Heritage Center. That was when I lived in Chicago over twenty years ago. I hope your friends in Dublin are able to help you.
Sincerely,
Mary (O'Brien) Burke"

Galway. And yet another example of handwriting that looked similar to the signature on Col's OBC. I also wondered why Mary found it important to mention she had no middle name. Neither of Col's letters mentioned the middle name Margaret on the OBC. If she was our bm, perhaps she'd added that name in 1958 as a deflection.

Maybe she discussed Col's letters with one or more of her four kids, who did a little snooping of their own and found one of Col's Facebook posts, or even Pinky McDermott's newspaper article, both of which said we were seeking a Mary "Margaret" O'Brien.

Or she was innocent and just a person trying to help us.

Didn't matter; either way things were getting curiouser and curiouser. It didn't take long on Ancestry.com to see what I was pretty certain was her GRO birth index information. The birth was registered in Galway City in the 4th quarter (Oct.–Dec.) of 1938, making her the approximate age to be Col's bm.

Our bm, according to Caseworkers Cashman and Dooley in their letters to Col, had three siblings and Mary Burke said she was one of six. However, we'd been told by some that it was not unusual for the Catholic Home Bureau to actually provide seekers with "Non-Identifying Background Bullshit" to try and throw them off. Was that the case here?

Or had Col's bm provided Fran Cashman an altered back story in 1958? We had no way of knowing. All I could do for now was keep looking deeper into our strongest lead to date to see what fell out of these now fifty-six year old trees.

Soon after, I told my friend Andy Miller about the search. We met in the mid-1980s, doing theatrical projects. At the time he was writing and directing. I did some production work for him.

When I showed him Mary O'Brien Burke's handwriting sample and the OBC he saw similarities, but said if I was interested, he'd ask his mother, Kit Miller to have a look at them. It was hard to say no to that offer.

Though now retired, Kit was the past Midwest Chapter President of the International Graphologists Association. Fancy for handwriting. She had testified in court cases because of her expertise in handwriting analysis. Kit said she'd be happy to have a look.

While I waited for those results, it was time for another visit to The Newberry. It was mid-spring and the weather had improved enough to skip public transit.

When the next convenient day came along, I whipped up a peanut butter and pickled jalapeno pepper—even better than pickle—sandwich on some kind of healthy bread, tossed it in a bag with some tortilla chips, a carrot and an apple, both organic of course, and a pocket-sized spiral notebook for scribbling notes. I stowed it all away in the handlebar bag of my trusty two-wheeled steed, more recently baptized Mary Ellen Cannondale, and pedaled downtown.

Different staff was on duty this time, but they were equally helpful and I had what I wanted right away: Chicago White Pages residential phone books from 1956 through '61, and the always valuable—but unfortunately only two available—Criss Cross books from 1953 and '55:

It looked as if the Burkes did not live on Chicago's Southwest Side when they first married. They lived on the West Side, on Lamon Avenue, in Chicago's Austin neighborhood. In her second reply, Mary O'Brien Burke had stated she and Anthony married in 1961. I did find it a little odd that Anthony Burke had a phone listing at the Lamon address in 1956 through '59, but not in '60 or '61.

Records indicated the Burkes moved to South Talman Avenue in '63, which made sense. By '63, Chicago's West Side was changing, and very quickly. It was becoming predominately African American.

When I mentioned to Gwen Burke Brennan where Anthony lived until at least '61, she was floored. Austin was her old neighborhood. It was where she grew up and lived until she married. She offered to ask around about Anthony Burke to find out if any of the folks her age remembered anything about him.

Links to a Distant Past

The Archdiocese of Chicago website showed that the most likely parish for the Burkes to worship when they settled on the Southwest side was St. Walter, at 117th and Oakley Avenue.

I'd never been to St. Walter, but I had known one of their former pastors, Father Francis Cisnieski, for as long as I could remember. He was a close family friend from Rogers Park, the neighborhood where my parents lived before we moved to Bridgeport.

"Father Frank" was a priest at St. Jerome's on Lunt Avenue, little more than a block from the "Abundant and Tasty" where I'd overdosed on carrot cake courtesy of waitron Angie O'Brien. The guy was like an uncle to us.

He remained at St. Walter until health issues forced him into retirement before passing away in the early 1990s.

I browsed the St. Walter website pages devoted to their various clubs: Holy Name Society, Youth Ministry, Women's and Seniors Club and more. No mention was made of the Burkes, but most of the posts and pictures were more current. I decided to pay a visit to the church to see if I could learn anything about them, without anyone knowing it was them who interested me.

Within a few days I'd carved out a Monday morning to visit the church office, along with the perfect ruse to get a peek at something that might aid me in this search. I brought along a camera with a lens capable of taking "macro" closeups and arrived at the church office midmorning.

Everything was typical. The office was connected to the rectory of this grand old church which, like St.Ignatius in Rogers Park and many others in Chicago, appeared to have been built in the early 20th century. I confidently sauntered into the office. The woman at the front desk was likely born mid-20th:

"Good morning. I'm Paul... Paul Terrazino. I grew up in Rogers Park."

A white lie. We'd moved away when I was six months in the womb. I stretched the truth:

"Father Cisnieski was a priest at St. Jerome's when my parents got married. He was a great guy. My family was wondering if you've any old pictures of him that I could make copies of. He and my parents were very good friends."

"Oh, Father Frank! I wasn't living in this parish when he was pastor, but it sounds like he was very well-liked. I have the 75th Anniversary Memorial book from 1983. There might be photos of him in it."

I took a seat in the vestibule and breezed through the magazine that had been created for the '83 event. There were a few pictures of Father Frank scattered throughout the glossy fifty or so pages.

To make it look good, I took a picture of one that showed him best. No photos identified any Burkes, and the only mention made of them was on a list of those who'd contributed money to the event. I gave the book back to the receptionist.

"Thanks very much. There was only one picture worth taking."

"Did you try the office of the grammar school? It's right around the corner."

"No, I hadn't. I'll head over there now. Thanks again for all your help."

St. Walter's Grammar School. The Burke children probably went there. I headed around the corner to the main entrance of the school, thinking up a new back story along those fifty yards. "Father Frank" would no longer do.

I gambled that the receptionist at the rectory had not preempted my arrival with a phone call to the school office. If she did, differing back stories might get me shut out. I approached the waist-high reception/security counter, where I was greeted by Julia, a woman about the same age as the rectory secretary. Stretching the truth would no longer do. It was time to slather on the bull:

"We moved to this neighborhood just after I graduated from grammar school, but my brothers and sisters went to school here and they would like very much if I could take some pictures of their friends to send them. They all live in different parts of the country now. I'm the only one who still lives around here. Does the school have any yearbooks or anything else I could take pictures of?"

"Sure! Right around the corner, take the hallway to the left. We have graduating class pictures on the wall going back to the 1960s."

"Thanks! I won't be long."

The hallway had all the annual class photos I would need. Father Frank was in a lot of them. Quick mental math told me that the Burke's oldest, Mary, would have graduated grammar school in about 1974.

Sure enough, there she was. And there was James, in 1976. I also found the youngest, Michael, who'd graduated in 1981. But I didn't see Kathleen, who would have been between James and Michael.

Mary and Michael were easy enough, but my problem with James was lighting. The fluorescents in the ceiling were reflecting on his photo and any adjustments I made created glare from the sunlit windows. I really wanted his because boy, did he resemble Col's son Thomas.

I didn't want it to seem like I was making a big deal out of a couple of old grammar school photos. I had to get a step stool or something, so I could stand higher and change the angle of reflection in my favor. I did not see anything nearby that would work and I did not want to start requesting things—and possibly involving more people, in this venture.

With my professional-looking camera gear, I was already getting strange looks from passersby in the hallway. One guy, whose casual garb indicated maintenance or engineering, but for all I knew was the current pastor in "street clothes", even commented:

"Now, don't go posting these on Facebook."

I did not need this kind of attention.

Julia was busy and didn't notice me leave as I ran out to my car to grab the plastic "milk crate" that houses rags, snow brush, a quart of oil, hand tools, a corkscrew/bottle opener and other travel essentials. I dumped the contents out in the trunk and made it back to the hallway.

She didn't blink when I said I'd forgotten something in the car. Her counter was high enough that if I held the milk crate low with one hand and swung my arms equally as if they were both empty, I could probably walk right by her and she wouldn't notice.

It worked. I took the picture of James that I needed. I still had not found Kathleen's. Who knows, maybe she was sick on "Picture Day", and thanked Julia as—fake empty arm successful again—I walked out.

Back home, I dug up my notes and sure enough, Kathleen Burke would have graduated in '78 or '79. I wanted to go back to St. Walter's School and make sure I had not just missed her for some reason, but that might raise eyebrows. Unless I created more back baloney.

In order for this new addition to my growing list of crap to seem slightly believable, I decided to wait a few days before returning. I also hoped Julia would not be on duty this time. I guess instead of merely hoping I should've considered temporarily rejoining the flock by praying:

"Hi Julia, remember me?"

"Yes, of course." She curled one eyebrow into a nonverbal question mark.

Uh oh.

"Well, I got home and sent the photos of my brothers and sisters and their classmates to them, and I realized I hadn't gotten one of my youngest sister Patrice's class. I'm sure you know how a sibling can get when he or she feels slighted!"

Even with the little wink I added for good measure, she wasn't impressed.

"Sure, go ahead. You know where they are."

"Thanks. I won't be long."

Her brow didn't budge. I felt her eyes boring holes in my shoulder blades as she tracked me until I was out of her periphery.

This time, I did find Kathleen Burke's. It was in the '78 class picture and I hadn't caught it before because it was quite faded from sitting on the wall in direct sunlight for thirty-five-plus years. The name, "Kathleen Burke" was so faded I could barely make it out.

I took the best picture I could—thankfully no milk crate—and got the hell out of there. Julia was busy on the phone and I did not wait around to thank her. No matter what happened, this would be my last visit to St. Walter's. I had definitely worn out my dance card with her.

Back home, I was able to load the photos into my computer and blow them up for a better look:

The youngest, Michael, did not look at all like his siblings. His hair was almost blonde and his face was rounder, ruddier. Mary, Kathleen and James all had dark hair and longer, narrower faces. I pointed this out to Col. She mentioned that it was not uncommon for a couple who had given up a child for adoption, perhaps because they weren't married yet, to adopt a child at a later date to raise as their own, as a sort of "pay back" for their lust-filled sin.

It was reaching a bit, but did the Burkes adopt as a way of paying back for the child—in this case possibly Col—they had given up when they weren't ready to raise a family in '58?

This was definitely a scenario I was creating to suit my needs and had to be taken with a grain of salt. Blood-related, natural siblings don't always look alike. And these were not the greatest of photos. Grainy, sun-washed and smaller than the do-it-yourself photos we used to take in the booth at a mall or movie theater, I didn't want to put too much stock in them.

But the resemblance between James Burke and Col's son Thomas was unmistakable. On the other hand, Gwen Burke Brennan put it best when I messaged her a pic of my stepson Thomas and James Burke side-by-side:

"I see resemblances. But we're Irish. We're all cousins and we all look alike."

I would get a well-deserved beating for saying something like that, but Gwen is as Irish as they come and therefore allowed to poke fun at her own people.

Gwen suggested I have a look at the Facebook page of their other son, Michael Burke. Amongst his photos were two of who had to be his mom, Mary O'Brien Burke.

Her face did appear to have the same general shape as her three darker-haired kids, Mary, Kathleen and James. I didn't see any resemblance between Mary O'Brien Burke and Col or either of Col's two children. If The Cabbie back in 1984 recognized Col because she was a ringer for her bm... well then, based on what I was seeing, Mary O'Brien Burke was not Col's.

Additionally, Col's two kids are the product of her first marriage to Michael Schmidt. Col didn't have any pictures of Michael's ancestors for comparison. So I could look at photos of these possible relatives until the sky turned paisley and unless someone really jumped off the page and was a ringer for Col— really a ringer—all this didn't mean much.

But I did not want to scratch her off the list based on appearances only. I needed to keep digging about this lead. It was all I had. If I kept digging, maybe another clue would surface that would point towards, or against her.

It was time to reach out again to former schoolmate and lawyer, Bill Finch. I wanted to find out about the apartment building that Anthony Burke lived in prior to, and what I guessed were the first few years after, marrying Mary O'Brien in 1961. I gave him the address, 436 North Lamon Avenue, and he promised to get back to me.

It didn't take him long. By day's end he emailed me two transactions. Anthony Burke apparently lived as a renter in the building until he and Mary O'Brien Burke purchased it, not long after they were married.

Phone records had already shown me that the Burkes moved to 11503 South Talman Avenue in about 1963. However, they did not sell the apartment building at 436 North Lamon Avenue until 1968. They sold it to a man named Willie Gates.

Not that it mattered, but Willie Gates was probably African American. By 1968, Chicago's West Side was almost entirely "Black". This would've been fairly typical for that chapter of demographic history. The only other item I found interesting was that Mary O'Brien Burke was listed as a co-owner of the property.

Had the purchase of their first home been made possible because Mary had a dowry to help with the down payment, or more? It would be hard to figure that one out. But a closer look at Mary O'Brien Burke's relatives in Ireland might be worth it.

I reached out to my Facebook friends with the ARA in Ireland. They suggested I have an online look at the Griffith's Land Evaluation records of Ireland. And, in true Irish "help your neighbor" fashion, ARA member Sandra O'Hara did the work for me.

She said the records indicated that Mary O'Brien came from a farming family that, though perhaps not mega-rich, had done pretty well based on the acreage, number and type of livestock they owned, and the fact that they had at least one boarder listed as "domestic help" in the 1911 Census.

So, perhaps Mary O'Brien did have a dowry that Anthony Burke used as part, or all, of what was needed to get them started "living the dream" in the United States. This was all well and good, but none of it did anything to support or nix that she was Col's bm. It was just information. Stuff.

I needed to keep digging. I asked Bill to pull any real estate records for what became the Burke's home for about fifty years: 11503 South Talman Avenue. A couple days later, he emailed me the result. Nothing unusual here. They bought the place in early 1963. He told me that I could find out more from the Cook County website.

I went online and was able to see that the home did change hands in August 2012, a few months after Anthony Burke died. It was sold to a Victor Ramirez. Not long after, Mary moved in with her daughter Kathleen in Bridgman, Michigan.

I had to dig at this family from another angle. Online, Ancestry. com showed an index listing for Anthony connected to the United States Immigration and Naturalization Service. The index gave little information, but it did have a six-digit number and a year: 1954.

The United States National Archives has a Federal Records Center at their regional office on Chicago's Southwest Side: 7358 South Pulaski Road. I could order Anthony Burke's naturalization record online and it would be mailed to me. Only five dollars, but I opted to drive there and get it. I felt as if I might be on to something and I didn't even want to wait for United States Postal Service, "USPS" snail mail.

The next day, I drove out to the Records Center, where I was greeted by a helpful young woman behind the counter. I gave her the name and index number I wanted. She researched and provided me with the only paperwork related to Anthony Burke. It was his Petition for Naturalization. I paid the required five bucks and was so anxious to see it I read it walking back to my car, nearly tripping over a crack in the asphalt:

Anthony Burke was born October 9, 1928, in County Monahan, Ireland. He arrived in New York City as an immigrant on January 17, 1949, aboard the S.S. Brittanic. After living in the U.S. for the required five years, his Petition for Naturalization was completed and signed on September 10, 1954. His address at the time was 859 North Keeler Avenue, Chicago.

That address was a few blocks from the Landon Screw Machine Company at 4500 Augusta Avenue, founded in 1908 by my great-grandfather, Edward J. Landon. Anthony Burke listed his occupation as "polisher-steel". Was it possible he worked at Landon Screw Machine? Was this a sign that I was on to something here? Or was my imagination connecting coincidental dots that meant nothing?

Among many other fascinating operations, Landon Screw Machine did polish steel and other metals as one final step for many of their products. Then again, in a city the size of Chicago in the mid-20th century, there were probably lots of factories polishing steel. I had not talked to anyone at the company for almost twenty years.

Just for laughs I emailed them. In 1933, Edward J. Landon had sold the business to a different family, and it had been years since I'd visited the factory. I explained my connection to the Landons and inquired if they had any record that might help me find out more about my wife's long-lost relative, Anthony Burke.

I did not hear back, but didn't feel it necessary to pursue them any further. An employer is not required to hold records that long. My name-dropping and founding family pedigree didn't matter.

What did strike me as significant was the physical description that Anthony Burke entered on his petition: 5'8" tall, with a "ruddy" complexion, blue eyes and red hair. That did not at all fit the description of Col's natural father given by her bm to the Catholic Home Bureau. Both letters stated that Col's birth father was 6'1", weighed two-hundred pounds, with a fair complexion, blue eyes and brown hair.

This could mean a few things, among them that Anthony Burke and Mary O'Brien did not conceive Col before they were ready to marry. Mary O'Brien got pregnant by a tall, strapping policeman, gave Col up for adoption, and then married Anthony Burke in 1961 and they started their family. Another thing to consider would be that Mary O'Brien, in her interview with the caseworker, fed her a back story about the natural father that was total horse shit and Anthony Burke was the birth father.

Or, I was barking up the wrong tree and Anthony and Mary O'Brien Burke had nothing to do with Col. Mary simply happened to fit the bill because of her name, age, and date of immigration from a county in Ireland—Galway, the same Irish county as Col's genetic bullseye.

I felt I had to dig some more. There had to be something out there that would lead me to an answer. The first thing was to see if Federal Records in Chicago had a naturalization petition for Mary O'Brien Burke. If she emigrated in 1956, she probably would have applied for U.S. citizenship in 1961 or 1962.

After digging a bit via Ancestry.com and familysearch.org, I found the naturalization index listing with a number for Mary Burke. She should have been eligible for naturalization in 1961, yet she didn't apply until 1964.

Now, I was curious as to why she waited approximately three years after becoming eligible before applying for citizenship. At my next possible opportunity, I headed to the Federal Records office on South Pulaski Road once more.

Five bucks and a gallon of gas later I had a copy of her Petition for Naturalization. Mary O'Brien Burke was born March 27, 1938, in Carna, County Galway, Ireland, and was described as 5'4" and 122 pounds, fair complexion, blue eyes and brown hair. She married Anthony Burke on August 2nd, 1961.

Her arrival date and means of arrival to the U.S. did solve one minor mystery, one that meant I could check off a box from the earliest stages of the search:

Mary O'Brien Burke was my Pan Am Mary who, along with Roger Park Mary, were the only two Mary O'Briens on travel manifests headed directly to Chicago in 1956. She emigrated to the U.S. on October 24, 1956, and was checked in by the Customs Office in Detroit, Michigan. She had arrived on Pan Am flight 634 from Shannon, Ireland.

My Helper's Little Mother

A week later, I received a call from Andy Miller. He informed me that his mom, Kit, said that because fifty-six years had passed between the time Col's bm signed the OBC and the two letters Mary O'Brien Burke had sent Col, she could only give it a seventy percent probability that the samples were from the same person.

She did say that the handwriting in the first reply, in which she denied being Col's bm, indicated deception, and that in the second letter, when she gave some information about her town and siblings, indicated anger or irritation.

I considered seventy percent to be okay, especially when added to the other evidence that pointed in Mary O'Brien Burke's direction. As for the opinion that there may have been deception and even anger evident in the handwriting, I didn't put too much stock in that. Maybe she thought Col would go away and having to reply a second letter pissed her off.

And maybe she did have something to hide. Maybe she also gave a child up before she was married, but it wasn't Col. Anything was possible.

What I found most curious about her Petition for Naturalization was that time frame. She emigrated in 1956. She would have been eligible five years later—late '61, and could have applied and been done with the entire process by spring of '62.

Why did she not apply until 1964? Was she Col's bm, and were the caseworkers telling the truth and did she go back in late '58 and then return to Chicago at a later date, complete the required time in residence here and then apply for naturalization in 1964? Did Anthony Burke not have a phone listing in Chicago in 1960 and '61 because he was in Ireland, courting Mary O'Brien, and did they marry there?

The petition only gave a marriage date, not a location. I didn't feel any of this conjecture was a stretch, but it seemed a difficult theory to prove. I shared my thoughts with Gwen Burke Brennan. Her common sense reply brought me back to earth:

"It wasn't a hard and fast rule that you had to apply for citizenship as soon as you possibly could. Maybe she was busy with being a newlywed and then a new mom and just didn't get around to it."

I was beginning to feel that Gwen thought there was a good chance Mary O'Brien Burke was not Col's bm. Or at the very least she thought the odds were less than I thought. I was in the "low nineties". Andy Miller was, including the evidence beyond the handwriting, right around sixty-five percent. Was I shoehorning Mary O'Brien Burke into this role?

I felt the best thing to do was keep digging with what I had. That meant, for starters, seeing where Anthony Burke and Mary O'Brien married in 1961. It was not a given that it happened in Chicago, but I would have been surprised if it had not.

Tradition has it that a marriage usually takes place in the bride's church. I figured the odds were better that Mary and Anthony were from the same or adjacent neighborhoods or parishes. I got online with the Archdiocese of Chicago website and created a list of the most likely parishes that corresponded with their West Side addresses. The two that fit best were St. Martin dePorres and St. Francis of Assisi.

The West Side had changed a lot since 1961. The congregations had changed, too. And it looked like St. Francis of Assisi was either closing or getting ready to. I emailed St. Martin de Porres' contact address with my inquiry, stating only that I was doing "family genealogy" and that the Burkes were relatives. They didn't reply. There was no email address available for St. Francis of Assisi, so I called the only phone number that was listed and left a voicemail.

No reply. I went back to the Archdiocese of Chicago website and found a phone number to call. The woman who answered informed me that many church records were now housed at the Archdiocese office on the Near West Side. I was told it would take a week or so, but if I submitted to her by email the groom name and bride's maiden name, she would search any available records.

Gwen Burke Brennan suggested I go to the Cook County Building in Downtown Chicago and inquire there. If they were married in Cook County, there had to be a record. Rather than make that trip, I let my fingers do the walking and logged on to the Cook County website. If a marriage is fifty years or older, a copy of the application can be had for fifteen dollars.

But when I searched for a marriage record for Anthony Burke and Mary O'Brien, nothing came up. What could this mean? Unfortunately, there were a few possibilities:

The records are not guaranteed to be absolutely fool-proof. Theirs could have fallen through the cracks. Maybe they got married outside of Cook County, or even in Ireland, and that's why Anthony Burke had no phone for a year. But I had not found his or her name, maiden or otherwise, on any travel manifests or flight lists.

I found the church closest to the O'Brien farm in Galway, Cashel Church in Carna, and posted on the Adoption Rights Alliance Facebook Page:

"Do any of you live, or know anyone who does, near Cashel Church in Carna, Galway?"

One woman replied that she was not too far and would be happy to stop by the church office to see if they had a marriage record for my suspect couple. I thought it over and declined her offer. This is a rural area, everybody knows everybody, and online Irish phone directories showed Mary O'Brien Burke still had relatives living in the area.

I was concerned that someone on the church staff knew the O'Briens, or was an O'Brien. The last thing that I wanted was for Mary O'Brien Burke to be alerted someone was snooping around in Carna about her. She would know it had to do with Col and, if she was her birth mum, that would probably really tick her off and the consequences could be disastrous. And if she was not, I would feel awful if this innocent woman were to learn she was the subject of an investigation.

About a week later I heard back from the woman at the Archdiocese of Chicago office. She could not find any marriage record for Anthony Burke and Mary O'Brien in any of the churches I had given her.

Col and Gwen Burke Brennan suggested something that might fit: If a woman is "not pure"—not a virgin or had a child out of wedlock, the marriage might take place as a very private event in a chapel adjoining the church, and that record might not be included in the regular church record. Or, the marriage would not take place in a church at all, but again, as a very private event officiated by a priest, in the home of the bride or groom or even a relative. Or it would be a strictly civil event and have no religious component at all, in which case all would be struck by lightning.

Then, just for laughs, I tried something that I will forever kick myself for not having thought of sooner. On Ancestry.com, I had gotten into the habit of trying slightly different spellings of first names and surnames. When one searches these type of sites, what is usually shown is only an index created by a transcriber, someone who looks over what are often handwritten chicken scratches from days of yore. Typos and errors are possible.

I tried searching a marriage with different vowels, and there it was:

Anthony B-E-R-K-E married Mary O'Brien on August 2, 1961. That was the only information available online. I created the required letter, added the fifteen dollar check and mailed it off to the Cook County Genealogy Department.

Within ten days I received a copy of the marriage affidavit. It listed information I already had, and it gave Mary O'Brien's address when they applied to marry: 7509 West Coyle Street, Chicago. That's in an area of Chicago's Northwest Side.

So, even though they lived miles away from each other in Chicago, somehow they met and married. Nothing unbelievable about that. The Archdiocese of Chicago website showed the nearest parish to her Coyle Street address: St. Julian.

I called the parish office and told the woman who answered that I was doing genealogical research about my family and was interested in a copy of the marriage certificate for them. She took my phone number and promised to call within a few days.

I picked the right church. She did call back, and offered to read the information to me. Good enough. Paul Burke was one witness to the marriage. Earlier digging had told me this was Anthony's brother. I didn't recognize the name of a woman who was the other witness.

Always the Teacher

Now it was time to go back to The Newberry to determine who, according to the '53 and '55 Criss Cross books, lived at 7509 West Coyle. Yes, Mary O'Brien, if she emigrated in 1956, would not show up in them. I wanted to know who lived at that address, even if it was, at best, a year before she arrived.

A couple of days later, with a hankering for something more

yin than the yang of jalapeno, I tossed a peanut butter and banana—an Elvis Presley Special "hold the bacon" sandwich—on some sort of healthy bread, tortilla chips, a carrot, an apple, yeah, blah, blah, blah both organic and a single-serve yogurt into my laptop bag and headed for the CTA Red Line, arriving at The Newberry midmorning. The usual pile of books was delivered to my desk:

The only names that came up in the Criss Cross books for that address were a William and Abigail O'Reilly.

The Chicago White Pages phone books from '53 through '57 showed much the same. I did find it interesting that the O'Reillys had a phone listing at the West Coyle address through '57, and then they disappeared from the book. There was a good possibility they moved away and rented or sold the home.

But to whom? I'd already learned from Bill Finch how to get the "pinumber" for any address in Cook County, so I had the one for 7509 Coyle in my notes. But, the County website only provided data going back thirty years.

I needed to know more about the history of this property from 1957 through 1961, when Mary O'Brien met and then married Anthony Burke, but I didn't know how. Might as well head down to The Newberry vendetteria and enjoy lunch while I pondered things.

God bless Gwen Burke Brennan. Just as I sat down to dine, she called to ask how I was doing. I gave her a quick explanation of my current conundrum. Her timing could not have been better:

"Oh, Paul! Did you know that in the basement of the County Building they have all of those records? I stopped in there years ago and was able to see the whole history of my Dad's home on the West Side. The hours are basically nine to four during the week, and sometimes it's busy and you have to wait. But you should be able to find out what you want there. Look for the Recorder of Deeds Office."

If I hustled and got back through the turnstyle within a few minutes, my original train fare would not turn pumpkin, and it would only cost two bits to get to the County Building. I ignored my grumbling belly. Reliving the King of Rock n' Roll's eating habits could wait.

Chapter 6
Move over, Robin Williams

The Schmooze Strikes Again

I had to shag ass down to the County Building ASAP. Staff was likely limited midday, when they probably staggered lunches. I wanted to do a quick dig there and then eat.

Bolting from The Newberry, I half-jogged to the subway stop, making it just before my initial fare expired. I was further blessed with "Rock Star" commuting when the train pulled into the station as if I'd ordered it up personally. Thank you, Elvis.

I was downtown by 11 am. It was Friday and I figured County workers were more likely to be in a good mood with the weekend right in front of them. I hoped that the number of others doing property searches for tax, business, real estate, legal and other purposes would not be too outrageous.

Unless it was vital, I wouldn't want to be digging around in the belly of this beast on a Friday morning.

And the real estate records are, indeed, nestled deep in the diverticular bowels of a twin-headed, money-devouring dragon. The central office of Cook County, Illinois, which wraps its greedy arms around Chicago and many of the city's suburbs, occupies the same building as Chicago's City Hall, taking up a rectangular half-block right in the middle of "The Loop".

The ornate, marbled, pillared and gold-leafed common lobby has brass-doored elevator banks lining both sides. Anyone familiar with Chicago area political history would find this fitting. For well over a hundred years the County and City have enjoyed an incestuously unholy relationship.

In a twisted way, sharing a building makes sense. It's more comfortable to just walk back and forth with sacks of untraceable green-backed payola without having to brave our often inhospitable climate.

The Cook County Recorder of Deeds Office is on the first floor of this massive, tall-windowed early 20th century structure. I inquired with the gentleman at the front desk of the Recorder's area, right off the lobby. He struck me as a true Grinch of a low-level bureaucrat as he gruffly grunted me down a winding staircase to the basement.

There, in a large triple-classroom sized, low-ceilinged room, were file cabinets of various types and vintages containing the property records for the entire known history of every piece of land in Cook County.

My Holy Grail, replete with an inner earworm of angelic eunuch cherubs in full voice.

Large, wide metal drawers in various institutional colors—grey, olive, beige, much like those seen in a draftsman's or blueprinter's office, are stacked about forty inches high, probably to make it easier to spread out the massive ledgers within. They're ganged together in whatever configuration works, back to back, side by side, creating aisles and makeshift kiosks that, when I looked at the numbering system on the placards adorning each drawer, held a sequential rhyme or reason that meant nothing to me.

It was obvious the few people I saw with those large books spread out in front of them, their noses buried in whatever they were digging for, were fellow citizens who understood the secret code in this secluded urban grotto.

I had to know how to crack the code. These were governmental workers, and I needed to befriend one. I didn't want to get the wrong person to teach me. Time to eavesdrop.

A narrow, chest-high formica counter with a few vintage computer keyboards paired off to monitors with even greyer whiskers was personned by a large, burly male in his thirties and a short, pleasingly plump Hispanic woman in her mid-to-late forties.

Both wore powder blue "lab coats".

Using an old, well-worn wooden bench that was within earshot of them, I pretended to organize the contents of my laptop bag that I had already organized during that ten minute train commute. I did need to make sure the insulated tote bag that housed my lunch had not turned vertical during that short, rattly underground trip. Nothing worse than a peanut butter hemorrhage.

The woman was helping a guy who, based on his overalls, fancy phone and briefcase, appeared to be a general contractor or home builder. Her accent said she was probably first-generation Chicago with "Tex Mex" or maybe even "Mex" parents. If need be, I'd play the part of the charming, "blue-eyed diablo" her parents had always warned her about.

But the more I eavesdropped, the more it sounded like this would be a piece of cake and I wouldn't have to bat as much as an eyelash. This chick had to be half-Jewish. She was a true "mensch".

I approached the counter. The name plate on her work smock said she was "Connie S." I decided she was either Consuelo Sanchez or Constance Schwarzburg. I knew to not commit the cardinal sin of being overly chummy by greeting her right off the bat by name. Too familiar too early can backfire.

"Hi! I understand I can see property records down here? I've never done this before. Can you help?"

"Do you have the pinumber?"

Another true Chicagoan.

"Sure. 7509 West Coyle, Chicago. Here ya' go."

I gave my yellow legal pad a 180 degree swivel and she copied from my notes to an index card. I pointed to a few other self-scrawled addresses that interested me.

"I have two, maybe three other addresses I might want to look at."

She didn't even look at them.

"OK, honey. You have others you want to look at? Take it

from me. Get all your eggs in one basket. The first thing we have to do is find out the lot numbers by matching them to the pinumbers and addresses. We'll create an index card for each."

"If you don't have the pins for those you need to head up to the third floor to get 'em. Take the stairs up to the lobby. Take the elevator to three, go through the double doors on the county side and you'll see a hallway leading to a drinking fountain. Go past the fountain, make a left and you'll be on a walkway. Along that walkway is an open area with a counter on your left. There's two computers that should both be logged on to our website. Use either one."

"On a day like today, you probably won't have to wait. Determine your pinumbers, jot them all down, come back and I'll show you what we do next, sweetie."

Honey? Sweetie? I was "in like Flynn".

"Thanks."

"But I might be at lunch. If I'm gone, whoever's here can help."

"I'll bear that in mind. Thanks again."

I found it odd that with obvious internet-connected gear on her counter, it wasn't permissible to just look up the "pins" right there. Oh well, our tax dollar hard at work. Gotta' feed that dragon.

Not wanting to lose Connie only to be stuck with—who knows?—the Grinch's basement County counterpart, I casually strolled to the doorway until out of her sight and, ditching the elevator bank for the stairs, dashed up to the third floor. That meant I had to rearrange Connie's directions a little. I only took one momentarily wrong turn.

Neither computer was in use, and the process was easy. I was back downstairs in about ten minutes, almost sighing audibly when I saw Connie wasn't yet on lunch.

She swiveled her monitor around to show me the process. This involved using the pinumber to find the onscreen page that would, literally, be a bird's eye line-drawing view of a few, or more, square blocks of city.

You then have to find the address and determine which subdivision and lot number(s) apply to that address. That gives you a series of numbers and page number(s) which then get matched up to one of the file cabinets, and which massive book of the dozen or so within the dozen or so drawers of each cabinet contains the information for that property.

Then, pull the right book and go to the page number you want. Once you find the property, the records are chronological. Sounds easy, right?

Not exactly. The toughest part seemed to be making absolutely certain you had the right plot number—that everything I would be viewing would be for 7509 West Coyle and not the house next door, or maybe part of an adjacent lot that had been divided at one point along its history.

That part of the process was something that Connie did on her screen. After that, digging up the right ledger in this huge room full of file cabinets full of drawers full of them was not so tough.

Every entry of the thirty-odd since 7509 West Coyle was built in 1921 was handwritten. And each time it was in a different hand, using different utensils—pen, pencil, felt-tip pen—and it was obvious at times those making the entries didn't care if things were completely legible or not. But what usually got entered clearly was the transaction number.

Once I had the book and page and saw the information, there was an opportunity to view books containing additional documents about the transaction. These huge books are nothing more than a list of the date, peoples involved and type, according to any number of secret abbreviations in one column. Connie gave me a printed list of what those abbreviations stood for: Sale, mortgage release, etc..

For 7509 West Coyle, it looked as if William and Abigail

O'Reilly bought the home from a Martin Schlemmer in 1955. Then a Patrick O'Grady and his wife Sarah bought the home in '61. I jotted down both transaction numbers.

The next step was to fill out a request for both down the hall, where someone would pull the microfilm for them and pass them off to another room, where I could retrieve the films and then use one of the many microfilm readers in that area to have a look at an image of the actual documents.

Upon entering the microfilm reading room, I picked up the faint odor of vinegar. I was famished and it got me thinking of salad dressing, but otherwise I paid it little attention. I would learn later I was smelling the acetate-based film decomposing. This is known as Vinegar Syndrome.

I wanted to know who else lived at that address when Mary O'Brien gave it as hers in 1961, when she applied to marry Anthony Burke. The images they brought out for me indicated it was the O'Gradys, and that they had just bought the home in April, and Mary O'Brien was living there in August.

Did the O'Gradys rent the home from the O'Reillys, starting in 1957, and did they later decide to buy it in 1961, and was that why the O'Reillys no longer had a phone listing after '57? Was Mary O'Brien living there, as a family friend or boarder, when Col was born in '58? Hard to tell. But when she lived there in August of 1961 it was probably as a boarder to the O'Gradys.

There were O'Gradys who were Facebook friends with Mary O'Brien's sons and daughters, and Irish records found on Ancestry. com showed the O'Grady surname in the same area of Carna in County Galway as the O'Brien farm. With a name as common as O'Grady, that could have been pure coincidence.

Now that I had a handle on how this type of dig worked and an even more audibly growling stomach, I left and, to lessen the possibility of prosecution regarding eating on the CTA's immaculately clean—yes that's sarcasm—trains, skirted the rule a bit by inhaling lunch in a few gulps as I rode home.

Back at the ranch, online digging revealed obituaries for William and Abigail O'Reilly and listed the names of their three children. More digging revealed two had obits of their own. The oldest, Christine, was born in '51 and she passed away in 2008. Next was Raymond, born in '53, who'd passed in 2011. Only the youngest, John, was still living. He was born about '56, and I found an address and phone listing for him. It was in Iron River, Michigan, a town in Michigan's Upper Peninsula, often referred to as the "U.P.".

I persuaded Col to send a letter to John O'Reilly in Iron River, Michigan. In it, she said only that she was seeking a long-lost relative named Mary O'Brien, that her research showed that she may have lived with them on Coyle Street when he was a toddler and, even though he may not have had any personal recollection of her, if he had ever heard his parents or older siblings talk of Mary.

For the price of a stamp, I felt we had absolutely nothing to lose. I also felt we would probably not hear back from John O'Reilly. And we didn't.

Cashing in Our Chips

By the summer of 2014 we were at a true standstill—not even spinning our wheels. Stopped cold. If Mary O'Brien Burke was our bm it seemed there was nothing we could do about it. She would take her secret, if there even was one, to her grave. A denial is a denial. Her generation would bury an event like this so deep that it would be as if it never happened.

Perhaps she was Col's bm, her family knew all about it and knew we were on to her, and they agreed with their mom that she should simply be left alone. I imagined a collective quotation from all four of them:

"Colleen, in your letter you said your adoptive parents provided you with a wonderful upbringing. Let it go, leave our mom alone and go away."

On the other hand, I knew it would bother my conscience if I were to deny being a natural parent, knowing that my birth child was continuing to spend additional unneeded time and resources.

It was time to let this lead rest. Until we came up with something that positively identified Mary O'Brien Burke as Col's bm, it would probably be best to set her aside for now. And to keep right on digging as if she was not.

A couple of weeks later, it was suggested we contact "CIS": Confidential Intermediary Services of Illinois.

A Confidential Intermediary would be allowed to see the sealed records of the original adoption agency—in Col's case the Catholic Home Bureau, and any other sealed court records pertaining to her case, to try and determine who an adoptee's birth parents are. If successful, he or she would try to contact either or both birth parents.

By law, without written permission, the intermediary cannot share anyone's identity with any of the parties involved. I went to their website and snooped them out a little bit. CIS is a branch of Midwest Adoption Services, a for-profit adoption agency in Des Plaines, a Northwest Suburb of Chicago. Their CIS division is financially subsidized by the State of Illinois, and there is no fee for that service.

We had always wanted this to be a personal quest, with Col reaching out directly to one or both of her birth parents. But, after much consideration, we decided to contact CIS and begin the proceedings.

In Illinois, for a Confidential Intermediary to be appointed, it must be approved in the same jurisdiction as the adoption, in this case, the Circuit Court of Cook County. A judge had to determine that Col had good cause for the intermediary to unearth these skeletons. We figured that for medical concerns alone Col would qualify, and we had been told that the court had been increasingly more willing to make a positive determination without grilling the adoptee. Col didn't even have to be present for the hearing.

Col contacted CIS and they linked her to the attachments containing the document she would have to file, along with—that money-sucking monster is insatiable—a nominal fee payable to the Clerk of the Court of Cook County. She was also told that if approved, her case would be handled by CIS Intermediary Kathryn Decker. The court would then put the request into the court schedule for a hearing, and the presiding judge would determine if Col's case warranted the time and taxpayer expense of the intermediary services.

We did not know how long it would take for our request to be heard by the court. I contacted Bill Finch. He worked in the same building and offered to hand deliver the request for us.

I don't know if Bill used his influence or not, but within a few weeks our request got "on the docket" and was heard and approved by—what a name—Circuit Court Judge Ponce DeLeon.

Not long after, Confidential Intermediary Kathryn Decker contacted Col by email and set up a phone call. In the call, Kathryn explained that she would try to find either birth parent. If successful at locating both, she was only allowed to contact one of Col's choosing.

The best outcome would be a birth parent willing to waive anonymity and wanting Kathryn to share his or her identity with Col. If not, Kathryn would then ask if that parent would agree to an anonymous exchange of medical information.

If she couldn't locate either parent, or if she found that one, or both, had passed away, but she did locate any children of either, she was allowed to reach out to one from each. In the case of any children, it was up to Col to decide which child Kathryn would try to contact. We provided Kathryn with all the information we had on our only solid lead, Mary O'Brien Burke.

A Better Bucket

We then learned a rather interesting fact from Gwen Burke Brennan: It was her understanding that the Ancestry.com DNA database is slightly more U.S. centric than its competitor, 23andMe. 23andMe is limited in that it does not provide the search platforms and wealth of data that Ancestry.com or familysearch.org does, but Gwen felt it was more likely we would find closer relatives in Ireland if Col submitted her goober to them, and she offered to treat Col to the test.

After receiving it by mail, Col, politely as always, turned her back to me, made her contribution to the vial and mailed it to the 23andMe spittoon.

As we waited for those results, I started trying to find a "Copper Bar", a tavern frequented by policemen, near the Burke's parish, St. Walter, on the far Southwest Side. It was a long shot, but I wondered if a policeman from their parish fit the bill as birth father. Not knowing where to begin, I contacted friends who are, or were, Chicago coppers, but most of them were from other neighborhoods and police precincts, and could be of no help.

Another of those coincidences that makes one wonder came along. One of our good friends from Canaryville, Denise McKinley, moved to Florida years ago. Every summer, she comes back to Chicago to visit. A meeting place and time in Bridgeport or Canaryville is always pre-determined, and many of Denise's friends, including us, get together to catch up with her over food and drink.

The venue selected for the 2014 soiree turned out to be nowhere near Bridgeport or Canaryville. Tommy's Place on 122nd Street and South Western Avenue, barely six blocks from St. Walter's. Denise knew nothing about Tommy's. She picked it because a former coworker of hers worked there. Other than that, none of us, including our mutual friends, knew anyone from that neighborhood.

It was as if my prayer for a bar in that neighborhood was answered just as I had started looking for one. We met Denise and others at Tommy's. It didn't change the oddness of it, but it turned out Tommy's wasn't a "Copper Bar", and there was no new information to be had.

About five weeks later, the results were in. Within the 23andMe system we were able to see and reach out to natural relatives of Col's whose DNA was in their database.

Two looked promising: a man named James McManus, who lived in the Providence, Rhode Island area, and a woman named Mary Dennison of Sparks, Nevada, both shown as 2nd–3rd cousins. There were also about thirty 3rd–4th cousins. From there on, the rest were all labeled "distant".

I sent internal 23andMe messages to McManus and Dennison, and to the thirty-odd closest others. Many answered with towns, villages, and areas of Ireland that their ancestors were from. But neither McManus nor Dennison replied.

Geographically, their responses were much more telling. Some had also submitted DNA to Ancestry.com. We recognized a lot of the same surnames and usernames of matches. There was a high concentration in the south and west of County Galway.

The 23andMe DNA test was, like the Ancestry.com test, autosomal. Therefore we still didn't know who was related to Col's birth mum or dad. We only knew they were related to Col. Tim Sullivan had said he was certain he was related to Col through his mother.

That's because Tim's father was from a different part of Ireland. The concentration of DNA "hits" was high along the west coast of County Galway, where Tim's mom hails from, and again in the area just north of Galway City.

Were both of Col's parents from County Galway? Sure looked like it. Did her birth parents know each other on "the auld sod" before emigrating? That would be tough to answer just yet.

And guess who else's goober was swirling around in the 23andMe bucket? Mad Dawg Bobby! Robert Lynch, the man Tim Sullivan mentioned as being from a long line of coppers who, like Tim, has roots in the western part of County Galway.

He came up a 3rd–5th cousin with 23andMe. In sending out the messages, I didn't notice because I'd seen so many Irish surnames that my eyes were spinning like a slot machine. This time, Mad Dawg reached out to Col.

I replied as her, not bothering to mention "I'd" messaged him months earlier via Ancestry.com and he had not replied. No harm. No foul.

"Colleen" started messaging him back and forth via the Yahoo email address we had set up for the search under Mary Eileen O'Brien.

Mad Dawg turned out to be a real character. Retired from the Northwest Suburban Arlington Heights Police Department, he was in his late sixties, but apparently robust. Into Aikido, and according to one pic I found on one of his profiles it appeared he flew airplanes.

Acting as Col, I mentioned that "...my husband Paul's brother Bill and his wife" are very much into Aikido, operate an Aikido school in their area in northern California, and recently spent time in Japan, studying at one of the famed Aikido schools, called "dojos". Mad Dawg said he had been there recently to study under the masters, too. Of course he wanted to know which dojo. I asked my brother for the name and passed it along to him.

He never replied whether it was the same dojo. It would have been freaky if it had been, and with my penchant for putting too much stock in the feeling there are no coincidences, I almost felt better at this point that he didn't answer. Like a true copper, let's keep it to the facts. "Dragnet's" Joe Gannon would've approved, Officer Mad Dawg. Good call.

The Lynch family in the Chicago area has so many members who plied or still ply their trade as law enforcement types that they could probably have a Fraternal Order of Police Lodge dedicated solely to themselves.

Bobby attached some pics of his ancestor Mary Greeney, who he thought Col resembled. I saw what he was saying. There were similarities in the general facial shape and chin. The towns and villages he mentioned his ancestors were from were in far western County Galway and off that same coast, on Inishbofin Island.

Now armed with this new information about Col's genetic heritage, I couldn't resist—just for rhythmic laughs, coupling it with her misspelled middle birth name. She was now "Eillen of the Islands". A "selchie", the mythical, "dark Irish", half-human, half-seal of ancient Irish lore.

Col was amused. She swims only slightly better than me. I tread water like a boulder, flailing arms windmilling in a downward spiral as I plummet to the depths. And her physical appearance is the opposite of the dark-haired folks of Celtic legend.

Maybe our mysterious "Galway Girl" was pure selchie, and Col was her half-breed daughter. Our bm had commiserated with a "fair" Irishman and Col popped out brown-haired and blue-eyed, a dud in the selchie world, and that's why Col was put up for adoption.

Having had my fun with this, I decided these Lynch connections could be set aside for now. Mad Dawg Bobby seemed to have shared all he knew about his DNA ancestors. It didn't appear there was a lead in the lot.

So... "Colleen" kept reaching out to DNA connections. Looking for an O'Brien. Looking for anyone who might remember an O'Brien or, for that matter, anyone, regardless of surname, who had emigrated to the U.S. after WWII and then returned home. She met many distant cousins by email and message systems of Ancestry.com, 23andMe and a third data-base, FamilyTreeDNA.

O'Brien was, probably, the least common surname of all. But, here and there, an O'Brien branch of a family tree would be revealed to us by a distant cousin who invited Col to browse over theirs.

Many of the stories shared by these DNA cousins were similar: Grand or great-grandparents who had emigrated to the U.S. between the mid-19th and early 20th centuries. Almost all from Counties Galway or Mayo. No one had anything to share that caused as much as a raised eyebrow. There were no solid connections to Chicago at all.

And there was even a Mary M. O'Brien on one of those trees we were privy to. Born in 1937. Perfect. I did a little digging online. Her birth had been registered in the 4th quarter of that year, in Galway City. She had brothers, sisters, other relatives. I contacted Jim Cahill, the creator of that family tree, who shared with me that this Mary M. O'Brien had moved in 1956:

To the great beyond. He wasn't sure what had taken her young life. This took the immaculate conception concept to a level I couldn't wrap my head around. So much for her.

Accessorizing For a Beard

It was by this point in the search that I started to notice some changes in me that had me wondering:

With the exception of those who knew us personally, in all of my internet communications—email, Facebook, messaging platforms within websites, I had acted as if I was Col.

I felt I would get more sympathy and get a lot further if the folks I was connecting with thought they were reading Col's texts and not her husband's. At first, I didn't expect this to be a big deal. For my "beard" to be successful, I just had to make sure I didn't accidentally sign off using my real name or refer to myself or Col in an improper tense, or use any phrases or words that are historically considered "male".

Sometimes it could get complicated. I did find it entertaining when any of the women I was messaging with via Facebook groups or websites would start bashing and slamming men in their related comments. I went along with it.

These folks I was communicating with had an impression of what type of person they thought Col was. But they were actually learning what the version of me pretending to be Col was like. A couple of the "blokes" even seemed to take a shine to Col and I could tell they were trying to determine through our cyber communications if I—what'd I tell ya', Col—was single and available.

I resisted the urge to lead them on, only to then crush their dreams after they started having fantasies about my cute Celtic bride. Would've been fun, but I needed these people. It was a bizarre feeling that would get more intense as time went on.

I started thinking like the person I had created. Occasionally, long after I was done working on the search for the day and it was safe for me to remove the beard and be myself again, I would catch myself continuing to think like my feminine alter-ego.

Much like a method actor forced to shake off his character when not in the role, was I even worse off? Would I wind up in therapy, like the master improvisor Jonathan Winters, because the feminine persona I'd strapped myself with was taking me over? Winters had many funny characters up his comedic sleeves. His "in drag" curmudgeon, Maude Frickert, suited me more than Dustin Hoffman's or Robin Williams' cross-dressing roles.

It never got the point where I considered slipping into a cocktail dress, but something in midnight blue, almost sheer with spaghetti straps but thicker, linguine-gauged, would have been my first choice.

Chapter 7
Valentine's Day
Payback Time

Five weeks later, Col received a call from Confidential Intermediary Kathryn Decker. She had found the man who she believed was Col's birth father! All she could legally share was that he had passed away within the prior ten years and left behind three children: two boys and a girl.

She offered to contact one of these offspring, who would possibly be Col's half or even full siblings. Col declined, telling Kathryn that for now she'd take a pass. If her birth father had passed away, and if Col's conception took place when he was married, she didn't want to upset his children and, if she was still alive, his widow. Col told Kathryn she felt it best to wait and see what might turn up in the bm search, and take it from there.

I immediately set about doing as much as I could with the information Kathryn Decker had shared with Col in their brief phone conversation.

The only thing that fit Mary O'Brien Burke was that, like the birth father, Anthony Burke had died within the prior ten years. But, if Pan Am Mary Burke was the birth mum, this meant Anthony was off the hook as the birth father. The Burkes had four children, two of each gender. Col's birth father supposedly had three, two boys and a girl. Any scenario that would change any of this involved creating dots just so they would connect. The Burkes would remain in their cubbyhole of a stalemate.

I went online and found the website for the union representing Chicago police officers, the Chicago Fraternal Order of Police, Lodge 7. The home page has links to their "Departed Members" section, where I could search for police officers who had passed away.

Of those ten years, 2005 and 2013 were missing. And each year's list was only that—a list of names and ranks. I then took each name to Legacy.com and searched the obituaries.

There were shortcomings in searching this site and scouring obits. The possibility existed that the birth father passed away in one of the missing two years, 2005 and 2013. It was also possible that there was an entry error or the birth father had a surname that didn't stand out as being Irish.

Moreover, some people stipulate in their will that they don't want an obit published upon passing. This site was only for Chicago cops. What if Col's father was a suburban cop, or in some other law enforcement agency? It wasn't even a requirement for a Chicago copper to be a member of F.O.P. Lodge 7.

But I felt I had to do it. If he was on that list and I made the match it would be worth it. I would then have a name to work with—I know, good luck. Even though it was tedious I didn't mind.

It didn't go too badly after I determined a system as efficient as my feeble mind could manage. I bounced back and forth between the F.O.P. Lodge 7 and Legacy.com websites and came up with two who had the right offspring combo:

According to his obituary, retired Chicago policeman James O'Donnell's age at death indicated he was, within two years, the right age to be Col's birth father. The church and funeral home were in Norridge, a suburb a few miles south of Edison Park, Pan Am Mary O'Brien's neighborhood when she lived on Coyle Street prior to marrying Anthony Burke in 1961.

Because the obituary listed O'Donnell's parents' names, I was able to match them to what I figured was the O'Donnell family in the 1940 Census, when they lived in Norwood Park, a Chicago neighborhood sandwiched between Edison Park and Norridge.

There was James, listed as one of their sons at nine years old. The obituary gave the maiden name Joan Gallagher as

James O'Donnell's widow, so I was able to find an index for their marriage. It was in 1954, and all information indicated this couple never split up. That would mean if he was Col's birth father, he was a married man when he conceived her.

I wanted to dig up more information on James O'Donnell, but we both agreed if it did pan out, we shouldn't contact any of his children. If we were right, it might be upsetting to his widow and kids. If we were wrong, we were better off.

The other Departed Member of Chicago F.O.P. Lodge 7 who fit the bill was a Terrence Sweeney. Through census records I was able to find his neighborhood in 1940, when he was eleven years old.

It was Rogers Park, home neighborhood to Rogers Park Mary, the early lead that did not add up because she was an American citizen by 1956. It would be straying from our "givens" to now think that Rogers Park Mary was the birth mom just because of that geographic connection.

And once again, even if we thought Terrence Sweeney was the birth father, we had to hold our tongues as far as making any contact with his surviving children. He had married a Nora Connolly in 1948 and, as far as I could tell, they were then off to raise their family. We just didn't want to go there. Not yet, anyway.

Resurrection of Mad Dawg Bobby

Then, Col heard from Mad Dawg Bobby Lynch again. He'd uncovered a first cousin named Gerald Lynch, who had passed away in 2013. His cousin "Gerry" was almost a generation older than he. Born in 1926, Gerry was in the range to be the birth father and in the right profession. A copper. Chicago P.D..

His survivors included a wife and three children. Two boys and a girl.

It interested me that Mad Dawg said Gerry had retired in the early 1970s. In 1984, The Cabbie told Col he had to retire from his regular field due to an "on the job injury".

In his next email Mad Dawg informed me that he learned it was more than rumor amongst the Lynch clan that Gerry's wife had been his "ex" for many years because of his repeated marital infidelities. He added that those dalliances and his apparent unwillingness to give up the "player lifestyle", even after being caught red-handed on numerous occasions, had contributed to their divorce and his somewhat early retirement.

I dug up his 2013 obituary from Legacy.com. It mentioned he had been a member of the V.F.W. (Veterans of Foreign Wars) Post #7363 in Southwest Suburban Oak Lawn.

Well... perhaps Mad Dawg didn't know his cousin Gerry, but I had a hunch my brother-in-law, Tom "Uncle Dunkle" Boroski did. He's Col's adoptive sister Maureen's husband and a recently retired detective, Oak Lawn Police Department. His rhythmic nickname sprang from an evening of beer-ing and bonding with our son-in-law, Kevin.

You can walk to the V.F.W. Post from the Boroski home, nestled in that bedroom community just outside the Chicago city limits. I immediately reached out to him:

"Gerry Lynch? Oh, sure. Nice guy. He tended bar at the V.F.W. Post for years. I heard he passed away. The last time I saw him he was slowin' down, but he was so well-liked they let him stick it out as long as he could, helping out at the bar, small cleaning projects around the post, that kind a' stuff. Talk to Sylvia at the bar. She works most weekends."

"Thanks, Uncle Dunkle. Say hi to Maureen for me."

A couple of days later I called the V.F.W. Post. Sylvia answered and I explained that I was Tom Boroski's brother-in-law, my wife was a relative of Gerry Lynch, and that Gerry's cousin Bobby (Mad Dawg) Lynch wanted some pictures of Gerry and, as Gerry was a member for years, figured there would be some at the post.

Bobby Lynch asked that we take some pictures for him, if any were available, so he would have pics of his cousin.

She readily obliged, and said she'd be around that weekend. No bullshit involved this time. I was just spinning the truth to fit my needs.

The following weekend we headed to Post #7363. As we drove up to the half-paved, half-not parking lot, it appeared this facility was like many V.F.W., American Legion and Elks Club facilities I'd been in over the years. Often older and single-leveled, this one was quite old and wooden framed. Shingled originally, but the current layer of siding was picket fence white vinyl. It was obvious additions had been made to what probably started out a farmhouse over a century ago. Figuring it would be relatively quiet, we chose a late Saturday afternoon.

Upon entering, we heard the unseen epicenter of good-times noise common to any gathering place. Aural bloodhounds, we sniffed our way to the origin. The bar.

I wouldn't have called it gang-bustin' busy, but there was a sporting event on TV that looked to be college basketball, so the area was fairly crowded. Sylvia, a short, quick-moving middle-aged brunette, was busy. I politely elbowed my way close enough and introduced us. She remembered my call from earlier that week.

"Well, there's probably other pictures of Gerry around in boxes or files, but the meeting room has pictures from over the years and you'll find a few of him there. He was Grand Marshall of our Veteran's Day Parade about five years ago."

"Thanks, Sylvia."

She "no problemed" me over her left side, diving right shoulder-first behind the bar for whatever her thirsty patrons needed next. Wanting to plop down a "tip" for her time, I was going to buy drinks, but it was at least "two deep" and she was swamped. Our more polite move—leaving, relinquished Sylvia to her throng.

We were on a mission. We wanted to see the images of Gerry

Lynch. Sylvia didn't have to tell us where the meeting room was. We'd noticed that on the way in. Right off the only hallway in the old farmhouse.

And there he was. We finally had a face to connect as a candidate for birth father, a "bf" in Adoption Rights Alliance lingo. The photos were large enough. They were color. There were two that were worth taking a pic of, and in both he was in military uniform.

Very handsome, he reminded me a bit of the actor David Niven. His eyes and facial shape were very much like Col's son, Thomas James. Though greying, it was apparent he was dark-haired and blue-eyed. I took the best images I could. Auto mode. Manual. Flash on. Flash off. We thanked Sylvia again and headed home.

The drive built up my thirst so, beer now in hand, with images of Gerry Lynch loaded into our desktop computer, I began viewing them alongside those of Col's two kids. I couldn't help but think of what Gwen Burke Brennan said, back when I was seeing similarities between Col's kids and the Burke's. It seemed like ages ago, but her dry comment was only several months old:

"We're Irish. We're all cousins and we all look alike."

Enough of that bad gag already.

Gerry Lynch had a couple of facial features, in pictures taken when he was in his seventies, similar to Col's son, who was half that age. That didn't connect anything that even qualified as a penciled dot.

More importantly, I felt we had to take at face value what was given to us by both DNA spittoons. Ancestry.com and 23andMe both said Col and Mad Dawg were at least 3rd–4th cousins. If Mad Dawg's deceased 1st cousin Gerry was Col's birth father, Col should—should because nothing is perfect—have come up a closer relation to Mad Dawg than 3rd–4th cousin in both the Ancestry and 23andMe DNA tests.

As fascinating as these pictures were, we were already starting to view Gerry Lynch not as a long shot, but as a mid-fairway iron away from the putting green. So, while the spittoon giveth, it also taketh away.

Based on the names in Gerry Lynch's obituary, it was an easy dig to determine who his kids were and their current addresses and phone numbers. Still in the area, his two boys and a girl were younger than Col, enough so that without even having to dig for his marriage year, it was likely Gerry was unmarried when Col was conceived. Hip hooray. We considered reaching out to the oldest, Gerry Junior, but opted not to.

I did not want to burn any more energy on this lead. About the only thing left to do with Gerry Lynch was to hope a solid, non-erasable Sharpee'd dot to connect would surface, one that would trump the scientific findings of both spittoons. A (sorry) "lynchpin".

Mad Dawg Bobby agreed.

Virginia Cavalry to the Rescue

A few months elapsed. I kept going over all my notes to date, to the extent that I could view them in my mind's eye at any given moment. There was nothing psychic or visionary about it. I would see notes and surnames and village names in my dreams.

Then in late 2014, Col decided to contact Confidential Intermediary Kathryn Decker and request that she contact one of the likely birth father's surviving children. Col had to make what was essentially a blind choice of sibling that Kathryn would attempt to contact on her behalf. We both agreed that the best choice would be the oldest son.

It was a tough call. A woman, in this case his daughter, might be more sympathetic to Col's cause. But we felt the oldest son might know who his dad "got into trouble with." And he might be willing to share her name or help in some way or, if nothing else, unknowingly disclose a clue.

It was more likely that he shared this secret with his oldest son than with "Daddy's little girl". A guy to guy thing. Warning him to be careful out there lest he get saddled with an unwanted child, or one that would have to be given up for adoption or even, heaven forbid, abortion:

"So, take it from me, young lad, if you're going to tap on the lassies, be extra careful. Double up on the condoms, whatever it takes. Pulling out and the rhythm method don't always work!"

Back to reality. Col contacted Kathryn Decker, who emailed the form she would have to fill out. In it, she agreed to allow Kathryn to share any of her contact information with the oldest son. Done deal. Kathryn said she'd get things moving right away. The next day, she informed us she had sent out a letter of inquiry to him.

Then, a woman named Kathleen Hogan Manuel of Alexandria, Virginia approached Mary Ellen O'Brien (me) via her Facebook page. She asked if she could help. She wanted to look at Col's profiles and genetic matches on Ancestry.com and 23andMe.

I gladly forked over the IDs and passwords for both. She started looking at the two closest matches, 2nd–3rd cousins James McManus of Providence and Mary Dennison of Sparks, Nevada.

James McManus still hadn't returned our 23andMe message of a couple months prior. Mary Dennison had. She was quite gracious. Said she had a distant, deceased relative who had been a Chicago police officer, named James O'Donnell. She didn't know much about him. Was this the same James O'Donnell I'd seen on the F.O.P. Lodge 7 list? Kathleen Hogan Manuel did some digging and found that it was quite possibly him. But it was the James McManus matchup that intrigued her. She messaged me:

"I really want to have a closer look at the McManus' of

Providence. It's a shame James McManus didn't return your 23andMe messages. Can you confirm that his birth year was 1951?"

Although it seemed she was light years ahead of me at this stuff, I confirmed James' birth year through the usual methods.

Beneath Our Feet

And Kathleen Hogan Manuel was right. Though Col never heard from him, 2nd–3rd cousin James McManus turned out to be the key to half of our puzzle.

First, she sent me a cut and paste of an obit from the online site of a Providence, Rhode Island newspaper. It was for James McManus' father. The obituary was very complete and effectively laid out the skeleton of his family tree. Kathleen used that information to dig through genealogical search sites and pieced together what she could of James McManus' family.

She found that he shared a great-grandfather, Michael Francis McMahon, with a man named John Valentine McMahon. Second cousins share great-grandparents. It's rare for men to change their surname, making them easier to trace back. In this case Kathleen was looking at a great-grandfather.

The variance in the surnames—McMahon/McManus—was not surprising. Things changed when people entered their new country. Sometimes it was a misinterpretation by the official at the customs office. Sometimes the immigrant changed it because he or she felt a different surname might be more accepted by Americans. Less commonly, someone fleeing their homeland for political or other more nefarious reasons might want to cover their tracks a bit. Naturally, I liked the adventurous romance of that finagling.

Kathleen then pasted out another obituary she'd found. Although it didn't give the middle name of Valentine, she was certain this was John Valentine McMahon. This obit was published in the Chicago Sun-Times on May 5, 2012:

> McMahon, John, Retired CPD. Beloved husband of Moira (nee Smith). Loving father of Angela (Jeremy) Butler, Francis (Lisa) and Liam. Dear grandfather of Maureen, Patrick, Michael and Robert. Fond uncle of many nieces and nephews. Proud Veteran of the US Navy. Visitation at Kenny Brothers Funeral Home, 3600 West 95th Street, Evergreen Park, Monday from 3 to 9 p.m. Funeral, Tuesday 9:15 a.m. to Most Holy Redeemer, 9525 South Lawndale, Evergreen Park. Mass at 10:00 a.m. Interment Holy Sepulchre Cemetery. Native of Oughterard, Co. Galway, Ireland.

So John Valentine McMahon was a 2nd cousin to James McManus, who came up a 2nd–3rd cousin to Col. John was, according to the online Social Security Death Index, the correct age, born in the summer of 1927, to be Col's father. He left behind three children, two boys and a girl, just as Kathryn Decker, without revealing any identities, had told us. And he was retired C.P.D.: Chicago Police Department.

Kathleen Hogan Manuel also emailed some information she uncovered via peoplefinders.com. If correct, John's oldest, Angela, would be about forty-three years old. Next was Francis, around forty. Youngest was Liam at thirty-six. If we were on to the same birth father as Kathryn Decker, it was Francis who she'd sent a letter of inquiry to just a few weeks prior.

I found Jeremy and Angela Butler's home. It was in Oak Lawn and I couldn't help noticing how close it was to Col's adoptive brother Pat Garrity's doorstep.

Googlemap estimated it at one thousand feet.

None of the digging Kathleen and I did revealed that John V. McMahon had a marriage to anyone prior to 1968, when he married Moira Smith. That would mean, if he was Col's birth father, she was not conceived as the result of an extramarital affair. At least on her father's side.

We figured it unlikely the bm was married at the time and she claimed to the caseworkers she was single. Or that she was married, and the caseworkers knew this and lied to Col to spare her the grief of living forever with the fact that she was conceived by a married woman whose husband was not the father.

Another item uncovered by the same search of his family was that John's widow, Moira Smith McMahon, was only about fourteen years old when Col was born. That made it highly unlikely that Col was born to John and Moira in 1958, and more likely that the caseworkers were telling the truth when they said that Col's birth father was single and that both parents had been dating awhile but had no plans of a future together.

Kathleen also said it appeared John V. McMahon had an older sister in the Chicago area, Philomena.

Kathleen was certain that John Valentine McMahon was Col's father. I was cautiously confident. Col was a little hesitant. I couldn't blame her. She wanted to be certain and to her this was not one-hundred percent proof. She did not want a repeat of the Mary O'Brien Burke affair, which I think she felt was a dead lead.

As I was pretending to be Col in all of these communications, I felt I had to represent her truthfully. So I indicated to Kathleen that I wasn't totally convinced. She was willing to bet money she was right. I told her that was not necessary.

Maude Frickert's gut told Paul she was right.

Then, within a few short days, Kathleen shared with me the results of an Ancestry.com communication between McMahon family members that she'd run across while researching the McMahon/McManus tree. Her email directed me to something she wanted Col to see:

"I can't find a marriage record in Providence for Michael

Francis McMahon, but it's interesting that the guy who supplied this information below and might be a first or second cousin to you, or I suppose even a brother, lives in Chicago. Take a look at one of the Ancestry.com blog links I sent you previously -- scroll about halfway down or a little further to a post from April, 2008 signed by 'Johnny'."

I followed her instruction. My jaw hit the floor so hard it almost bruised.

"Johnny" was an old friend of mine, Johnny Kafferly. I'd gone to grammar school with him at St. Mary of Perpetual Help in Bridgeport.

Johnny graduated in 1969, a year after me. His older brother Daniel was in my older brother Bill's class. I had not seen Johnny since the 1980s. Nice guy. I'd heard he was now an Assistant Corporation Counsel for the City of Chicago.

In the post on Ancestry.com, Johnny was describing his ancestors to a Peggy McMahon. Most of the information he was sharing was details Kathleen and I had already pieced together on our own. But his last comment on the post captured our attention:

"The only one of my mother's siblings still alive is my uncle John. He is a retired policeman and lives in Chicago."

I knew contact with Johnny Kafferly was in the offing, but first it was time to do a bit of digging. I needed to get back to The Newberry. I wanted to see who lived where in 1958. If John McMahon was Johnny Kafferly's uncle, I was almost certain Johnny's mom was John McMahon's sister, Philomena.

I slapped together a peanut butter and something with all the usual sides and headed to The Newberry:

Chicago Residential White Pages showed the Kafferly address in 1958 as 3428 South Parnell. I remembered it as the Kafferly home and recalled at least once, in the late 1960s, hanging out on the front porch with Johnny Kafferly and other adolescent street urchins. A decade later, when I dated Col in 1978, she was sharing an apartment with my sister Maria in the very next block, at 3347 South Parnell. She lived there for two years.

It also showed John V. McMahon had his own phone listing at the same Kafferly address through 1967. Therefore, this would have been the house he was living in when he and Mary Margaret O'Brien conceived Col in early 1958. Then I found the next likely address for John V. McMahon, in 1969, about a half mile away on South Lowe in Canaryville. I couldn't determine when he left that address, but I did find a third address on the Southwest Side that seemed to be the one he lived in with his wife Moira until he passed away in 2012.

That made sense. Philomena McMahon was John V's older sister and she married Peter Kafferly. She may have even been John's sponsor. John lived in the Kafferly house until he got established, married and moved out, probably in about 1968.

Later, I hopped aboard Ms. Cannondale and rolled over to Col's old Bridgeport address and, just for laughs, used her very precise digital odometer as a tape measure to determine the space between Col's 1978 apartment and the Kafferly home:

Five-hundred feet. In 1978, Col was living five-hundred feet away from the home her birth father lived in when he'd conceived her in 1958.

Her birth father's sister, Philomena McMahon Kafferly, was still living there in 1978, and would until she passed away in 1992.

For over two years that included those few months I dated Col, she was living five-hundred feet away from her paternal natural aunt.

And how fitting that Col, born with a hole in one chamber of her heart, an unsealed channel in another, and what her doctor later termed a "heart-shaped" uterus, had a birth father with the middle name Valentine.

I wanted to see if there were any pics of John Valentine McMahon or his kids, Col's half-siblings. If his funeral was at Holy Redeemer Church, it was likely that was their parish and those two boys and a girl were educated at Holy Redeemer Grammar School.

My timing couldn't have been better. According to their website, in a few short days the school would be hosting an "Open House".

Perfect. Unlike my visit to the Burke's parish, I wasn't going to bring any pro-looking camera gear. I wanted this to seem innocently impulsive.

We couldn't pass ourselves off as parents, but we could easily claim to be grandparents checking out the school for our granddaughter. We were simply gathering information for Mary T and Kevin. What made this even better was that we couldn't be struck by lightning. At that time, they were actually shopping for a school for Sharon.

Also, Col mentioned to me that she went to high school with a Cynthia McMurtry who had grown up in Holy Redeemer parish. I wanted Col to come with me to provide camouflage, and a reason to dig a little. I'd already told her I would use the McMurtry connection as an "in". I hoped it would get us what we wanted.

We arrived that Saturday and found the school not crowded. Teachers wanted to meet us, and they were pretty good salespeople. A couple of them tried to get us to put Sharon's parents on their mailing/emailing lists. We wouldn't capitulate, informing them that our daughter and her husband were looking at so many schools they were feeling bombarded.

We listened to their pitches, thanked them for their time and accepted their brochures. I made sure the teacher who seemed the most aggressive overheard my question to Col:

"Say, Colleen, didn't you tell me you went to high school

with one of the McMurtrys, but they were from Holy Redeemer parish?"

"Yep, Cynthia. She had a couple of brothers, too. Jim and Terry."

I extended my hand to the teacher. I figured she'd help if we gave the school a favorable review when we reported back to our daughter and son-in-law:

"You've been so kind. Thanks for all your help. We'll make sure to get this information to our daughter."

Turning to leave, I dusted off my fictional "Columbo" hat, feigning afterthought, rubbing my Roman "schnoz":

"Say...before we go, does the library have any old yearbooks we can browse?"

"Actually, we brought a lot of them out for people to enjoy. They're right down the hall in the Science Room."

"Great. Thanks again. I bet we can see the McMurtrys in those books, Col."

Wink-wink.

We headed for the mother lode. The Science Room. And there they were. Yearbooks going back thirty years or better. Based on the ages of John V. McMahon's three kids, I had already determined the likely years they'd graduated grammar school.

I was right on the money with all three. No one paid any attention as we browsed away, all the while talking about the McMurtrys when anyone came within earshot. All three of Col's half-siblings were dark-haired, very Irish-looking, and bore some resemblances. No big deal there.

But I just knew we were on to something. Ungluing my feet from the manure I'd been spreading—might as well leave the Science Room an imaginary experiment, we headed home.

Meanwhile, I was hoping we would get a positive reply to Kathryn Decker's inquiry letter to the birth father's oldest son. I was certain it would turn out to be Francis McMahon, and my digging told me that he was living in the Nashville, Tennessee area. Kathryn had indicated that any communication CIS did by mail was done in a manner that wouldn't arouse suspicion, so we added a few excruciating days for what was probably an inconspicuously snail mailed letter.

Success. Col got a call from Kathryn about two weeks later. She had spoken to the oldest son. He'd received her letter and apparently was very surprised. Kathryn wanted to confirm that it was okay to share Col's contact information with him.

You bet it is.

A couple of days later, Col received an email from her half-brother. The email was sent by an "fmcmahon", and he signed it "Frank".

Maude Frickert was glad he hadn't taken up Kathleen Hogan Manuel on that bet.

It was very brief and concluded with an invitation to a phone call in the near future. A few days later, Col talked with her natural half-brother, Frank McMahon. He said they had no idea of Col's existence, but that Dad didn't talk about his "single" days. No, Dad hadn't been married before.

He was going to talk to his siblings and arrangements would be made so that Col could meet her half-sister, who we knew to be Angela McMahon Butler of Oak Lawn.

Frank didn't share anything about his brother, Liam. Col did not share just how much we knew about the McMahons, including Angela's address and that we had learned Liam had followed in his father's footsteps and was a Chicago policeman. She did share that I went to grammar school with his cousin, Johnny Kafferly.

Col made sure to tell Frank that none of us was sharing any of this with anyone. Frank said he and his siblings wanted their anonymity preserved. Of course we would oblige them. Frank said he was sure he'd be talking to Col again.

It was now high time to call Johnny Kafferly. I couldn't locate his current phone number online. But peoplefinders.com did show that he still lived in the old neighborhood. Right around the corner from classmate/lawyer Bill Finch.

I gave Bill a call and asked him for Johnny's phone number and he gladly obliged. I left Johnny a voicemail that simply asked him to give me a call at his leisure.

The following day Johnny returned my call. We exchanged the usual pleasantries that old schoolmates always share and then, as calmly as I could, given what I was about to reveal, I explained that Col was an adoptee and that our research indicated his uncle John was her birth father. There was a pause:

"Well, that's not surprising. My uncle was a very popular guy... for all we know there's another cousin or two floatin' around out there."

I asked him if he'd ever heard of any specific incident of John getting a woman "in trouble" back then. He said no, but that he was sure some old-timer in the neighborhood would know.

I mentioned that my dad, who'd passed away recently and was a very active parishioner at "Perpetual Help" for over fifty years, had often mentioned names of some of those old codgers.

Sensing that Johnny now realized I was going to keep digging, I took the plunge:

"Do you remember any mention of anyone in particular your uncle John was dating way back when?"

Another slight pause that seemed eternal:

"Well... there was Teddie Shaw's sister, but she went back to Ireland."

Chapter 8
Tumblin' Walls
A Local Legend

"BUT" she went back to Ireland?

Johnny Kafferly said it as if Teddie Shaw's sister going "back home" disqualified her. I felt like I'd just hit it big in the Irish Lotto. I don't think he sensed I was now grinning ear-to-ear and needed to pause before answering:

"Do you mind if I send you something in the mail that may interest you."

"No, not at all. Do you mind if I talk to my sister, Ellen, about this? She's sort of our family historian."

"G'right ahead. Tahk t'ya' soon."

I love Chicago-ese.

Johnny was mailed a copy of Col's OBC, and of the first letter she'd received from Caseworker Fran Cashman in 1979.

I hadn't heard the name Teddie Shaw in at least thirty-five years. He was the co-owner of Murphy's Tavern on Pershing Road, on the border of Canaryville, Col's old neighborhood—and Bridgeport, mine.

Now that's a gin mill I was familiar with. Now long out of existence, but in my grammar, high school and beyond days it was THE Irish tavern in the area. Once when not legally old enough, I recall having a beer or six in the place. Might've even been Teddie who served me. At eighteen, I was well-versed in Chicago tavern etiquette:

You lay more than enough cash down on the bar (credit card, you're joking) and order. The tender returns with your beverage, pulls out what payment he needs and then sets the change down next to your drink. It's usually best to tip the tender for that first purchase by laying a tip in the "rail" of the bar. That signals the tender it's his and that you intend to tip again.

Stick around and have a few more and there's a good chance you'll get a drink "on the house". In forty-plus years of pub crawling in other cities I've never seen the ritual performed quite like this.

All I remember from Murphy's is following that prescription and a burly bartender one-handedly popping open—not easy in the days of "pull tabs" that required total removal—a can of some cheap adult "soda pop" swill, at the time illicitly delicious, and plopping it down on the bar while offering up an empty water glass with his other bear-sized paw. I declined. A quick flick of his wrist tiddlywinked the tab into some unseen receptacle as he somersaulted the glass back under.

Right where it belonged.

St. Gabriel Parish, where Col and her adoptive siblings worshiped and likely received great educations, was the parish to the south of Murphy's. St. Mary of Perpetual Help, where I pretended to worship and know I got well-schooled, was to the north. I had to learn more. The St. Gabriel Parish Facebook page seemed the more active. I created a back story for my question:

> "I have a friend who is languishing in a local nursing home (true).
>
> The other day we got to talking and he brought up Murphy's Tavern (pure bullshit).
>
> I did most of my early beer-quaffing in other joints. I didn't have much to offer him. Can any of you help me with any history?"

The responses were immediate. The tavern was owned from 1956 through '78 by Timothy "Teddie" Shaw and Francis Murphy. Teddie was a Chicago policeman who had risen to the rank of Captain before retiring in the mid-1990s. Francis Murphy was a fireman. Although Teddie owned the majority interest in the tavern, it was in his partner Francis' wife Martha's name because Chicago police and firemen are prohibited from owning taverns. Murphy's was also called "The Bridge", a moniker supposedly created by Teddie.

Teddie and Francis were married to, respectively, Peggy and Martha Russell, two sisters from Mallow, County Cork, Ireland. Peggy passed away in 2000. Initial digging indicated the sisters didn't know the men from "back home". It appeared the Russell sisters came over prior to World War II, and that Francis Murphy and Teddie Shaw came over after.

And I'm not kidding when I say this was THE Irish tavern. Every year, right around St. Patrick's Day, the locally famous Irish Rovers Bagpipe Band would show up and entertain.

Like many Chicago taverns, Murphy's was more than a bar. It also had a back room for parties, where many a bachelor or retirement bash was held. From the stories that were told, the place could get pretty wild.

As one Facebook respondent put it:

"Murphy's. A serious bar for serious drinkers."

Another half-joked:

"I think I was conceived there."

If only that contributor knew the real reason behind my query.

Murphy's would also use the back room to sponsor peaceful, community-oriented events to balance out the rowdiness that the joint was sometimes known for.

Colorful history aside, Facebook respondent Dierdre Bridges offered up the clue that would break the search camel's back:

"Teddie's a Galway boy. He's from Clifden."

Clifden! Where Col and I had stayed, at the Bay Mist B&B, for three days in 2007. In my beloved underdog region of Connemara.

So much for that long-held image of Col singin' and dancin' barefoot over the spongy undergrowth of the auld sod. In Connemara that'd be a penance worse than scaling rugged Croagh Patrick. To help her navigate the rocky, dry slopes along the Wild West of the Wild Atlantic Way whilst not spilling a drop of Guinness, I thereafter placed a good pair of hiking shoes on that visual.

Another St. Gabriel respondent guided me to Teddie's current address:

> "He still lives in the same house he has for the last sixty years. On Princeton near 50th Street."

If my gut was correct that our bm lived with her brother Teddie in 1958, this would mean I now knew the home she lived in when Col was conceived.

Even though I couldn't find a current phone listing for him, it was fairly easy to find his address:

5024 South Princeton, less than a mile from the Garrity home Col grew up in.

Even closer "as the crow flies", as one has to go out of the way a bit to the nearest crossing to traverse a set of freight train tracks, and to skirt the cyclone-fenced grounds of—go figger, a long-shuttered orphanage.

Johnny Kafferly had not mentioned Teddie Shaw's sister's— Col's very likely bm's—first name. If Teddie was her brother, this meant that the name given as the bm on the OBC, Mary Margaret O'Brien, was pure sheep shite. The O'Brien part anyway. She was likely a Shaw.

We ran this idea by Col's adoptive brother Kevin, who'd found his bm in fifteen minutes about a year prior. He called Trudy in Florida, who replied, "no way". She claimed she had to show valid identification to be admitted to the same hospital, St. Francis, in June 1956, when she birthed Kevin.

With a brother and birth father in law enforcement, getting a phony "ID" for a one-time usage, especially in 1958, before chips and holograms and bar codes existed, would have been fairly easy.

A month later, Col and I met her newfound paternal cousin Johnny Kafferly. He selected Pershing Place, a trendy restaurant and bar that occupies a two-story building on the corner of Pershing and Wallace, right up the street from a manicurist's salon that once housed Murphy's Tavern.

When Johnny and I were kids, Pershing Place was a family-oriented, neighborhood eatery called Ma' Fisher's. Lots of chrome and formica, much like The Abundant and Tasty in Rogers Park. I think the only thing I ever had at Fisher's were their good, basic 1960s-style cheeseburgers. No frills, American cheese only and on a cheap, slightly grilled white bread bun with a smattering of sesame seeds glued to the top.

Back in my adolescent days, I was involved in at least one "dine and dash" caper with my fellow "droogs" there. An exit next to a booth along the Wallace Avenue side was hard to resist. We'd "draw straws" to see who would be the last to bolt out that side door, thereby putting themselves at the greatest danger of being corralled by the collar trying to commit the crime. None of us got pinched for these "munch 'n runs". I don't think Johnny Kafferly was ever with us.

I hadn't seen Johnny in over thirty years. I ran into him walking down Halsted Street about 1982. At the time, he was a tall, good-looking young Irishman. The Johnny Kafferly I saw waiting outside Pershing Place to meet his cousin for the first time was a tall, good-looking older Irishman.

It's a good thing I dated Col back in 1978, when she was single and living a mere five-hundred feet from the Kafferly home. Johnny was single then, better-looking on his worst day than me on my best and, if not still living at home, was still in the area. Col could have wound up marrying this first cousin, about three years her senior.

I didn't want to press him over Teddie's sister's name. We enjoyed our slightly expensive drinks and engaged in neighborhood small-talk.

Always thinking about The Cabbie, I did ask him at one point if his uncle John "moonlighted" driving a cab in around 1984. He said he didn't recall his uncle ever driving a cab—that he worked side jobs in security and construction. After one beverage apiece, knowing we'd be seeing Johnny again, we parted ways.

Behind The Celtic Curtain

In the span of little more than a week, it was as if a wall, a chimera, dissolved:

Through online Irish Census records, I found who I was fairly certain was Teddie's father, Cornelius, living in 1911 as the thirteen-year-old son of farmer Malachi Shaw and his wife Honore, with an assortment of children, in the village of Shanakeen, a few miles northeast of Clifden.

I only say "fairly certain" because, just as expected, the 1911 records showed other Shaw families in the Clifden area. One in particular was in the village of Glenkeever, with another Shaw male the right approximate age to qualify as the bm's father. My gut commanded me to focus on the Shaws of Shanakeen.

Cornelius and Mary Donahue Shaw registered the birth of Timothy Shaw in Quarter 1 of 1928, meaning "Teddie" was probably born between late 1927 and early 1928. But the same search also revealed Teddie's mother died, and her death was registered the same year and quarter.

She probably died during childbirth. So, is Teddie Shaw actually our bm's half-brother?

It looked that way and even more so when I found a marriage registration index for one Cornelius Shaw to an Eileen Costello in Quarter 3 of 1931. Col's OBC gave her the name Mary Eillen O'Brien. The bm's mum's maiden name was Eileen Costello, and her half-brother Teddie's mum's maiden name was Mary Donahue.

Col's bm might have requested the nuns name the child she was giving up for adoption "Mary Eileen" in tribute to those two women, Mary Costello Shaw and Eileen Donahue Shaw.

Or, the Irish nuns at the hospital made up both Mary and Eileen out of the clear green because they are very common and ring along nicely with the apparently fabricated Mary Margaret O'Brien. Others I then conferred with mentioned that sometimes it was the attending nurse/nun who signed the OBC as the bm.

So much for finally getting to see your natural mother's handwriting.

If I could do anything to pay back for all the lying to church and school employees, digging into people's Facebook pages, school yearbooks, real estate records, and any more eggs we were most certain to crack along the way to finish this omelette, I would be a champion for something that would lead to legislative changes allowing an adoptee to know the names that should be on any "Original Birth Certificate":

The real ones.

I fired off an email to the adoption rights advocate, Illinois Congressperson Sarah Feigenholtz. The reply from her aide contained the usual rigmarole... but at least he didn't add me to the Feigenholtz spam list. Yet.

Continuing, I searched for an Irish birth registration index for the most common female names of the time with Shaw as the surname. I started, of course, with Mary. None.

But Margaret came up immediately.

Margaret Shaw, whose birth was registered in Clifden in Qtr. 1 of 1938, was found on a specific volume and page number in GRO records. I passed this information along to Kathy Finn.

On her next trip to Dublin she would provide that information, have that birth cert pulled and would, after taking a pic of it and shooting it to me, snail mail me a copy as well.

A few days later I got it via Facebook Messenger: Margaret Shaw was born to Cornelius and Eileen Shaw on August 11, 1937. Eileen Shaw's maiden name was listed as Costello, confirming we had the right parents for Teddie's half-sister.

The record also showed Margaret was not born at home. Many babies born in rural Ireland through the mid-20th century were. She was born in a nursing home in Clifden. Was it possible Margaret's mother, Eileen, had difficulty bearing children? If so, was it due to the same heart-shaped uterus that Col had? Genetic properties often skip generations and Margaret's mother, Eileen Costello Shaw, was Col's maternal grandmother.

Now a dog baring its gums, jawing a bone so tight it would forfeit its own "canines" before letting go, I had to find Margaret— Teddie Shaw's half-sister. Col's likely bm. Any letter Col sent had to go directly to her. She probably had married and had a family and with it a different surname.

One of the many people in Ireland who I had met online through the Adoption Rights Alliance is Therese Norris. She messaged that she could dig up a few things on her own. I told her the approximate age of our bm, and to look for the first name Margaret, but that she was probably no longer a Shaw.

A few days later she sent an attachment with many descriptions of property in the area around Clifden that involved Shaws of both genders. A lot of them referenced condos along Galway Bay and in other parts of Galway County. There were even a couple in the next county south, Clare.

None mentioned a Margaret, and none had anything to do with the village of Shanakeen that was the Shaw homestead where Teddie was born and I had a hunch our bm still lived.

I went online as Mary Ellen O'Brien and posed a question on the ARA Facebook page:

"Anybody out there live around Clifden, County Galway?"

I received a response from a man named Oisin (pronounced "Oh Sheen") Anderson. I had seen his posts on the ARA page before. In fact, he had just recently found his bm and was in the process of some early communication with her.

Oisin lives in Clifden. We started messaging back and forth. At first, I was pretending to be the "Mary Ellen O'Brien" Facebook identity, but—Maude Frickert still hard at work—I told him right away that I was actually Colleen Garrity Terrazino.

I explained that I was trying to learn more about any current inhabitants of Shanakeen. All I could see on Google Satellite Maps was what looked like a group of homes. He explained why:

The village is just that. A crossroads with a few homes. I told him Margaret was still alive, that she was probably living in Shanakeen, but that her last name was probably not Shaw.

He replied that he knew someone. A sympathetic clerk of sorts who he hoped to have something from in a few days.

While that was happening, Therese Norris of the ARA messaged. She had found a record of a 2009 real estate transaction in Shanakeen. It appeared this involved a plot of land connected to a Padraig (pronounced "pour uhg", Patrick in Yankee-speak) Flaherty.

The land included a small stone building about the size of a three-car garage. Therese sent me a link to a phone listing and photo of the building. It was a business:

"Paddy Flaherty Sheep Shearing and Factory Crutching". No website. Just a phone number. And a woman's name:

Margaret Flaherty!

I passed that name along to Oisin Anderson. He said he would inquire about Margaret with his friend. As I waited, I just had to find out what the heck Factory Crutching is:

In a nutshell—no pun intended, it's cleaning and preparing the area around a sheep's tail and nether regions between its rear legs, making all clean and suitable for "the factory" and perhaps ultimate slaughter.

Oisin messaged a day later. His connection informed him that Margaret Flaherty "is who you're looking for".

I now had a married name to work with. But I still wanted to confirm this and could not find a Margaret Shaw emigrating here in 1956. Then, I let the search widen a little bit and got the "hit" that I was certain was her.

A "Mary" Shaw was on a flight manifest, listed as entering the U.S. as an immigrant, headed for Chicago from Shannon, Ireland in mid-November 1956. The original image was blurred and whoever transcribed the flight manifest decided it was Mary.

Out of curiosity and nothing else, I clicked my way along in the online flight manifest images and looked over all the passengers to see if there were any other Shaws onboard. None.

Just for entertainment, I kept going and found the first page for that flight. It offers, among other information, the type of aircraft. It wasn't a jet. It was a Lockheed Constellation, a four-engine propeller driven airplane. I imagined what that flight must have been like. The noise level. Probably got cold, passengers wrapped in blankets. No in-flight amenities—I wonder if they let you smoke? Times sure have changed.

And it was time for a return trip to Connie/Consuelo Schwarzburg/Sanchez at the Cook County Recorder of Deeds Office. I wanted to know where Teddie lived with his family when Col was born.

A few days later I bagged up all the usual stuff for lunch and headed downtown. Now that I knew the drill on digging in this dragon's intestines, I didn't really need Connie. But I knew it would go smoother with her. If I played it right, and she took her lunch break at the same time, I'd have an hour.

The subway cooperated and I was there in half that time. There was no one at the counter on the ground level. The Grinch from my first visit must've been off delivering payola to his boss. Didn't matter. I knew the way to the property records dungeon and walked downstairs like I owned the place.

And there she was. Same smock, same smudges, same "Connie S." nameplate. I still felt it would be too familiar to call her by name:

"Hi, remember me?"

"Oh, sure. What's up now?"

"I need to look up another address or two."

"OK. What're the pinumbers?"

Same slang.

"Here ya' go. Thanks."

As it turned out, the St. Gabriel parishioner who claimed Teddie had lived on Princeton "for the last sixty years" was a little off. According to the records, the mortgage "closed"—finalized as a contract—on July 8th, 1959. Teddie had only lived on Princeton fifty-six years, and the Shaws were not living there when Col was conceived or born.

The Shaws moved to Tom and Mary Garrity's neighborhood four months after the Garritys took Col home from the orphanage.

So, where did the Shaws live when Col was conceived? I would need to get home to dig on that one. I thanked Connie and bid her farewell. Her curiosity must have gotten the better of her:

"This must be really important to you. What is it you're trying to find?"

"Actually, it's not a 'what'. It's a who. My wife is an adoptee and I'm trying to find her birth mother."

"Oh, boy. Ya' know... sometimes when it comes to those kind of things, it's really better to just leave well enough alone."

Hmmm... Her Jewish-motherly vocabulary and attitude from

my first visit impressed me as a Schwarzburg. I was now leaning toward the more repressively Roman Catholic Sanchez.

My next comment informed her it was way too late in the game to walk away from anything:

"Yeah, well... I do appreciate what you're sayin' but sometimes ya' just gotta do what ya' gotta do."

Yes, I know it reads like Gary Cooper in the classic Western, "High Noon". Only "Coop" was the epitome of cool—it came out of me dorky.

When I got home, I immediately logged on to Ancestry.com and started digging about Teddie Shaw. I found an entry on a flight manifest that had to be him. This included an image of the card he filled out at the Customs Office at the Detroit airport:

Timothy Shaw entered the U.S., as a U.S. citizen, from Shannon, Ireland, on January 20, 1958. He must have gone home for a visit. I could find no other Shaws on that flight. He listed his address as 4316 South Francisco in Chicago—the Brighton Park neighborhood just southwest of Bridgeport. The date of birth he offered was December 28, 1927.

Now there's an easy one to remember! I was born twenty-six years later, on December 28, 1953. What a wonderful coincidence. But what I found most intriguing was the date he arrived back in the U.S.:

Nine months and one week after Teddie arrived back in Chicago, on the other side of town at St. Francis Hospital, "Mary Margaret O'Brien" would give birth to "Mary Eillen O'Brien" and the nuns would whisk the newborn away. 120-odd days later, the Garritys took her home, and—legal technicalities aside—her life as Colleen Garrity, including those eyesight and life-saving surgeries, commenced.

Was Teddie overseas when Col was conceived? Possibly, "when the cat's away..."

I went to the best platform to learn more about people after learning their identities—Facebook, and found Shanakeen Sheep Shearer Paddy Flaherty. Not very active on social media, he hadn't made a post in a couple of years. Looked to be in his mid-forties, built stocky and with a rounder face than Col.

By looking to see who his Facebook friends were, I found two who were probable siblings:

John Thomas, who went by "J.T." Flaherty, and a Diane Flaherty, who it appeared spent a lot of time in Philadelphia, and by some identifying catch-phrases seemed quite the "spiritual" type. New Age-y stuff. I could not tell what their ages were.

Diane's face was shaped more like Paddy's, but J.T. had a narrower face and eyes that were similar to Col's. There was an obvious resemblance. I looked at every image available for each and didn't see anyone who might be their mum—and therefore Col's.

Next, I informed Col of this latest development. I told her Margaret Flaherty was definitely Teddie's sister and I was certain she was our bm. Much like Kathleen Hogan Manuel, our search angel from Virginia, when certain John V. McMahon was our "bf", I just knew Margaret Flaherty was our "bm" and was willing to bet on it.

The DNA connections leveled their lasered fingers that way, too. Just as there was a higher concentration in County Galway surrounding Oughterard, birth place of Col's birth father, there were distant relative DNA hits clustered around coastal Clifden.

A Silver Lining

I showed all of this to Col. I wanted her to know why I was so certain, and I wanted her to mail a simple and straightforward letter to Margaret Flaherty.

I was keeping our Irish friends abreast of everything we did. Kathy Finn of the ARA suggested Col send it in some traceable way.

But that's a little tougher when sending a letter overseas. The USPS will only keep track of a letter until it gets to Ireland. So we'd probably have to use FedEx or UPS International or DHL to trace delivery all the way to the recipient.

Had Margaret ever shared her secret with her husband? If not, and if he was still alive, and she wanted it to remain a secret, that would be tough with an official-looking letter arriving.

Col and I both felt that with this letter going to a village this small a multi-colored missive like that would stick out like a sore thumb. Anyone seeing it would want to know what was so important coming from the States.

But, if it was a standard Air Mail, USPS letter, she could always tell her husband, or any others who might be curious, that Col was a friend from her days in Chicago and they'd become pen pals. After all, she had lived in Chicago for two years. She must have made friends. It went snail mail:

> "Dear Margaret,
>
> My name is Colleen Garrity Terrazino. I was born in late October, 1958 at St. Francis Hospital in Evanston and given up for adoption. I have been searching for my birth parents for many years. My research tells me you are my birth mother.
>
> I am sure you made what was the best decision for you at the time. I feel no ill will towards you. My adoptive parents were wonderful in raising me and my five siblings, all of whom are adoptees, just like me.
>
> It would fill a hole in my heart if we were to make contact with each other. I am including some pictures of me, now and in previous years, and a recent picture of my family.
>
> All of my contact information is below. Thank you very much for your time.
>
> Sincerely,
>
> Colleen Garrity Terrazino"

Once again, we were playing the waiting game.

A few weeks later, Col got a call from Confidential Intermediary Kathryn Decker. She had sent an "outreach letter", as they call them, to a woman in Ireland who she thought was the bm's sister.

The sister had not responded, but a week later, she got a call from a woman who said that she was the person "we" had been looking for!

Col said that Kathryn seemed careful to relay the exact words the bm used in their conversation: The caller told Kathryn she was sorry and very upset about the situation, but that she did not wish to have contact with Col at this time.

She also said she did not want to share any medical information, but that in the future, if it became necessary, she might do so then. Kathryn expressed regret that things had not turned out as Col had hoped.

On the surface, this might have sounded discouraging. To us, it was anything but.

Her bm said she was the person "we" were looking for. That meant we both had the same person and—hallelujah!—the search was over. She said "at this time" she didn't want any contact. It's not unusual for bms to initially respond negatively to having contact, only to turn it around at a later date. Can't blame 'em.

On the tough side, she said she was "very upset about the situation". That could be interpreted a couple of ways. Was she upset she'd been found? Upset that she didn't, or for some reason couldn't, have contact? Both?

For all we knew, she may have told Kathryn she was upset, but she might have been just plain old pissed off. As Col put it, in her authentic-sounding brogue:

"The bitch found me."

It was a shame we didn't know Kathryn Decker had sent a letter to Margaret's sister. Depending on the timing, had she let us know she planned to reach out, Col would have asked her to hold off because we were on to something in our search and didn't want the bm to feel suddenly bombarded from two directions after fifty-seven years. On the other hand, we should have kept Kathryn informed.

It was obvious we had traumatized Margaret. Now, we had to step back and let her process all of this and hopefully come to terms with the fact that she had been found.

It was now late summer of 2015. Col sent a completely innocuous—if there is such a thing in this case—birthday card to Margaret in early August.

Again, no reply. I suggested she send a letter to Teddie Shaw. We felt that, after fifty-seven years, others had probably strongly suspected, or perhaps even been told, of this long-ago event. But we had to play it as if, with the exception of Teddie, no one had ever been informed.

Col mailed a straight-forward, concise letter to Teddie, explaining she had learned his sister Margaret was her birth mother and that she had not replied her letters. She said she would like to have contact with him.

About ten days later, Col received a call from a Mary Shaw Ryan! She was Teddie's youngest, and in order to help out, had been living with him.

Teddie had received Col's letter. Mary said she saw it on the kitchen counter, opened. She read it and asked him about it. He became noticeably upset, said he had not meant to leave it out and told her to throw it away. She did, but later she noticed he had fished it out of the wastebasket and tucked it away with some other papers.

A couple of days later, she saw it again, on the dining room table, with his reading glasses next to it. Two good signs.

Shortly thereafter, Col met Mary Shaw Ryan at a Hyde Park Starbucks. Col returned from that meeting more energized than I had seen her in a while.

She said she immediately felt comfortable with her newfound cousin Mary, as if she had known her all her life. Considering they grew up within a mile of each other, I was not surprised. They may have crossed paths many times over the years.

Yes, Margaret still lived on the family farm in Shanakeen. Her nickname is "Molly". She didn't elaborate, but she said Molly had had a very tough life. She married in the 1960s and she and her husband raised seven children.

Seven! I'd only found three: Paddy, J.T. and Diane. But it turned out Molly and her husband Thomas had raised seven. Four girls and three boys.

Marie is the oldest, about three years younger than Col. She lives near Shanakeen.

Next is Sandra, married to David Collier. They have children and live near Galway City.

Then there's Catharine, who lives with her significant other and their child in Bensenville, a Chicago suburb in the shadow of O'Hare Airport.

Diane is Paddy's twin sister. She is also married with children and lives in Philadelphia.

Padraig, "Paddy", lives with his wife and children in Shanakeen, down the road from the sheep shearing shop.

Second youngest is John Thomas, "J.T.", in Pueblo, Colorado.

Jimmie is the youngest. He also lives in County Galway with his wife and children.

Mary Shaw Ryan also said her father Teddie's business partner in Murphy's Tavern, Francis Murphy, had passed away many years ago, and that Francis' wife, Teddie's sister-in-law Martha, was in a local nursing home near Chicago. Martha's memory was slipping a bit; she was not always certain of the year, those sorts of things. Yet she was still spry and had recently taken up embroidery.

Col realized she knew Martha Murphy! They were neighbors for eight years, from 1984 to '92.

She and her then-husband Michael Schmidt were raising Thomas and Mary T. They lived in Bridgeport, at 3157 South Throop (correctly pronounced "Troop"). Martha Murphy and her son Jim lived three doors north, at 3153. Col told me Martha used to scold her son Thomas when he was out playing in the street. She remembered one such incident, reenacting it once more in her linguist-approved brogue:

"Thomas James, stop throwin' rocks before ya' break a winda' and get back home right now and put'cher coat on!"

I didn't even need Mary Ellen Cannondale's freakishly accurate digital odometer for this calculation. The average single lot property width in Chicago is thirty feet:

For eight years Col, her husband and two kids lived ninety feet from her birth uncle's sister-in-law, the widow of his former business partner in Murphy's Tavern.

Col knew them as Martha Murphy and her son Jim, and they knew her as Colleen Schmidt and family. She said the kids on the block called Martha "the lady with the dogs" because she had two that she'd walk regularly. According to Col they actually walked her, pulling the diminutive Martha along.

Diminutive? So was The Bookworm.

Martha's sister Peggy, Teddie's wife, passed away in 2000, around the time Col had that experience at the Hyde Park Borders Book Store.

In 1984, The Cabbie recognized Col as Molly's natural child. Surely, he knew Martha. Did he tell Martha who he thought her neighbor Colleen was? And, since Col had moved from Martha's block in 1992, did Martha see Col eight years later at the bookstore and—thinking Col was alone—decide to approach her in confidence about it, only to bail out and dash out the door when she saw Mary T rushing down the escalator?

Mary Shaw Ryan also revealed that in later years her mother,

Peggy Shaw, told them their aunt Molly was pregnant out of wedlock when she lived with them in Chicago in 1958 and that the child, a boy, was adopted by a couple in England.

Col's newfound cousin was having a cup o' joe with that "boy" who was a girl who grew up right down the road from her and would, for eight years, live a young kid's thrown stone from her Aunt Martha's windows.

And legend had it that a certain Connie Coneely, not John V. McMahon, was Col's birth father. It was an easy dig to find that Connor "Connie" Coneely was also Chicago Police, deceased since 2003. He was probably one of the bar patrons at Murphy's.

One of the guys, just like John Valentine McMahon.

My digging also told me Connie was a married bar buddy years before Col was born. His son, Connor Junior, is also a cop, or retired cop, and the Coneelys were from the next neighborhood south of Canaryville, called Back of the Yards because it includes the infamous, but now long-shuttered for livestock butchering Chicago Stockyards.

Mary Shaw Ryan said she would begin including her siblings into the fold. Col and I both felt the best thing to do was something we were getting pretty used to at this point.

Wait.

Deja Vu Rendezvous

It helped pass some of that time when Col and her birth father's firstborn from his marriage, Angela McMahon Butler, started some communication that culminated in a physical meeting.

First, Angela and Col had a phone call that wasn't very long or involved. Angela told her that she had always viewed her father as elderly. Understandably, as John was in his early forties when she was born. Col told Angela she had learned her birth mother's identity but felt it best to not share her name.

Angela revealed what she could about their father's medical history and the specific conditions that led to his passing away in 2012, all of which Col made note of. Col shared the serious medical problems she was born with.

Angela emailed Col a pic of the father they shared. It appeared to have been taken in the early 1950's. She said it was the one used for his passport photo. It was likely taken within a few years of when Col was conceived.

It was a good portrait. And a handsome devil he was. A large mop of wavy brown hair. Large, dreamily sensitive eyes and a slight cleft in his chin. He was, I'm sure—echoing his nephew Johnny Kafferly, "a very popular guy" back in those days when he was a young, unmarried Chicago copper.

I have a class picture of Col's daughter Mary T, taken when she was about fifteen. If I hold it next to John V. McMahon's pic, they look like versions of the same face to me.

Angela and Col arranged a meeting at a different Starbucks on yet another corner in Hyde Park as the Mary Shaw Ryan summit. Angela said she might be able to bring her brother Liam along. Great.

A few days later, Col arrived at the appointed time. She was waiting in line for her usual Vente White Mocha Latte Skim "easy whipped" (I'm glad I'm not her barista) when she heard the squeaky-hinged Starbucks door behind her open. With the sunlight streaming in through it, all Col could see was silhouette. It was a tall man, in profile.

Col said everything about him from his hair, frame, posture, even to the way he carried himself, told her it was her son, Thomas James. She had no idea he was in town from Michigan.

She was about to ask him why hadn't told her he would be in Chicago when a woman behind him stepped up. It was Angela McMahon Butler, who introduced herself and then the tall guy who Col thought for a moment was her son.

It was her half-brother, Liam McMahon.

They sat in Starbucks a while. Both Angela and Liam agreed that if questioned about his premarriage days their dad would get quiet. Liam said it was as if he "fell out of the sky" and married their mom and that was that.

At one point, when Liam and Angela got to talking about some of their dad's old friends, Col said Angela, in passing, dropped the name Connie Coneely into the conversation. She said her dad and Teddie Shaw and Connie and others would get together and play cards.

Col said it seemed Angela was injecting Connie's name just to see how she would react. I figured by now they had snooped into things and been told the fairy-tale of Teddie Shaw's sister Molly and Connie Coneely. As Liam is a copper, Angela may have dropped Connie's name for his benefit so his training could better interpret what nonverbal responses Col made when she heard that name.

Angela seemed to question Col's initial claim that John V. McMahon was her father. Col explained the DNA connection, that she shared a 2nd cousin with their father—her birth father.

Col had a copy of her Original Birth Certificate to show them. It seemed important to Angela that the section dedicated to identifying information regarding the birth father had been rubber-stamped "legally omitted". Col explained that her birth mother was on her own and was under no obligation to divulge the father's name for inclusion in the OBC, and that any name entered as either parent is not valid unless signed by that person.

According to Col, Liam's nonverbal clues indicated he agreed with his until-recently unknown sibling on that one.

Col felt all she could do was offer to pay for a DNA test for either one of them. They declined.

For now, all that could be said had been. Liam said Col would be hearing from them again. Angela shot him a dagger-filled look indicating that was not what she had in mind.

Over the next several months, Col would reach out to Angela a few times, requesting that they talk again, and requesting any other pictures of the man who created her than the one she had shared. No reply. Col did exchange a holiday email with their brother, Frank. He replied to the holiday greeting, wishing her a good one as well.

That was that. Col never heard from either of these three paternal siblings again, leaving her with a six-decade-old j-pegged pic as the only visual memento of the birth father she would never know.

Beer Beats Coffee

It was now early November. Mary Shaw Ryan called Col. All of her siblings were now in the loop. A date and place were determined: We would meet Mary and any siblings who could make it, for drinks at Gaelic Park in Oak Forest on the night after Thanksgiving. Friday the 27th at 7pm.

We arrived on the correct date and time and walked into the bar area. It was crowded and we didn't see Mary Shaw Ryan. But I saw one woman seated at the bar just as her eyes almost popped out of her head.

"I think they found us," I said to Col as we wiggled and waded through the crowd towards them. The unknown woman pointed to Col, keeping her finger trained on her. As we got closer, she flipped her hand over and changed the pointing finger to a beckoning one, curling it upward repeatedly in a "come hither" motion. She spoke first:

"Hi Molly!"

"My name's Colleen."

"I know. But you look so much like her. I knew as soon as you walked in that you're a Shaw and that you are my aunt Molly's daughter."

Yep. So did The Cabbie and The Bookworm.

Mary Shaw Ryan arrived, and introductions were made. Two of her sisters and her brother had made it, but Teddie and Peggy Shaw raised nine kids.

There was the oldest, Robert "Buddy", who had followed in his father's footsteps and was a Chicago policeman. Kathleen, owner of the beckoning finger, is about Col's age, and there was Bridget and her husband Rick Milovic.

The remaining five were all women: Maeve, Olivia, Betsy, Rene and Siobhan (roughly pronounced "Shivahn"). Other than Mary Shaw Ryan, I didn't know how they all fit into this puzzle chronologically.

I learned later that all eight girls attended St. Barbara's, now "co-ed", but at the time an all-girls Catholic high school in Bridgeport, and that Buddy was shipped off to boarding school for his four years of secondary education.

I'm not sure if this was Buddy's request, if parents Teddie and Peggy Shaw first made the suggestion, or if it was a consensus. But were I the lone male amongst eight sisters, being in mere proximity to that level of developing estrogenic fumes would've sent me running for the hills.

Col ordered her usual "Jamie" and Diet Coke. I didn't notice any giggling. I perused the beer on tap selection: Guinness, Harp and Smithwick's. Buddy ordered a Smithwick's and I had the same. He explained he liked it better than Harp because it's not as filling. I mentioned I had never thought of it that way, but that I simply liked the taste better.

I don't recall what the others were drinking. But boy, what a nice group of people Col had just learned were only about half of her maternal cousins. Very down to earth folks that we both felt comfortable with.

Go figure. They'd been right in our backyards the whole

time. Literally, as the Shaw girls would often cavort in the same Canaryville playground as the Garritys.

The more we talked of those we knew from both neighborhoods, the more we realized how little separated all of us. Even Bridget's Bridgeport-bred husband Rick, who'd gone to grammar school with my sister Patrice, brought up names and friends' names I'd not heard in years. Out of the corner of my ear I heard them talking about the Kennedys of St. Gabriel's, a family I had often heard Col talk of.

Col's adoptive mom, Mary Agnes Garrity, was good friends with Mrs. Kennedy. The Kennedys had many children, and there was a Kennedy in each of her five adoptive sibling's classes as well. The youngest girl, Katie Kennedy, used to babysit for Col's kids. Several years ago, we'd stopped in at a local Bridgeport bar, and Col introduced me to a Peter Kennedy, who I'd guessed was about my age.

It was "ears wide open" when we were then let in on some Shaw family history:

The Shaws began farming land in Shanakeen in the mid-19th century. Descendants Cornelius and Mary Shaw bore two children: Andrew was born mid-1926, Teddie at the end of 1927. Not quite Irish twins—when siblings are born within a year—but close. Mary Shaw did perish, of complications from birthing Teddie, in mid-January 1928, about two weeks after he was born.

So, like Col but for a different reason, Teddie had never known his natural mother. When Teddie was about three years old, widower Cornelius Shaw married Eileen Costello. Together they had four. In 1931 Teresa was born, followed by twins Mary and John in 1933. Molly came along in 1937.

In 1942 Andrew, then only fifteen, died in an automobile accident. Molly emigrated to the U.S. in late 1956. Little more than a year later, at the end of 1957, her older sister Teresa lost her life. She had an infection, perhaps "mumps", and when the doctor lanced a boil near her ear to relieve the pressure, the "pus" got into her bloodstream and she died of acute sepsis. Poisoning.

That explained why I saw Teddie Shaw returning to Chicago from Ireland in January of 1958. He had gone home because of the death of his sister.

Nine months later Molly gave up "Mary Eillen O'Brien" for adoption and returned to Ireland. A couple of years passed before she married Thomas Flaherty. They raised seven children.

About five years ago, Molly's husband Thomas Flaherty suffered a debilitating stroke. Now in a nearby nursing home, unable to move, speak or show much in the way of emotion, Molly still visits him at least once a week.

Mary Shaw Ryan couldn't have put it better when she said her aunt Molly's life had been tough.

She also said that Teddie told her John V. McMahon "swore up and down" he was not the father. John claimed that Connie Coneely was responsible. Connie denied it, and he and Teddie even came to physical blows over it.

Did Molly and then-married Connie Coneely have some sort of relationship beyond friendship? Or, were they friends, but just enough to raise that suspicion, handing John V. McMahon good reason to think he could get away with alleging Connie was Col's father?

I wanted to straighten that one out with the Coneelys. Even though Connie had passed away a dozen years ago, I still felt it important to clear his name.

Next, the discussion took a turn toward the future. The consensus among the Shaws was that Col should reach out to her half-siblings, Molly's seven kids.

Col and I agreed with the Shaws, but in the hopes Molly decided to tell her kids they have a big sister they never knew about, we wanted to give her more time to think it over.

We wanted it to be a year from when Col first contacted Molly to the time, if there was still no response, she would reach out to her newly discovered seven half-siblings. That would be April 2016. Five months away. It had been fifty-seven years. We felt that was being respectful to Molly.

We were in a tough spot. The Shaws and Flahertys seemed close-knit. We wanted to stall those few months more, during which time the Shaw cousins would have to keep this knowledge to themselves. Or, at least try to.

It was a very relaxed get-together, lasting ninety minutes or better. Toward the end, Mary Shaw Ryan suggested that the next step might be for Col and me to join Teddie at his home for Sunday dinner, which was always at 4:00pm. She said a Sunday in January would probably work best.

On the drive home, I brought up the Kennedys of St. Gabriel's parish:

"So, I didn't hear the whole conversation. How do the Shaws connect to the Kennedys? The Shaws went to St. Basil."

"They know the Kennedys from the neighborhood, and a lot of the Shaw girls are about the same ages. Do you recall Johnny Kafferly mentioning his younger sister?"

"Yeah. He said her name is Ellen, and she's the keeper of the Kafferly family tree."

"Well... Ellen Kafferly is married to Pat Kennedy. Mike Kennedy was in my class. Pat was a little younger. He was in my sister Eileen's."

Col's natural paternal cousin had married one of the Kennedys, a family that she had talked about for all our married years.

I felt the world squeezing my rib cage.

Chapter 9
Teddie Vetter

Watchful Eye(s) of Irish Royalty

"Dear Margaret,
All of my adult life I have wanted to know and meet my natural relatives. Please grant me my Christmas wish.
Love,
Colleen"

That was the simple note Col included in the tastefully traditional holiday card she sent to Molly in Shanakeen. We were hoping she'd received hers about December 20th, the same day as our friend Oisin Anderson confirmed he got his in Clifden.

Our holidays went well. We drove to Michigan to see our son Thomas, his wife and three and a half kids. Erica was midway through gestation with their fourth.

In early January we heard back from Mary Shaw Ryan. How about dinner at her father Teddie's on Sunday, January 24th? 4:00pm. Leg of lamb will be served. We brought a pound of butter cookies from our favorite Hyde Park bakery, Fabiana's.

Coincidentally, had she not passed in 1983, January 24th would have been Col's adoptive mom Mary Agnes Garrity's ninety-ninth birthday.

We parked outside the old, two-story stucco white frame home with green trim that I'd driven or bicycled by whenever I was nearby just in the hopes of seeing him, and walked up the few short steps to the doorway.

Mary greeted us. Kathleen, who we'd already met at the Gaelic Park meetup in late November, was there. And there were two new sisters to meet: Olivia and Betsy. We made our way into the interior of the place Teddie Shaw had called home for five-plus decades.

And there he was. Small, wiry, grey-haired, thickly bespectacled. It was obvious he had trouble walking.

He stood up from his seat at the head of the dining room table and shuffled his way to us. Other than noticing the Blue Ridge topography of veins on his long hands I don't recall how the introductions went. But I'll never forget one of the first things he said to Col:

"Well, you sure do look like her, that's for sure."

We'd still not seen any pics of Molly but yes, we do keep hearing that.

We all sat at the dining room table. I sat on one side of Teddie, Col on the other. Teddie was "old school", no doubt about it. But he had lived stateside long enough—since the late 1940s according to my digging—that I felt he was probably used to and tolerant of "new school". Molly would probably not respond to Col unless she got a nudge from someone, and I felt Teddie might be the best person for this. But I knew we shouldn't ask for his help.

What did matter was that Teddie "vet" Col. But as time went on that evening, I felt as if I had jeopardized our chances of Teddie and his kids being any more helpful than they already had been:

Six weeks before, I had an unplanned medical procedure. Like many men, I avoid all medical professionals as if they carry the plague. Naturally, my pulse and blood pressure might be elevated. But my reading that day gave me cause for concern to take action.

I realized I'd been averaging too many beers a day and was stepping into Starbucks for more than the usual cup or two of "leaded" throughout a typical week.

Wanting to get my "bp" readings down without prescription "meds", I decided to pay more attention to my sodium intake, lay off alcohol entirely and caffeine with chocolate and green tea being the only exceptions.

I also wanted to be at my best when I met this neighborhood

icon, so I went to the gym for an intense workout just before we drove to Teddie's for dinner. I knew my system well. I'd abstained for over a month. One adult beverage and I would be the exact opposite of my very best.

I'd be scouting out Teddie's most comfy couch for a Sunday afternoon nap.

So, what did I do? I waltzed into the home of Col's uncle Teddie, an old school Irishman from everything I'd been told, and former co-owner of THE Irish tavern in the Canaryville/Bridgeport area, and when he asked which of the many beers I'd like—naturally all Irish—I declined and insisted on a glass of water.

His lower lip actually trembled along with the "fish eye" I got through his multi-layered lenses.

What the heck was I thinking? It would not have killed me to break my self-imposed alcohol fast for one night. It's not as if I was a "twelve-stepper". I was only experimenting to see if it could lower my blood pressure.

Once more selfishly and without regard for our cause, I declined his second attempt to give me a real man's drink. But—figuring an absorbent belly blanket would keep me awake and off his couch—I went for a consolation prize:

"I'll have one with dinner."

When Mary Shaw Ryan brought out the salad, she quipped:

"Whatever you two do, don't ask if we've any olives."

Her sisters chuckled over this. Teddie replied to my questioning look:

"When I came over in 1949, it was by boat. Cheapest ticket I could buy. The weather was rough, the trip took longer, and the only thing left for us in steerage was part of the cargo. Olives and root beer. I was seasick as hell. That's all I vomited for two days. To this day I can't stand either. You won't see them in this house."

Good thing I hadn't requested a root beer in lieu of the real thing.

Teddie then talked about the history of Shanakeen. He said in the early 1920s, his father Cornelius, Col's grandfather, volunteered to fight with the rebellious Irish Republican Army, the "IRA". They declined his offer, instead recruiting him as an unarmed courier, smuggling messages in his shoe during the early "Black and Tan" Days.

The Black and Tans were a military group, so named for the color combination of their uniforms, formed in Ireland in 1919 by then Minister of Defense Winston Churchill. Yes, that one. Often violent and with little regard for the law, they worked for the British to fight and attempt to destroy the IRA.

Legend had it that the Black and Tans thought Cornelius had direct knowledge that implicated them in the well-publicized murder of one William Durkin, a highly-respected Irish citizen who the Brits thought was working for the IRA.

They planned to kill Cornelius and burn his home to the ground, but as the villages of Shanakeen and nearby Glenkeever held similar Shaw clans, they weren't quite sure which Shaw they needed to target.

Rather than terrorize the wrong village, the Black and Tans opted to abort the mission.

He chuckled as he concluded the story:

"Connemarans... we're all crazy. Even the IRA didn't want anything to do with us."

The world got smaller and smaller that night. Olivia said that she and two of her sisters remembered my brother, Joey. When they were teens, he was their manager at the Huck Finn Doughnut Shop on Archer Avenue. Teddie even knew my deceased Bridgeport cousin, "mobbed-up" gambling bookie Tony Freda.

Everybody knew Tony.

When the leg of lamb and vegetables and potato medley—all fabulous—came out, I requested a Smithwick's, even borrowing

Teddie's son Buddy's reason for why he prefers it to Harp. From that point on, I proceeded to chug away like a twelve-stepper who'd fallen off the wagon. Making up for lost time.

Teddie was happy to oblige. He had one with me and I poured half of one of mine into his glass. I wound up having three and a half beers in an hour and a half. Certainly not bingeing, but what did these folks now think of me? More importantly, what was I thinking?

Apparently, I was not. Adding insult to this injury, when I loaded up a second helping of leg o' lamb and then discovered a dime-sized, harmless varicose spider of edible marbling in the center of the perfectly cooked cut, I carefully carved it out and left it on my plate.

Out of the corner of my eye I could see Teddie, quadruple fish eyes and all, witnessing this Italian wimp refusing to eat a tiny piece of lamb that wasn't totally lean.

Teddie would soon realize I couldn't clean my plate because I was too busy working out how to cram both feet into my mouth for dessert:

The girls were off in the living room, looking at some of the family photos on the walls.

Teddie and I were alone at the dining room table. He now seemed comfortable enough with me that I didn't see any harm in posing a question:

"What do you think will happen with Margaret, Teddie?"

His answer was direct and unflinching.

"Let me tell you right now, I don't want to get involved in this. This is between the two of them."

My tongue had loosened up from the Smithwick's and I'd asked a question I shouldn't have. Too late now.

I had blown it. Really blown it. I never should have brought Margaret up in our first meeting. Had I not had three-plus beers by that point, I probably would not have. But as the Latin saying goes, "in vino veritas".

That evening should have been strictly for those present to get to know one another. For Teddie to "vet" Col. If he accepted her, and it seemed he had, I should have just enjoyed the company of this generous family and let him think it all over. Instead, I got the impression that he now thought I was just out to get him to talk to Molly.

Of course, had he offered on his own to talk to her we would have accepted.

But it came out wrong and I was tasting shoe leather instead of Fabiana's meltaway butter cookies. I had to bail out and make my question seem less important:

"I agree, Teddie. I understand."

"You know, this is still a very shameful thing over there."

"Yes, I suppose it still is."

"It will work out for the best."

I wasn't sure if he meant in general, or if he was implying that he knew in time Molly would come around.

Thankfully, the evening did not end on that note. The girls returned and Teddie gave us a tour of his finished basement. The walls were adorned with family photos of the Chicago Shaws. I didn't notice any that may have been of Molly.

We went back upstairs and sat around the dining room a little while longer. It became obvious things were wrapping up. One of Teddie's daughters bid farewell, then another did the same. We sensed it was getting time to leave, and I was hoping enough time had elapsed since I made the stupid mistake of bringing up Molly. In bidding us farewell as he shuffled us to his doorway, he said, "Please, don't be strangers."

Did he really mean that, or was he just being polite? Was it a "throwaway line" by a good tavern owner and bartender? I had only met him a few hours earlier. I had no way of knowing, but figured I'd keep it light:

"Well, I'm glad you said that, Teddie. We've got a few things out in the car and I'm sure you've a spare room for us."

He laughed. I found out later that my quip may have tapped his funny bone a little extra because, starting in the early 1980s, he had taken in three of Molly's kids, Kathleen, Diane and J.T., when they emigrated to the States from Shanakeen.

I felt that I had covered up my earlier screwups enough that we would hopefully be seeing him again. At least I hoped Col would get to see him again because while getting in the car, I realized that the entire evening, save for the moments I was eating, drinking or twisting my feet into my mouth, I never shut up for more than a minute.

I was enjoying Teddie so much that I'd dominated the conversation. It was probably just nerves. But what the heck did I have to be nervous about? I should have let Col talk to Teddie. She was his niece. I was just supposed to be along for the ride.

Teddie vetted the two of us. Col passed as default because he didn't really get to know her thanks to my endless jaw-flapping. I failed. Miserably.

I should have accepted Teddie's offer of a drink without hesitation, cleaned my plate like a good boy, and I never should have brought up Molly. Who knows? I may have even managed to bury my head in my butt at some additional point and failed to notice it. Good thing I'm adept at "Self-Factory Crutching".

My work was done. Teddie was right when he said the rest was up to her and Molly. It was then that I realized what was happening:

The search was over, but I was still acting as if I was Col. Until this point, I had found it humorous that I would sometimes react to things like Col instead of myself.. She appreciated that I would freely offer my opinions and that I'd been helping her write letters.

But, if anyone should have posed any question about Molly to

Teddie, it should have been Col. I felt terrible—especially because I felt there wasn't jack I could do about it. The only thing I could do was to go sit in the corner and shut up. But it was driving me bonkers. I wanted the Chicago Shaws to like me and if they didn't, to not judge Col over it.

I wanted to call Teddie on the phone, apologize and let him know that I wasn't trying to bring him into the situation—that I just wanted to know what Molly was like. I wanted to offer to stop by and visit so we could talk about anything under the sun but the situation that had brought all of us together.

But I couldn't. All I could do was wait.

Not knowing what Teddie was thinking, I opted to do one more thing. I sent him a "Thank You" card for accepting Col as if she was family, adding that it meant a lot to her, and left it at that.

It was after I'd dropped that card in the mail that I realized I'd followed up the monkey wrenches of Sunday dinner with a tire iron:

Guys don't send guys, especially when the recipient is a retired copper and old school Irish tavern owner, a Thank You card. Real men just don't do this. The only cards we know get shuffled and dealt while smoking cigars and chasing down Cheetos with hard liquor.

An Italian wimp? By now Teddie probably thought Col and I were "new school" American and I was her bisexual husband. Take a back seat? Heck, I'd eclipsed Tommy Duffy of Westport. At least he didn't try to drive from it.

It was high time to thrust a javelin-length stake made of centuries-old Connemaran turf, petrified diamond-hard by the lightning of St. Patrick's septre, through the hearts of my alter egos, skewering all, from Mary Eileen to Mary Ellen to Maude Frickert to Cyber-tootsie to Mrs. Doublefire or any others I'd dreamed up into an eternal, blood-dripping shish kabob.

In time, I would manage to shrug all this off. I began using

Teddie's own words as a personal, multi-syllabled mantra:
"Itwillworkoutforthebest...itwillworkoutforthebest...
itwillworkoutforthebest..."

A Dangerous Gamble

Our lives went on for a few more weeks. I posed a question to
Col:
"I don't think Teddie wants to get involved. Can't blame him.
You should consider sending a letter to Molly, letting her know that
you plan to contact her children, your siblings."

Col agreed, but didn't want to do it right then or any time in
the immediate future. I expressed we shouldn't dillydally around
too long about it and left it at that. I knew I would be reminding
her now and then.

That was in late February. A few weeks later, Col sent Teddie
an Easter card. Just a howdy and hope to see you soon card. You
know, the kind of thing real women do.

I felt it important for Col to send that letter to Molly. This is
a tight-knit family. Many of Molly and Teddie's kids are friends.
Teddie's kids, Col's first cousins, had learned of Col's existence by
a fluke. We had no idea that Teddie's daughter, Mary Shaw Ryan,
lived with him and would read the letter. She had now brought in
her brother and seven sisters. Mary Shaw Ryan may have been our
heroine. What if Teddie had pitched the letter in the garbage and
never said a word to anyone?

Another theory jigging around in my noggin' was that Teddie
asked Mary to read it to him as a segue to include her. She struck
me as a nurturing soul and may have been a confidant.

The complications presented by Molly's brother, nephew and
eight nieces knowing of Col's existence, even meeting half of the
ten before Molly had so much as uttered or written a word to Col,
was one of the more bizarre dichotomies I have ever experienced.

Enough skull-scratching. The Shaw cousins had suggested we reach out to Molly's kids and that they would go to their mother about it. But Col didn't want to "rat out" Molly to her own children without warning her.

After Easter, I ran the idea by Col once again, this time explaining why I felt we needed to move quickly. We couldn't just leave the Chicago cousins, and Teddie, hanging. Col wanted to wait until after our next grandchild was born. The due date—pre-determined by caesarian section for the pre-named Jameson Thomas Schmidt—was April 5.

She determined to write a letter, letting Molly know that she intended to contact her siblings, but giving her at least a month to think it over.

I pieced together a few sentences of what I thought might be important for Col to say to Molly. Even though she didn't know her, she had to be warm and non-threatening.

Col appreciated my thoughts and would think it over and compose her version. She thought that it would help personalize things by sharing Jameson's birth stats. All we had to do was wait.

Jameson Thomas officially entered the world, right on schedule.

It always drove me crazy when Col would spend a few days—or more—mulling over the actual content of any letters that had been sent to Mary O'Brien Burke or Teddie and now Molly. But this was one time when I was glad she did.

The more I pondered what I had originally suggested she write, the more I didn't like it. My version was too heavy in the sharing of medical history, and not emotional enough.

We decided to downplay the medical angle. We didn't want Molly to think that was all Col cared about, or that she was still needing expensive medical care and even though legally Molly had no financial obligation, this was just a "quid" quest on Col's part. The final version was much simpler and, given the intent, as warm as it could be:

> "Dear Margaret,
>
> I hope all is well with you and your family. We just welcomed our fourth grandchild into the world. Jameson Thomas was born on April 5, weighing 8 lbs. 9 oz. and 20 1/2" long!
>
> As I said in my Christmas card, I want to know my natural relatives, including you. At the end of May, after Mother's Day has passed, I plan to reach out to your children, my half-siblings. Knowing my family medical history, and them knowing the history of my children, could be of benefit to all.
>
> My door is always open to you. Please do not hesitate to contact me.
>
> Sincerely,
>
> Colleen"

It was now time to play the waiting game. This was always tougher on me than it was on Col.

The snail mailed letter was postmarked April 12, one week after Jameson Thomas' birth. Prior experience told us that Air Mail was getting to Dublin or Shannon in a week. Adding a few days to Clifden would make it just over a week.

That meant Molly would probably get this latest communication by Monday, April 25th. If she responded by mail immediately, we might receive something from her by early May. Mother's Day in the U.S..

We probably wouldn't hear from her. We'd probably have to reach out to all seven of her kids. That carried with it the risk that we would drive Molly away.

Col's Shaw cousins had all said that Molly's kids would be thrilled to know the person a few had heard whispers of was straight out of their American cousins' neighborhood. But that didn't predicate that they would be open-armed about this revelation.

Col was stressing out a woman in her late seventies and that woman was their mother.

A few days after Col posted the letter, I asked:

"Is there a part of you that is ticked off at Molly for not responding?"

"Yes."

"Me, too, and she's not even my mom. It's not wrong to be a little pissed at her."

"I know. But I think the thing I'm most worried about is that I'm upsetting her. She's angry with me and I don't blame her."

I nodded in agreement. We were probably causing a stranger—albeit one who was half-responsible for Col's existence, a great deal of grief.

With Col's latest communication, if we considered an actual communication between Molly and Col the peak, this adventure would be reaching a pre-summit within the next six weeks or so.

By the last week of May we still had not received a reply. Col thought it would be best if all seven received her letter at the same time.

She sent out the following on May 26th, snail mailing each of the five siblings who had addresses in the village of Shanakeen. Her intention was to mail to J.T. in Colorado on June 3rd, and to complete the task with Catharine Flaherty in suburban Bensenville on the 4th. If it went well all seven siblings would probably receive their letters no later than June 6th:

"Dear _____,

My name is Colleen Garrity Terrazino. I was born in Chicago in 1958 and given up for adoption. A little over a year ago, I discovered that my birth mother is your Mom, Margaret.

My adoptive parents, Tom and Mary Garrity, who passed away over thirty years ago, were terrific in raising me.

In the past year, I have written to your Mom four times, without reply. More recently, I contacted your Uncle Teddie.

His children have since learned of me. I requested they temporarily keep this knowledge to themselves. I felt it best that, after leaving ample time for your Mom to approach you first, I should then contact you directly.

I bear absolutely no ill will towards your Mom. It pains me that her knowing I've found her is likely causing her distress. However, all of my life I have felt a strong emotional need to know my natural relatives. As it's information that could be important to you and future generations, I also feel you should know my medical history,

In mid-April, in my most recent letter to your Mom, I told her I would be contacting you and your siblings at the end of May. This letter has been sent to them as well.

I would very much like to have contact with you.

I hope to hear from you soon.

Sincerely,

Colleen"

Battling Boredom

While we waited for the letters to arrive in Shanakeen, I distracted myself by emailing a Freedom of Information Act request, a "FOIA" request, to the City of Chicago.

I still wondered if Teddie Shaw was The Cabbie back in '84. The Shaws said they didn't recall Teddie moonlighting as a cab driver, but that doesn't mean he did not. Or, perhaps Connie Coneely was The Cabbie. I decided to start with Teddie.

With Martha Murphy being unsure of the year and embroidering away in a nearby nursing home, I knew I'd probably never find out if she was The Bookworm, but if Teddie Shaw was The Cabbie, at least that mystery would be solved.

The email response was almost immediate:

"May 28, 2016

Dear Mr. Terrazino,

On behalf of the City of Chicago Department of Business Affairs and Consumer Protection, I am responding to your Freedom of Information Act ("FOIA") request received in our office on May 27, 2016 for the following documents:

"Trying to determine if Timothy Shaw held a Chauffeur's License in 1984."

The Department of Business Affairs and Consumer Protection has no documents responsive to this request. We do not possess records from that time.

Sincerely,

Michael H. Toporek

Assistant Commissioner

Freedom of Information Office

Department of Business Affairs and Consumer Protection"

They simply don't keep the records going back that far. It wouldn't matter what name I gave. 1984 was too long ago.

I didn't want to contact Connie's son, Connor Junior, to ask if his old man moonlighted driving a cab over thirty years ago. He was a stranger to me, a copper too and would be understandably reluctant unless he knew why and vetted me first.

Enough already. I'd peeled open so many cans of worms I could open a bait shop.

Then I remembered something: In the 1980s, I'd done some technical work for the Phoenix Theatre Company, on Halsted Street a few blocks from Teddie's home. Their Artistic Director, Mark Williamson, worked for the City of Chicago.

And I was almost certain he worked for the Department of Business Affairs and Consumer Protection. Just because they don't keep records back that far doesn't mean they don't exist. They aren't required to keep them under FOIA guidelines, but they might be buried somewhere.

Maybe Mark knew. I hadn't seen him in years. I sent him a

cordial letter, explained that I was writing a book based on a true story that had roots near "the Phoenix" and that I wanted to know if a key character had driven a cab in 1984 and if he might be able to direct me to someone at the city who could help.

I never heard from him.

But I was added to the Phoenix Theatre Facebook Page notifications and email spam list.

Chapter 10
The Peat Hits the Fan
What Stuck to the Wall

I was in that soothing, transcendent state just before waking, when the conscious and sub slap backs before parting ways for the day. Lounging in Col's lingering scents, I was unaware she had already risen until her voice filtered through the misty grey:

"I got a call from Ireland."

Col's primary physician is, naturally, Dr. (Christopher) Ireland. In my half-awakedness, I thought she meant he had called. Grumbling through the pillow as I one-eyed the alarm clock on the nightstand, I saw it was 5:35am:

"What in hell does he want this early?"

"Not the doctor. The country."

In four beats, my pulse doubled as I literally fell out of bed.

It was a voicemail from Diane Flaherty, Molly's daughter and Col's sibling! Soft-spoken, sweet-sounding. Quite Irish. It went into Col's cell phone mailbox at 5:30am Chicago time, 11:30am Irish time. She gave no details except that she had received Col's letter and wanted to talk to her about it.

Holy shite! What happened? Col had snail-mailed them on Friday May 27th, the day before the three-day holiday weekend celebrating Monday, Memorial Day in the U.S.. There is no mail delivery on Sundays and national holidays.

We figured they'd be lucky to make it out of the U.S. before Tuesday, but it was Tuesday the 31st, the day after Memorial Day, and the letters were already delivered.

How did they get there so fast? Were they stowaways on a FedEx flight? Did a Connemaran leprechaun with a jet engine lashed to his back fly across the ocean and parachute the mail over

Shanakeen, just to mess with us?

Oh, well. Col told Molly she would reach out to her siblings at the end of May. I guess the last day of May qualifies. Not exactly the logistical result we had wanted, but now it was done.

Had Molly intended to contact Col and ask her to not contact her children on that day?

Doubtful.

Had Molly stuck her head in the sand hoping that Col would not follow through?

Probably not. Instead, I thought Molly, perhaps subconsciously, wanted to be outed, but didn't want to be the one to do it. If she did nothing, she would be outed by Col, and the guilt and shame she had been feeling all these years would land on Col's shoulders for ratting her out to her seven kids.

So much for conjecture. Col called Diane back. Diane said the entire village of Shanakeen had gotten her letters. She had suspected for a long time that her mother left something behind in Chicago and wanted to know who the father was. Diane said she had heard the name John V. McMahon but knew nothing of him. She also said she'd heard the name Connie Coneely.

Diane wanted to know a bit about Col's upbringing. Col shared that she grew up in the Canaryville neighborhood, not far from their uncle Teddie. Col made sure to let Diane know that we had met Teddie and that he didn't want to get involved. She told Diane I was from the same area, too.

Diane was quite curious as to how we found Molly and Col explained in general terms, without mentioning Johnny Kafferly. He had only mentioned that his uncle John dated Teddie's sister at one time. For obvious reason, we were the ones who ran with it.

Col and Diane promised to talk again very soon. Col headed off to work.

A little after 9:00am, my cell phone rang. It was Col.

"I talked to her. I talked to my mother."

"How'd it go?"

"She called my cell phone as I was walking into the office. It was hard to understand her. She was crying a lot."

"She chewed me out for reaching out to my siblings so quickly. I told her at least she knows I'm a woman of my word. She wanted to know if I'd met John, my father. I told her no, that he'd passed away in 2012."

"At one point, I didn't know what to say and I was silent. She asked if I was still there and I let her know it was a little difficult to talk in the office. Then she calmed down a bit. We talked a little more. She said that she had been mourning her sister Teresa's death and that John V. McMahon had taken advantage of her and she had succumbed to his desires."

"She said that when she learned she was pregnant, abortion (illegal then) was discussed and rejected. She said after she gave birth, the nuns would not even let her hold me. She was assured I'd be placed in a good home."

"She said she'd errands to run but wanted me to call her back. That's when things got fuzzy. She wanted a call back 'at nine' on Friday but didn't make clear what time zone she had in mind. Then she said this Friday was not good, because she wouldn't be home. She hung up at that point."

We checked Col's cell phone. After fifty-seven plus years, she had finally spoken to her birth mother. From across the pond, for twelve minutes. She scolded Col, asked that she call her back in four days, then postponed the call indefinitely.

Col was officially family.

Faccia a faccia?

The next day, Col and Diane Flaherty talked again. Diane said that for years she had been wanting to find out more about the child many suspected their mom had given up for adoption. When she first moved to Chicago in the 1980's, she asked her uncle Teddie's wife, their aunt Peggy, for any information she might have. Peggy Shaw's answer confirmed that Diane had a sibling out there somewhere:

"Teddie would kill me."

At one point, Diane even hired a psychic to help spirit her way to the sibling her inner self told her existed. The psychic said she needed something to work with: a photo, anything. Diane had only whispered secrets and ancient family lore.

Diane wanted to know if Col had mailed out to their two siblings who were living in the States, Catharine and J.T.. Col said she had planned to in a couple of days. However, that had all changed when the letters to Ireland got there so fast. Now, the cat was out of the bag.

Diane requested Col not send those two letters just yet. She felt it best that we wait a bit, let things settle down with Molly and the rest of Shanakeen, and then bring in Catharine and J.T..

The only problem I saw this posing was that cousin Rene Shaw Lewis was, according to the other Shaw cousins, close to Catharine Flaherty. So far as we knew, Rene was holding back on revealing anything to Catharine about the existence of her newfound cousin.

Any Shaws we had met all echoed the same sentiment regarding Diane. They all felt she was the best choice among the siblings to communicate with Molly. Col and I agreed that, even though it seemed unfair that we were temporarily leaving two siblings in the dark, we needed to abide by Diane's request.

Molly had opted out of having an abortion and Col was placed in an excellent home and given a fine upbringing. Yes, it was an out of wedlock birth, but it was before any of them were born and the two participants were single at the time.

From my viewpoint, I could not wait to meet Molly to thank her for making the right decision. She had opted to carry Col to term. From her viewpoint, Col's conception and birth was an upsetting event that she thought she had buried forever, and now it was coming back to haunt her. Molly had not wanted to get pregnant. It was taken care of and never discussed again.

She then left within sixty days, returning to the auld sod that she had only left two years before. She had swept the event deeper than under the rug, leaving it behind, beneath the soil of America. Within three years she started a new life, with a husband and eventually seven children to boot.

A couple of days later, Diane Facebook-messaged Col. She said Sunday might be a good day to try calling. She was considering using her Skype account, so that it would be a video call and Col and Molly would meet face-to-face.

Sunday rolled around and we went about our usual routine. Big breakfast. "Meet the Press". Col was anxiously waiting for a message from Diane in Ireland.

Nothing. Then, about 2pm, she got one, but it was about two hours old. Must've gotten stuck in cyberspace.

"Now might be a good time to try calling Molly at her home."

We knew this to mean that Col should try calling Molly's hard line. Not via Skype. Either way, contact is contact. So what if it was .16 a minute instead of Skype for free?

Col called. Diane answered the phone.

"Now is not a good time. Can I get back to you?"

A short time later Diane called. Molly had reversed herself. One-hundred and eighty degrees. Shut down. There would be no call today. Skype or otherwise.

Double shite.

At first, I was fuming with frustration over this. What went wrong? Col was very patient. Molly, though pissed that Col had contacted her siblings "so quickly", had even requested that Col call her back.

Were we moving things too quickly? Did Molly freak out at the prospect of meeting her daughter face-to-face via Skype? Would the dinosauric dixie cup on a string of a phone call have been better?

Col had only been trying to follow through on Molly's request. She had wanted to talk. Now Molly was getting cold feet. I posted our plight to the Adoption Rights Alliance page. All the respondents voiced pretty much the same opinions that I've lumped into one collective quote:

"This happens all the time. She's still processing all of this. Once the dust settles, don't be surprised if she changes her mind again. And again even. But whatever happens, establish relationships with any of the seven siblings who are interested. If bmum has issues over being found, tough. She'll have to work her way through them—if she wants. Don't let her issues become your issues. You've done nothing wrong."

It was possible that in Molly's view, Col did do something wrong. A good Irish Catholic adoptee is supposed to accept without question that her adoptive parents are her parents and there is no value, and nothing but harm, in an adoptee wanting to know her natural relatives.

But I had read way too many accounts of bms who, after coming to terms with being discovered, realize that they were glad they got outed.

We didn't know Molly and should not be the ones to judge whether or not the dust had settled enough to try and initiate contact with her again. We decided to sit back and relax about all of this.

And, of course, wait...

A week or so later, Col checked in with Diane via text. Just a "How are things going?" sort of message. No pressure. Not even a mention of Molly. Diane's response was promising:

"Molly is doing much better and is interested in talking with you. Let's set up a time in the near future. I will be talking to her tomorrow night and I will get back to you."

A few days later Diane called Col through Facebook Messenger. Among other things, she mentioned that J.T. of Colorado was in Shanakeen now, and that Catharine of Bensenville planned to be there in September.

Another week passed. Still no word. Then Diane called again. There had been a death in their extended family in another part of Ireland. Molly would be away for the funeral and related events, so this week was not going to be good for Col and Molly to have a second conversation.

Holy triple shite. But patience is—supposedly—a virtue. So, we sat back again and waited. And waited.

A week passed. No word from Diane. Col mentioned to me she wanted to visit her old church, St. Gabriel in Canaryville. Even though neighboring St. Basil in Back of the Yards was their original parish, Teddie Shaw had recently decided to instead attend St. Gabriel. Mary Shaw Ryan said he went to the 10am Sunday Mass and that he liked to get there early and sit in the last pew.

Col messaged Mary that she would like to go to Mass with Teddie and she could make it Sunday, July 3rd.

I was so tempted to suggest to Col that she offer us up as helpers. We wouldn't mind at all picking up Teddie and taking him to church. But I didn't say a word. I felt that the relationship between us—especially the Shaws and me, was not yet at the point where they would be comfortable with that.

On Saturday, our five-year-old granddaughter Sharon was dropped off with us for the weekend. The next day, we took her with us to "St. Gabe's" for 10am Mass and arrived a little early.

No Teddie and Mary yet. We took our place in the last pew. With Mass about to begin, I stepped out to the vestibule to see if they were maybe just running late. Just as I crossed the threshold there was Mary Shaw Ryan.

"Dad can't make it. He's not feeling well. He's really been

failing the last month."

"I'm so sorry. Col and Sharon are inside. I'll be in soon."

I had always wanted to get a better pic or two of the original Garrity home than what the Googlemap vans provide from their cyclopian turrets. The homestead was less than two blocks away on 46th Place.

Sometime since we'd last seen it a decade earlier, this small post-WWII single story brick bungalow had been chopped off at the top of the brick line under the original roof and had sprouted into a multi-leveled "McMansion".

I took a few pictures from the front, then walked around back and, noticing that the gate was open, stepped into the backyard to get a pic or two from that angle. I realized after leaving that was a foolish thing to do. Even at 10am on a Sunday, in that part of Chicago I was lucky I didn't get shot as an intruder.

Just as I finished and started to head back the short distance to the church, I got a text from Col:

"Sharon wants you."

Col told me Sharon was always well-behaved in church—even intrigued by the theatrical kabuki of Catholic Mass. The night before we had explained to her that we really needed to go because Col hadn't seen her uncle Teddie in a long time. Sharon started out a trouper this Sunday but got itchy feet once Mass started.

It hadn't taken long for her to befriend her Nana's cousin. Resting her red-haired youngness against Mary Shaw Ryan's left side, she turned and whispered in my ear:

"Can we go for a walk outside?"

Gladly. She and I took a brief tour of the grounds around the church and waited for Mass to end. When Col and Mary exited, the four of us walked into the small adjacent garden to chat.

Mary had to get back to Teddie. She explained that he was acting more as if he was reaching the end of his life. Starting to make certain that anything mechanical in the home that needed fixing, even if it had been tolerated until now, was getting attention. He had stopped his newspaper subscription. All he'd been reading was the obits anyway.

He had also told Mary that he felt he was "a burden". Her reply?

"You're not a burden. You're just a pain the ass."

We had only met Teddie once but were certain he'd appreciated the humor on his daughter's part.

Mary also said that Teddie, upon learning John V. McMahon was definitely Col's father, was questioning just who his real friends were back then. Hearing that was tough on us.

He was eighty-eight years old and in poor health when we blindsided him, and we rendered him contemplating the validity of a relationship with one of his deceased friends. And he had expressed doubt, to the level of good old-fashioned fisticuffs, in his friend Connie Coneely's denial of paternity.

Was it not best that Teddie now knew the truth?

Mary also wanted to know how things were going with her cousins—Col's siblings, in Shanakeen. Mary felt things were going too slowly, what with Diane still wanting Col to not mail letters to Catharine and J.T. just yet.

We had honored Diane's request. Mary indicated she didn't necessarily agree that Diane should be calling all the shots.

I felt that we didn't have much of a choice. So far, Diane was the only of Col's seven siblings who had replied her at all. We didn't know what the other four siblings—the ones who had received Col's letter—thought of all of this. We figured those four had decided that for now Diane should be the go-between.

Diane planned to be in Chicago that month. Perhaps the rest of the siblings wanted Diane to vet Col first. Mary felt that Catharine and J.T. should be in the mix, just like the others. I agreed, but felt we had to honor Diane's request.

On the drive home, Col told me that when she was growing up, the Garritys always occupied the same back row, center aisle pew for Mass every Sunday. It was the same pew Col and Sharon selected as being the one Teddie Shaw probably used, and Mary Shaw Ryan confirmed it. Figures.

A couple more weeks went by and Molly's seventy-ninth birthday was approaching. Col had never heard back from Diane. We took a Sunday walk one morning, caught a matinee at the local movie theater and snagged a sensible, simple birthday card at the local drugstore. No flowery poems or jokes. There was ample blank space for a short note.

I suggested to Col that she not say anything pointed or controversial. She only asked if they could arrange to talk again. She mailed it a little late. It would probably not arrive until a few days after Molly's August 11th birthday.

The following weekend, we went to Detroit for Col's adoptive uncle Jack Garrity's eightieth birthday party. When we returned, a letter from Molly was in our mailbox!

It was a short, handwritten, note. In it, she apologized for not writing sooner, and for things turning out the way they did. She said she wondered how Col had figured out where her seven children lived.

She added that she would try to send a picture of herself, and repeated she was not in a good place to have contact at the time. But she ended the letter by saying that perhaps that would change some day, and that if Col made it to Ireland, she would arrange to meet her.

The letter was postmarked July 30. Molly had sent it before her birthday. The birthday card Col sent to her was en route at the same time. Col was worried it would upset Molly that she had sent her a birthday card reiterating that she wanted to have contact and that it might seem in defiance of Molly's desire not to.

I explained to her that it would be obvious that the birthday card and letter had crossed paths in the mail and that Col's request was not a pushy rebuttal to the letter Molly sent. But would Molly put that together?

Molly's letter had more positives than not. Unlike her phone call to Col, wherein she was upset and angry with her for reaching out to her siblings so quickly, the tone was cordial.

And contradictory. In one sentence, Molly said she would like to know how Col found out about her children. In the next, she said she did not want contact. Molly was torn. Perhaps a side of her wanted to accept Col while another didn't.

Understandable.

What I found most promising about Molly's letter was that she said she would arrange to meet Col if we ever made it to Ireland again. I thought, contradictions or not, that was golden.

Her offer was almost an invitation. But it would not be a good idea for Col to take her up on it immediately. It would freak Molly out if Col were to write back and say we'd kicked around the idea and would be in Ireland some time soon.

Maybe after the dust settled some more. I did not want to make a trip to Ireland unless Molly specifically desired to meet Col. I felt Molly wasn't quite there yet.

But, best not to set our expectations too high. It might not get any further than this. Col might never meet her.

It seemed as if Col was beginning to regret this whole adventure. The search. The letters to Molly's brother Teddie and her kids in Ireland.

When Teddie shared the letter that Col sent with his daughter Mary Shaw Ryan, we were left no choice but to contact Molly's children. If we hadn't, what were the Chicago Shaws supposed to do? Sit on this secret? That would have been unfair to everyone.

Col agreed with me. But I was sure it was still gnawing away at her. I felt as if Col, Diane and even Molly all needed to "grow a pair", get over it and move past the trauma of the whole exposé part of this.

As the next several days passed, we discussed the situation. For now, it was best to sit back and let things simmer once again. If Molly sent a photo of herself, Col should reply, thank her for it, and share something about herself in return.

It might even be appropriate to send a pic of our latest addition, Jameson Thomas. And I thought it most important that Col not mention any of the 1958 drama. "Here's our latest grandson. Isn't he a cutie? Have a good day!" And leave it at that.

If Molly felt no pressure to have contact...

Col waited a couple weeks and then, on a Sunday night in early August, she messaged Diane via Facebook and described the most recent letter from Molly.

She learned Diane and her siblings still had not told Catharine Flaherty and did not plan to until she returned to the States in September.

Oh, c'mon.

Digital Snafus

In late August Col received another letter.

Molly shared a little bit about herself, mentioning that it was a little tough to write at times because of arthritis. She closed the letter by sharing her cell phone number and offering up the best time to call her: 4:30pm "Irish Time" on the weekends.

Now the door was a touch more than slightly ajar.

Sharon was with us for a sleepover that weekend. Valuing every day we could see her so much that we wanted to enjoy every millisecond of it, Col decided to wait until the following weekend before giving Molly a call.

But would Molly get cold feet again? Would Col's timing be bad? We certainly couldn't expect Molly to sit every Saturday or Sunday with her cell phone at her side at 4:30pm Irish.

So what? Call anyway. If it gets delayed or if she happens to be in the midst of something, so be it. Leave a message.

C'mon woman, grow that pair.

Col planned to call Molly on Saturday the 27th. We had no idea how this call might go.

Had Molly invited Col to call only so she could tell her, once more, that she is not in a place to have contact with her and to go away? Or was Molly softening up a bit?

I wanted to see the half-full glass. There was no need to bring up the past. It was history. Time for things to move forward.

In her last letter Molly shared a little about herself. I suggested that Col just treat her as if she were a long-lost old friend. Tell her you're sorry she's having pains associated with old age and share a little about your own life.

Col dialed up Molly's cell phone number at precisely 4:30pm Irish. It went to her voicemail. A soft, female greeting in a thick brogue. She left a simple "hope all is well" and "call back if you like" type message.

Neither one of us expected her to return Col's call and we felt no animosity when she didn't. Col messaged Diane about leaving that voicemail. Diane called her and they talked for a while.

Navigating 21st century technology is not one of Molly's strong suits. Diane said she would get ahold of their sister Marie to see if Molly even knew she had a voicemail.

Diane had been in Shanakeen for a few weeks and was hoping to get to Chicago. She wanted to see her uncle Teddie, and she wanted to meet Col.

The following weekend was Labor Day weekend in the States, and we were again busy with granddaughter Sharon—in big time fun mode and over for the weekend.

Col had the following week off and wanted to "chill". She did not want a potentially emotional, high-charged conversation with Molly.

I couldn't blame her. But I didn't want Molly to think that after all the grief Col had caused, now Col was the one getting cold feet and doing the "one-eighty".

The third weekend of September rolled around, and we were once again having Sharon over for a sleepover. I was really hoping Col would try calling Molly. But it didn't look promising.

But Col got a message that I thought kept us on track. In a week's time, Diane planned on being in Chicago and would let us know where she would be staying.

That was great news. We wanted very much to meet her. We wanted to get things to the point that Catharine and J.T. would be let in. I thought it ridiculous that they were being kept in the dark this long. Catharine lived in the Chicago area. For Pete's sake on a good day I could ride my bike to her home. But Diane felt this was best.

Col was going along with the program. She had told me that Diane said she was pretty sure J.T. was now aware of things and she needed to talk to Catharine about this, that her sister had to be let in because it wasn't fair to her.

I agreed wholeheartedly, but felt my hands were tied and there was not a damned thing I could do about it. I wanted to message Diane and give her a piece of my mind. I was getting fed up with her holding the reins on this, and fed up with Col for continuing to go along with it. I imagined what I'd like to say:

"Diane, if you feel it's unfair to your sister Catharine, do something about it. She has the right to know her sibling. We need to be assured that J.T. knows, too. You only said you were pretty sure he knew. Sorry. Not good enough."

I bit my tongue and stood on the sidelines. Looking back on it, Maude Frickert was actually more pissed off than I was.

Diane said she would be in Chicago the weekend of September 23rd. On Monday the 19th, she called Col and told her she would not be coming in September. Her work schedule would not permit it. But, she said, she would be in Chicago in October for sure.

Multiple sheep shite again.

So, did this now mean that Diane was going to stall on letting Catharine in until October, too?

Enough already.

I felt that the longer the time gap between when the village of Shanakeen learned of Col and when her two remaining stateside siblings learned of her, the worse it would make things in the long run.

I said as much to Col. It didn't matter. She was willing to go along with anything Diane proposed. Hook, line and sinker. I thought Col needed to take over. This was her search.

I also started secretly wishing that Chicago cousin Rene Shaw Lyons, supposedly close friends with Catharine, would get fed up with Diane dragging her feet over this and would rat out her aunt Molly to Catharine.

I was thinking like them again. The stake of titanium-hard turf hadn't done its job. The alter-egos simply refused to croak. Like nine-lived cats, they kept resurrecting.

Then, on Thursday the 22nd, Col got another letter from Molly. This one was very positive. She said she hoped Col had received her last letter, repeated her cell phone number, and said that if Col would like to call to chat, it would be very nice.

So, on Saturday at 4:28pm Irish, Col sat down to dial up Molly. It was then that she noticed something:

The phone number in the most recent letter was one digit different than the one Molly had provided the first time.

Col had called the wrong number over a month before and left a voicemail with some female stranger in Ireland.

In the interim, Col thought Molly had gotten a voicemail while Molly was sitting around wondering why her firstborn daughter, whom she had given up for adoption and who had spent all this time and effort trying to locate her, had not accepted her invitation to call.

Voce a voce!

Col tried the latest version of the cell phone number. A cyborgian greeting kicked her into voicemail. She left a message for who she hoped was Molly and had just hung up when the phone rang.

It was Molly. She'd been outside and could not get to the phone in time. She was delighted that Col was calling her.

They talked for a half hour and it was all positive. I could only hear one side of the conversation, but later Col filled in the gaps:

She told Col that she'd had some time now to think about things and she understood that "times have changed".

Col comforted her. A couple of times during that half-hour phone call, I heard her say how grateful she was to Molly for making the right decision in giving her up for adoption.

Most of their conversation centered around their respective families. Molly wanted to know about Col's grandchildren—technically her great-grandchildren even though she probably didn't feel that way. Col was getting bits and pieces about Molly's children and grandchildren, too.

They talked like two long-lost friends catching up.

As they were wrapping up the conversation, I could tell by Col's response that Molly was asking about our 2007 trip to Ireland. Crossing my fingers and hoping for what might come next; Col's next remark told me the superstitious silliness had worked:

"Yes, we are planning to come over. We're just not sure when it will happen."

Molly said she would love to meet Col in person. This was better than golden. Platinum. It meant she wasn't afraid—or at least not enough to not let, a physical meeting happen.

In due time, Col wanted Molly to know that we would be coming to Ireland specifically to meet her. If we had any additional time to visit others—Col's adoptive relatives in Westport and any of the many "angels" who'd selflessly sacrificed their time and energy to help us, that would be a great "extra".

But our purpose was for Molly and Col to meet.

It was a good thing for a few reasons: time, money, winter around the corner, that we could not make it to Ireland for at least six months. Spring of 2017. Better to have Col and Molly communicate more. Get to know each other better.

So, keeping an eye on airfares—too early to be looking at that stuff but great for positive visualization—we went on with our lives.

Two weeks later, Col and Diane talked by phone. She said Molly was planning to talk to the whole family about Col when everyone was in Shanakeen for the Christmas holiday.

She also told Col that Catharine was in the loop. Apparently, she had become suspicious, maybe because of things Molly said when Catharine was home in Shanakeen over the summer.

Or, maybe one of the Shaw cousins had "dropped a dime". In any event, Diane said Catharine was the one to bring it up, asking her if their mother had another child. Diane replied yes, and told her that she'd known for a bit, but that she had asked Col to not contact her just yet because Catharine's life was pretty crazy at the moment.

In the end, did it really matter?

Nope. It mattered that Molly be in a good place. And it seemed she was.

Diane also asked if Col would like to meet Catharine. Of course. Diane felt it would be best if she were present for that meeting and she hoped to be in Chicago in the next two weeks. We would probably have our granddaughter Sharon the first weekend she might be in, of October 28th.

But things got stalled again. Diane had clients that needed her. It would be a while. An undetermined while.

How long were we supposed to drag this out?

When Catharine returned from Shanakeen to her Bensenville home after the holidays there should be nothing preventing Col from meeting her, and tough shite if Diane couldn't make it. What was this, grammar school?

On the bright side, Molly sent Col a birthday card. It arrived the 22nd of October. It was a beautiful, old-fashioned card. Lots of lace and flowers. "To a Wonderful Daughter". She also called Col on her birthday. Col said the call was brief. Just small talk. This was great.

One again, our lives continued. Diane was always in communication with Col. She was busy working in Philadelphia and still unsure of when she could make it to Chicago.

Our Thanksgiving holiday was uneventful.

Col went through her annual, womanly ritual of sending out holiday cards. Maude Frickert helped with addressing and licking envelopes. One was, of course, sent to Molly and one to Teddie. Col included a brief note to Teddie that mentioned we hoped to see him soon. We didn't hear back from him, but we knew he appreciated the thoughts.

Christmas came and went. Col sent Teddie a birthday card. Easy to remember as it was the same as mine.

On January 11th Col got a message from Mary Shaw Ryan. Teddie was not doing well. He was at Mercy Hospital. Diane would be in Chicago as soon as possible.

Mercy Hospital. Where Col worked for twenty years. Where for the last ten, her daughter Mary T now worked.

Col would finally get to meet Diane. Under tough circumstances. We both struggled with the possibility that, with our coming from out of left field, disrupting Teddie in his waning days, we had hastened that process.

Or, were we not that important and giving ourselves too much morbid credit?

Chapter 11
An Ancient Irish Prayer
Paradoxes of Poor Timing

Diane Flaherty arrived in Chicago Friday night, the 13th of January.

Mary Shaw Ryan texted Col. She and Diane would be at O'Grady's restaurant, on 95th Street in Oak Lawn. Could we make it by 7:30pm? Of course we could. Whatever it takes.

Blue is considered a spiritually calming color. As Diane seemed a New Age type, I created a multi-denominational ensemble, wearing a powder blue polo shirt under what I call my "Papal Purple" pullover.

I picked Col up from her office and we arrived at O'Grady's. Walking in, we saw that Buddy Shaw and who we would learn was his wife Nancy and their son Colin were also present.

Even though they had talked over the phone a number of times, it was different for Col and Diane to be meeting in person. They did a lot of hugging. All the necessary introductions were made, and we sat down at a small, round "high top" table for drinks and conversation.

Nancy seemed a very pleasant woman, guileless and with a dry-sly sense of humor. Colin appeared to be in his mid-twenties. Big, tall, polite kid.

From either adrenalin, the environment, those first two beers or all the above, it felt a bit warm, so I took off that Pope Francis sweater, revealing my relaxingly tinted shirt. Diane was wearing a white pullover. Surely she had to be roasting, too. I was not the least surprised when she followed suit, revealing a blouse of an almost identical, relaxing blue hue.

Yep. New Agey all right.

We were told Teddie had been in hospital since December 30th. But he had been failing for some time. This was not entirely unexpected. All indications were that if he survived, he would not be returning to his Canaryville home of fifty-six years. It would be off to "assisted living".

We'd only met Teddie once for that Sunday night dinner a year earlier, but my impression of him and comments made by his kids indicated he was the type who would rather perish than be carted off to one of those places.

We share more than a birthday. Ditto, Teddie.

We stayed at O'Grady's for a couple of hours that night. The Shaws refused to let us pay for anything.

On Saturday afternoon, we went to the hospital. At reception we were told Teddie had visitors so we hovered around by the cafeteria on the first floor.

Diane messaged that she was one of those visitors and that Catharine, Col's sister who lived in Bensenville and whom we'd never met, had just arrived and was already in Teddie's room.

A little while later, Diane messaged Col that she and Catharine were headed down. Col would finally meet her newfound younger sister, who lived two-dozen miles away in Bensenville. They were to meet in the cafeteria.

I opted to step aside for this one and parked on an institutional grade hospital-issue armchair in a waiting area that was exceptionally quiet and meditated.

Until the janitors arrived to vacuum the carpets.

I thought of the author and public speaker Dr. Wayne Dyer, who once described the challenges of meditating in a place that starts conducive, only to become so noisy it's the opposite. The cleaning crew has the same right to make noise as I do to meditate.

His solution? Surrender to it, let it become part of the meditation. Spiritual white noise.

That approach wasn't working for me. No transcendental

vacuum cleaner today. If it must be a motor, the preferred background music to my meditative ears would be the hopalong hymn of a perfectly tuned "Harley" at idle.

Just as I started seeking a new spot to isolate my ethereal self, Col, Diane and Catharine emerged from the cafeteria.

I recognized Catharine from Facebook pics I'd seen. She seemed a very nice person. Soft-spoken. Very polite, almost formal in a way. In every pic I'd seen her in, she was always dressed well. No blue jeans or t-shirts or gym shoes. In person, she didn't let me down on that one.

Teddie Shaw would not have cared how any visitor was dressed. But his niece Catharine Flaherty sure did.

The four of us talked in the hallway for several minutes. Catharine said Teddie was tired and falling off to sleep when she left his room. Col and I figured it best to let him rest. We didn't live far. We would get by there soon. We bid each other solemn farewells.

On Sunday, we met midafternoon with Mary Shaw Ryan and Diane at Medici Pizza on 53rd Street in Hyde Park. Though not with us, our granddaughter Sharon is especially fond of "Medici" because they encourage doodling graffiti on the walls and wooden booths.

It was obvious how tired Mary was. Given the circumstances, the four of us had a relaxing time. I couldn't tell you what any of us ate. We didn't talk about Teddie much. I think everyone knew things were not going well.

As always, I managed to stick—only one this time—foot in my mouth. I said that it was wonderful we were all becoming friends, but that what was most important was the next phase: Col meeting Molly.

Of course I didn't mean it to sound as if I was forgetting the reason Mary and Diane were with us. Mary was close to losing her father, Diane her uncle. But I realized after it springboarded from my lips that it sure could have come across that way. I opted to not apologize or explain anything. Better to leave it be and hope they understood what I meant.

Even the grumpy Maude Frickert would have been more tactful. Why couldn't I be?

We weren't at Medici long. Mary Shaw Ryan needed her rest and Diane needed to fly home to Philadelphia.

We wanted to visit Teddie but had to make sure it was at the right moment. We did not want to cross paths with a friend or relative from the neighborhood who might wonder what we were doing there.

Even though the Shaws were treating us like family, in a way we were not. We were newcomers in a most unusual way.

On Thursday, we learned Teddie declined enduring any surgeries that might prolong his life and had been moved to a nearby hospice. In the minds of most believers, regardless of stripe, he was now in the final step before his soul headed off on its next voyage.

We planned to visit on Friday evening, when Col got off work. On that day Col woke up at her usual time. We had just finished breakfast and were getting ready to leave so I could drive her to the train station for her commute.

"We need to see Teddie this morning. I don't care if I miss the train and I'm late for work. I'll catch the next one."

We arrived at the hospice center about 7:30am. Kathleen was keeping vigil. He was lying on his right side, his breathing short and labored, but we could sense he could hear us. Kathleen started weeping. Col hugged her. I started to choke up a little too and had to turn away and face a wall for a moment.

Col announced to him that we were in the room. We both thanked him for being so kind to us. Col sat down on one side of the bed. I stood at the other side. She held one of his hands for a bit and I touched the other as I thanked him one last time. We said goodbye to Kathleen, who was reaching for more tissues as we left.

We got down to our car. Just as we pulled out of our spot in the lot outside the door, Mary Shaw Ryan arrived and filled our vacancy. We circled back and exchanged a few pleasantries before she headed in.

I dropped Col off at the train station. We both went on about our day. About 5:00pm, she called:

"I just got off the phone with Mary Shaw Ryan. Teddie died at about 4:40."

It was a good thing Col's sixth sense was in fine tune that morning and we had made sure to see him that last time.

I now had to deal with the perpetual guilt of knowing Col would have no memories of Teddie beyond that dinner with the Shaws, when I couldn't shut my pie hole long enough to allow her to fully enjoy the experience.

But I had to cut myself loose from this self-imposed whipping post because we were faced with a new challenge. We knew we'd be going to the wake—easy to attend without raising suspicion. We could simply say we knew Teddie from the neighborhood and were stopping by to pay our last respects.

What about the funeral? We knew we would probably have to do a little dance here and there, but as long as it didn't ruffle anyone's feathers, we were in. The word we were getting was that several relatives would be coming over from Ireland.

The wake was scheduled for the following Tuesday, with the funeral the next day at St. Gabriel's. Diane's twin brother, Patrick Flaherty, would be arriving from Ireland, as would brother J.T. from Colorado. Col's Irish aunt, Mary Shaw Tierney, would be flying over, but her twin brother John Shaw would not be. Some of Col's cousins from both Chicago and Ireland would be there.

On Monday, Patrick Flaherty and others arrived. Diane messaged Col that Patrick wanted to meet her. They would be at Buddy Shaw's house that evening. Col was working until 5:30. We could be there by about 6:15pm.

When we arrived at Buddy and Nancy's medium-sized, two-story brick home on the Southwest Side, we were asked if we'd like to stay for dinner. As it just so happened, I was starving. Through the condensation on the glass-doored oven I spied what looked like a beef roast in the oven.

And boy, was it. Top sirloin I believe. When I got to the second helping there was a tiny bit of fat, barely the size of a petite pea, right in the center of the perfectly medium rare slice. I thought back to that leg o' lamb at Teddie's house a year before:

Buddy was sitting right next to me, just like his father. Out of the corner of my eye, I thought I saw him eyeing me. I ate that little piece of marbling, relishing it like the sugar baby prize in a multi-colored Mardi Gras King Cake.

Then, out came dessert. Diane contributed a cheesecake assortment that may have come with her from Philadelphia. Or she got it in Chicago. Nothing wrong with our versions either.

Then, as we were getting ready to leave, a woman named Ellen Carol stopped by with a contribution to the wake: two huge Tupperware containers of her homemade blueberry scones. Thinking that she may have been related to the Carol family I grew up down the street from in Bridgeport, I inquired:

"Tell me, is Carol your maiden name?"

"No, Ellen Carol is my first and middle name. I'm a Kafferly. Johnny's my brother. I'm a Kennedy now. I married Pat Kennedy."

Jesus, Mary and Joseph.

So here we were, standing in the home of Col's maternal cousin, meeting a sibling from Ireland for the first time, and her paternal cousin, her birth father's niece, shows up with scones.

Now we knew exactly who Ellen Carol was. Even though at Gaelic Park over a year earlier we had learned from the Shaws that she had married a Kennedy, I played coy:

"Oh, you're Johnny's sister!"

"Yes, I'm seven years younger."

"I remember Johnny from grammar school. My older brother Bill was in your brother Daniel's class."

Col piped in next:

"I remember all the Kennedys. I was in Michael's class in grammar school at St. Gabe's."

Ellen Carol shot us both a look that said:

"I know who you are, and I know you know who I am."

As Buddy's wife Nancy would dryly understate after Ellen Carol left:

"The world keeps getting smaller and smaller."

The next evening, I picked Col up directly from her office. I decided to not dress up in the least. As far as anyone was concerned, we were just neighborhood folk who knew Teddie Shaw. We were there to pay our respects and say a few kind words to his relatives.

It was an Irish wake, all right. Even though it was not out in the open, we were informed that if desired, there was a bottle of Jameson tucked away beneath the snack table. I noticed a good number of discarded plastic shot glass empties on counters, in wastebaskets and on crumbed-up throwaway plates.

Teddie had been ill for a long time. He had lived a good life. It was not a completely sad occasion. This had been expected for a few years. People were sad that he had passed, but happy to see their relatives, especially those from Ireland.

Col and I were feeling torn. We had not met Molly yet, but we were meeting all of these other long-lost relatives. This was good, but the reason behind it was the passing of the patriarch of this very large family.

As I come from a large family, it got me pondering my own mortality and that of my loved ones. I would be crushed if one of my six siblings should pass away and so, to avoid that suffering there's a side of me that wants to kick the bucket first. Yet, viewed from another angle, that means I'm the selfish one—that I would rather die than endure the grief of one of them passing. It's a paradox with no solution.

Way too much philosophical head-scratching. It's no wonder I'm bald.

We met another sibling! J.T. made it from Colorado. Nice guy. He'd emigrated in the early 1990s and, just like his sisters Diane and Catharine a decade earlier, stayed with Uncle Teddie until he got set up in the States.

A self-described "gypsy" since, he'd lived around the world, never married, but he had at least one child with a girlfriend way back when. He told me he had studied engineering in Ireland, and that he'd used that education to build his own adobe home in Pueblo.

As we drained our plastic shot glasses of "Jamie" he said one thing about Teddie that I will never forget:

"He was of a different generation. These were guys who worked hard and drank even harder."

We saw Molly's sister, Mary Shaw Tierney of Ireland. I'd seen pictures of her on Facebook, so I knew who she was right away. Eighty-two years old, at best an equal number of pounds soaking wet and barely five feet tall. Diane and Catharine kept placing themselves between Col and her.

We had already heard Mary was energetic and feisty. She seemed quite lucid and she started eyeing Col right away. The girls' "screen play" didn't last long. But there were so many people, at least seventy-five when we arrived, that we just kept moving around. An improvised "end around" play. Mary would glance at us now and then, but that was the extent of her curiosity.

We met hordes of people that night. At the funeral the next day, we would learn that some of the younger generation— nephews and nieces who were in the long receiving line stretched along the wall of the parlor, had been informed who Col was. That explained the obvious nods and winks when we were introduced.

Ellen Carol Kennedy's scones were the perfect texture and not too sweet.

I also noticed on the snack bar an abundance of pitted olives, both black and green, along with a two-litre jug of root beer. I would learn that, when in hospice, Teddie had said, since it would no longer matter, both previously forbidden items would be allowed at his wake.

On the drive home, we talked of how well things went.

Joycean Climes

The next day, we drove to St. Gabe's. In honor of Teddie, a Chicago Police Department squad car, its "Mars" lights flashing, was parked outside. Inside, several parishioners were finishing up the daily ritual: reading aloud the "Stations of the Cross".

We picked out a pew on the left side of the center aisle that would make us one of the crowd and got comfortable. People started making their way into the church for the funeral.

We were seeing many of the same faces we'd seen the night before. Col tugged on my coat sleeve the moment she opened the program that included the specifics of the service:

"Look who's one of the celebrants."

The celebrant is the priest. In this case, there were two. She pointed to the second name:

"Father Thomas Mulvaney. He married Maureen and Tom Boroski."

Uncle Dunkle.

Stood to reason. Father Mulvaney was a Fire Department Chaplain. Teddie and Uncle Dunkle had both been coppers. It was just one more insignificant connection that made the world shrink more.

Ellen Carol Kennedy came in, helping an elderly woman along. Col said it was Mrs. Geraldine Kennedy, matriarch of the

Kennedy clan. Had to be in her nineties by now. Joining them a moment later was Ellen Carol's husband, Pat.

It was a very good service. Teddie's grandkids were involved. Two of the older ones gave readings from Scripture. A couple of younger ones were "Presenters of the Gifts"—whatever that means. Buddy Shaw gave the eulogy:

"Our Dad was an old school guy, simple, proud, tough but fair. He instilled in us the importance of hard work and being pragmatic, respectful, honest, and most of all, he remembered you. He helped many a friend who was there when he needed him. He was a man who meant something different to each of us."

"We all knew a different side of him and are thankful for the parts he shared of himself. He doted over all nine of us, but as the only boy, he loved to include me in men's past times. He took me fishing, in Chicago and on vacation at the family cottage on Diamond Lake in Michigan. I will never forget summers with him there. He'd rise just before dawn, and began each day with his eye opener. Two jiggers of Jameson. When asked why two, he would always say, 'I have two eyes, don't I?'"

"He loved the small fishing boat he kept at the cottage. After he retired, he replaced the original motor with a four-cylinder racing engine that was almost too much for his old wooden craft. One day, as we sped across the lake, I asked why he decided to install such a fast motor. He said, 'I'm an old man now. I have less time left.'"

"He taught me how to skin a catfish at that cottage, and how to shoot a gun, when we'd take target practice out back with the twenty-two caliber Ruger that lived in the glove box of our station wagon."

"Being Irish Catholic and a policeman were central to the core of his existence. He was proud that he enjoyed keeping up with the news online, particularly of the Chicago sports teams."

"He liked to be punctual. He once made us stop the car a

block from church, so we could get out and run, instead of waiting to park, so we wouldn't be late."

"He loved being a policeman, worked up to the last day that he could. He made many great friends and mentored many. He was clever, funny, enjoyed a good sense of humor in others. Many people would tell him something he had said thirty years ago, and it still stuck with them."

"He was the source of a dark sense of humor, that now belongs to many of us. The dinner table was full of laughter, teasing, as he tried to pit us against each other, to who was the favorite child. He could be a prankster to fellow policeman and to his own kids and close family."

"He loved our mother deeply, and took care of her throughout her long illness with love and caring. He loved all his children, remembered all of our birthdays and never missed any of our school or church events."

"He really enjoyed his grandchildren and was very proud of each and every one of them. He tried very hard in the end to meet his first great grandchild. He loved his sisters and brother, nieces and nephews very much."

"Up to the end he continued to impress us with his open heart, as he expressed gratitude to the medical staff at Mercy Hospital, then later in rehab. He told his family constantly how proud he was of all of us. Finally, in his strength in leaving this world on his own terms, we are very proud of him. He was the greatest."

On the last couple of phrases, his voice faltered in emotion as he stepped away from the podium.

Following tradition, we waited after the service for the immediate family, as they accompanied the casket up the aisle to the church exit and the waiting hearse outside. We fell in line at the end, with the rest of the general congregation.

There was Johnny Kafferly, waiting aisle-side toward the back of the church. He gave a quick "hello" and shook each of our hands warmly.

When we got outside "old home week" continued. We were all outside the church, standing around in small groups and talking as the procession was being organized. The traffic cop assigned to stop traffic for the funeral procession was none other than Sammy Heinz.

I had known Sammy for years. We hugged and chatted very briefly before heading to our cars for the six or so mile drive to the cemetery.

The drive there got me thinking of the following paragraph, from James Joyce's "The Dead".

Even though the descriptions didn't match this blustery day, with what little snow that had fallen being blown about in a continual blender-like fury, it reminded me so much of Chicago cemeteries at more placid moments in the midst of our often brutal winters:

> "Yes, the newspapers were right: snow was general all over Ireland. It was falling softly upon the Bog of Allen and, further westwards, softly falling into the dark mutinous Shannon waves. It was falling too upon every part of the lonely churchyard where Michael Furey lay buried. It lay thickly drifted on the crooked crosses and headstones, on the spears of the little gate, on the barren thorns. His soul swooned slowly as he heard the snow falling faintly through the universe and faintly falling, like the descent of their last end, upon all the living and the dead."

There was no graveside service. Instead, the casket was wheeled into the vestibule of a small chapel and—as Teddie was a veteran, the ritual of folding the American flag that draped the coffin into a perfect triangle and presenting it to his son Buddy was performed. A few words were spoken, and we headed to our cars. Ellen Carol Kennedy walked nearby. I couldn't resist:

"You make a delicious scone, by the way."

"Why, thank you."

Then her husband Pat Kennedy saw Col.

"Colleen! Wow, it's been years! How are you?"

They hugged and Col asked if she could say hello to his mom, Geraldine, who had stayed in the car while these final rituals took place.

While Col reminisced with Mrs. Kennedy, Buddy and Mary Shaw Ryan emerged. They wanted to know if we were going to lunch as well, at Via Roma in the nearby suburb of Burbank. I was a little concerned. After all, this would be a different situation. We would stick out because we were not family. I stalled:

"Col is saying hello to Mrs. Kennedy. Let me ask her."

Col returned shortly thereafter. She said Geraldine was still sharp mentally and immediately recognized her—reeling off the names of Col's five Garrity siblings—and wanted to know how all were doing. When I told Col we'd been invited to Via Roma, her expression revealed some reluctance.

I recalled a story about a spiritual leader who perished because he'd been offered rice by a family that wasn't aware it had gone bad and turned poisonous, and that even though his physical senses told him the rice was bad, from a spiritual standpoint he had to accept the offering. The gist of the parable is that regardless of the consequences, he had to accept the offering of food. I made it my decision:

"Yes, of course we'll join you. I know where it is."

On arriving at Via Roma we realized we didn't need to worry about being noticed. Buddy Shaw had booked the entire restaurant along with a five-piece Irish string band. It was a party Teddie would have wanted.

We were among sixty-plus people. Open bar, so beer, wine and harder stuff flowed freely. Long tables had been set up for the Family Style Italian lunch. We hung out with those we'd already met.

We didn't see Ellen Carol Kennedy or her husband Pat. Were they not attending because our presence made her that uncomfortable? Did she not want anything to do with us because she—and perhaps the other Kafferlys and McMahons—wanted Connie Coneely to forever be considered Col's natural father?

Or, was it just that she and Pat couldn't make it and my own morbid selfishness was once again the villain? Was my mind's worst enemy my mind?

In 1958, when confronted by Teddie Shaw, John V. McMahon had insisted that Connie was Col's father. DNA evidence proved he was lying to Teddie. What sort of man did that make John? I struggled with that one. I'm sure Col did too.

It was not fair of us to judge him. His denial may have been his survival instinct kicking in because he didn't want Teddie to beat him to smithereens for impregnating his sister.

I felt there was nothing we could do. What's done is done. Yet, I kept getting back to the feeling that maybe, when I first learned that, in what was at that time the second largest city in the U.S., everything had happened right in our own back yard and involved people whose relatives and friends we knew from both parishes, we should have then walked away from it and left well enough alone.

Those feelings never lasted long.

As we worked our way around the restaurant, there was Mary Shaw Tierney, Molly's "five stone and twelve" sister. I could tell she was wondering who we were.

It was fun watching Col's Flaherty sisters block Mary's view a bit and distract her when she looked like she was about to approach Col. I was surprised she hadn't put two and two together because Col probably looked like Molly twenty years earlier. But, in her early eighties, maybe her eyesight wasn't so grand anymore.

Soon, it was time to eat. We opted to sit at a table with, among others, Kathleen Shaw Judge. Her husband, Jim, also sat with us.

The food was quite good. Pasta, salad, chicken and beef. I

wouldn't have called it Italian. Definitely Italian American.

We started talking with Kathleen and Jim, and I mentioned that I felt it was a good thing that at least we knew Connie Coneely was innocent. Even if he'd passed away a dozen years ago, a married man would no longer be to blame for this. Kathleen whispered across the table:

"You might want to keep it down. That's Connie's daughter, Marla, sitting across from you."

She tossed a glance at a dark-haired woman, probably in her fifties, not ten feet away from me on the other side of our table.

Holy quintuple sheep shite. The world will "fit in me hip pocket" if it gets any smaller.

Luckily, it appeared Marla Coneely had not heard me mention the half-century overdue exoneration of her father.

After lunch, everybody went back to drinking. It soon became apparent that this might go on forever. Buddy Shaw knew exactly what to do: He had the bartender shut down the "open" bar.

No more free drinks works every time.

Buddy asked us if we'd like to join him and other family back at his house. This was going to be a much tighter situation. We knew we would stick out but we both had a few cocktails in us, so caution was heaved wholesale into those fan blades:

Of course, we would love to join you!

It was back to Buddy's house, where we'd had that fabulous beef roast dinner just two nights earlier.

When we arrived the whole crew was there. Five of Col's Flaherty siblings. Many of the many Teddie Shaw girls were there, a couple with their husbands.

The Ireland contingent was composed of Mary Shaw Tierney and her daughter Sharon Tierney McAuliffe, who had flown over with her. Tierney's twin brother John Shaw could not make it, but two of his sons, John and Michael, were present, as was his daughter, Rebecca Shaw Gannon.

It was then that I learned Teddie's home, which was being used by the travelers as lodging these past few days, had been burglarized by "wakers":

Wakers are criminals who browse obituaries to find residences that make for easy targets while everyone is off to the wake or funeral. During the wake they broke in through Teddie's back door. Some cash was taken. What a way to greet visitors to Chicago.

We stayed a couple hours. A few kept glancing our way as if about to ask us two party crashers just who the heck we were. Mary Shaw Tierney was seated at the kitchen table, and whenever Col mulled around that area, I could see her eyeing her. It looked like she hadn't made the familial connection yet.

I also had a small degree of concern for Mary's nephew, John Shaw Junior. The guy is big. Really big. The size of a church door big. I sensed he wasn't against mixing it up with his ham hock-sized fists now and then either.

He and a couple other guys were standing around in the kitchen, beers in hand. He appeared to have a few in him. I thought I saw him giving me the eye, the likes of which I'd seen in my bartending days in Chicago thirty years hence—often just before a bloody fray erupts.

I knew nothing like that was going to happen here. But I got the feeling he may have had an inkling who Col and I were, and he may have been a little offended that we had not introduced ourselves.

Our plan all along—and we'd been following it—was to not say anything unless asked. And if asked, keep it to simple half-truths:

I knew Teddie from Murphy's Tavern. Col knew the Murphys from her eight years living ninety feet west of Teddie's sister-in-law, Francis Murphy's widow Martha. Nice and easy. I had a feeling that, soon enough and when the timing was right, everyone would know and love Col.

We had met some of the Shaws. Col had been in contact with her mother and her sister Diane. Now, we'd spent some time with more Flahertys and Shaws. I was getting to know and love these people. It was as if I had known them all along. Partly because I'd been researching their roots for a couple of years and partly because, in the case of the Chicago-based relatives, we were from the same general neighborhood.

It was time to move on. As my drunken digits fumbled for the car key, a small laminated "Mass Card" fluttered out of one pocket. It had a picture of Teddie on one side and an ancient Irish prayer on the reverse. The author was probably not describing the rock-pocked, windswept slopes of my beloved Connemara:

"May the earth be soft under you when you lie upon it, tired at the end of the day. And may it rest easy over you when at last you lie underneath it. May it rest so lightly over you that your soul may be quickly through it and on its way to God."

We would soon be on our way to an earthly destination across the ocean, our imaginary compass the contrail of a turbine-powered leprechaun.

Chapter 12
Seats Upright

The Summit

After Teddie Shaw's passing, wake, and funeral, Col and I were emotionally trashed.

The guilt of wondering if we had accelerated Teddie's demise when he learned his friend John V. McMahon had lied to him in 1958 by pointing the paternal finger at Connie Coneely. The slippery slope at four functions: the wake, funeral and both follow-up gatherings. The twin surprises of Ellen Carol Kafferly Kennedy's late night scone delivery and unexpectedly sharing post-funereal lunch with Connie's daughter Marla. It was all catching up.

What about Molly? She was who this was all about from the beginning, yet so much had happened that she had taken a back seat.

On the other hand, those events helped. Col got to meet a few more relatives. Got to be vetted some more. But what a backward way this had all come to fruition. From everything I'd read about others who had located their birth parents, both here and in Ireland, it was usually the bm who was found first.

We had identified Col's birth father first. Col met two of his three children. We identified Col's bm and met her maternal cousins, followed by her maternal uncle and then much of his extended family when he passed away, even meeting four of Col's seven maternal siblings before we were to meet the other three...

You just can't write this stuff. Hmmm... wait a second...

I would have crawled bare-chested across an ocean of broken glass to get to Shanakeen. Our plan was to go over as soon as we could after Col wrapped up income tax season on April 18th.

We booked our flights for a Friday night April 21st departure with a return on Sunday afternoon April 30th. An overnight flight, we'd leave Chicago about 8:30pm and, due to the six-hour time difference, arrival in Dublin would be about 10:15am Irish Time, Saturday morning the 22nd.

I immediately posted on the Adoption Rights Alliance Facebook page that we wanted to meet anyone interested for snacks and beverages—adult or non—in Dublin around midday on the 22nd before boarding the bus west for Galway City. Kathy Finn, Therese Norris and Bernice Wade responded favorably.

We booked a B&B, Villa Clifden, about a mile south of Shanakeen, for the 22nd through the 25th. Our plan was to go to Oughterard on the 25th to see Col's birth father John V. McMahon's home town. On the 26th we'd check out of Villa Clifden and visit Col's adoptive relatives in Westport, the Corcorans. After spending the night at their hotel, the Castlecourt, we'd return to Villa Clifden for the remainder of our trip, from the 27th though the 29th.

Col wrote to May Corcoran's daughter Ann and explained why we could only stay at the Castlecourt one night. It was common knowledge among the Westport relatives, particularly old-timers like May, that Tom and Mary Agnes Garrity had adopted all six of their children, but Ann was unaware of that part of the family history. We never brought it up when we met her during our first trip to Ireland in 2007. This time we did explain the primary purpose for our upcoming visit. Ann was understanding and looked forward to seeing us, if only for the one night and following day.

I also contacted Louise Munster, a member of the Adoption Rights Alliance who lives in Westport, to see if she'd like to meet us for a pint or two. She said the night we'd be in town, she had been planning to attend a play.

Entitled, "The Stolen Child", the protagonist is an adoptee searching for her birth mother. Go figure. I guess we picked the right day to visit Westport. I ordered two tickets online for the performance of the evening of the 26th. We planned to meet Louise and a friend of hers, fellow ARA member Grainne Shannon, at the show and for drinks afterwards.

Villa Clifden is owned by Doug and Irene Callaway. I had one concern: I'd seen the family surname Callaway connected to Shaw family history. If Doug was a cousin of Molly, it might get a little sticky if any of the Callaways saw who we were walking up the road to visit. Col contacted Diane Flaherty. She said Callaway was a common surname and that Doug and Irene were not direct relatives of hers.

That concern put to rest, we then literally counted the days from the time we bought the tickets and made our arrangements.

March 17th brought St. Patrick's Day. The contemporary Irish musician Ed Sheeran released the song "Galway Girl". One more funny coincidence. But the subject of his song seemed a bit of a "barfly", better at drinking, gambling, throwin' darts and shootin' billiards than Sheeran, and from what little we had learned, nothing like the "Conomara cailin", the Connemara colleen we were due to meet in less than two months.

Now that things were getting close, fear started creeping in. What if Molly got cold feet after we got over? What would we do?

We decided to not change anything. If she wimped out, we would not wimp out with her. We would remain at her "beck and call", a mile down the road at Villa Clifden, the two exceptions being our overnight foray to Westport and day trip to Oughterard.

That was unlikely to happen. Diane Flaherty passed word along that Molly was anxious yet looking forward to our visit. It was a huge plus that Col and Molly had been talking and writing back and forth for several months now.

We didn't want to entertain any expectations about the reception we would get from Molly, or anyone else. It sounded as if Col's siblings that she had not yet met, Marie Flaherty, Sandra

Flaherty Collier and Jimmie Flaherty, didn't harbor any adverse feelings for us sending out letters to the whole village, slinging all that turf into the fan.

At this point, we also weren't sure what Molly's twin siblings, Mary Shaw Tierney and John Shaw, knew. When she returned to Ireland barely sixty days after giving to birth to Col in 1958, wouldn't there have been physical signs that people—especially her sister and her mother—would have noticed?

It was hard to swallow that this secret was as secret as it was. People love to talk.

Especially about secrets.

If Peggy Shaw told her kids, when they were growing up, that their aunt Molly was pregnant in 1958, surely this must have gotten back to Shanakeen.

But, to hell with the past. What mattered now was the present and presently Molly's sister and brother probably knew about Col.

And they'd probably learned we would be there to visit soon. Would we be meeting these Shaw twins as well? It appeared they lived in the same general area. I guessed, soon enough, we'd find out.

Spittoons Regurgitate

On a different note, one day in late March, I checked the Mary Eileen O'Brien Yahoo email account:

A 23andMe message from a Peggy McMahon of Providence, Rhode Island! She was putting together a family tree and had her DNA tested. Col came up a 2nd cousin, but Peggy had no idea how Col was connected to the McMahon clan.

Of course not. No one was supposed to know her father was John V. McMahon.

Peggy's actual surname is McManus but as we'd learned, the original family name in Ireland was McMahon. So people—

especially those in Ireland—would recognize it, she used McMahon on the family tree.

Peggy invited Col to have a look at the McMahon tree she was piecing together on Ancestry.com. It proved a very thorough one, and it took very little scrolling for us to see how she and Col were related. They share a great-grandfather, Michael McMahon, making them 2nd cousins.

Until this point, I had never considered that with the increasing popularity of DNA testing, someone fairly close on Col's father's, or, even worse as she was still alive, Molly's side who didn't know the filthy little secret might submit DNA and wonder just who Colleen Garrity Terrazino is.

It would matter—a lot—if a cousin or other close relative on Molly's side who had not been told of Col's existence took a DNA test and didn't know what to make of this mystery match.

So far I'd seen some DNA matches that, by the surnames and villages mentioned in their profiles, were very likely distant relatives from Molly's side. Thankfully, we had not yet been approached by any of them.

I had not seen any DNA relatives with the last name Shaw, or any that listed that surname on their profiles on those sites. I did see some Costellos and Callaways, but they were distant so at this point I wasn't losing any sleep over them.

But I figured it would only be a matter of time before this happened on Molly's side. We would have to protect her secret as best we could. And we'd have to have faith that if anyone did put it together and figure out Molly was Col's natural mother the secret would be honored, and no one would approach Molly about it.

Without revealing names, we emailed Peggy McManus the truth. We told her Col was an adoptee and of our upcoming plans that included a day trip to see Col's birth father's home town, Oughterard. If possible, we wanted to meet any paternal relatives who might still be around. If we did meet any our plan was to keep it vague: Col knew she had McMahon roots, but was a distant cousin, unsure of the precise familial connection.

Peggy could not have been more accommodating. It was apparent she had figured out Col's father was John V. McMahon. She said she understood the situation and the need for confidentiality. She immediately sent photos she took when she last visited Oughterard, in 2011. There were pictures of the family tavern, Crosby's, now owned by another cousin, Elizabeth Crosby, and operated by Elizabeth's son, Paul.

A phone call was arranged. Col and Peggy talked a bit. Peggy said she had contacted Elizabeth Crosby and that Elizabeth was looking forward to meeting us in April. That was great! We'd get to meet natural Irish kin on Col's father's side.

Not so fast. Peggy then informed Col that Elizabeth Crosby is not really "blood kin". She's also an adoptee!

Why was I not the least shocked?

By early April, it felt as if I was starting to count the hours, let alone the days remaining until we'd finally get on that Dublin-bound flight. Our lives went on, but there was barely a moment I wasn't pondering our upcoming adventure.

For better or worse, this was the culmination of what had been a ton of work and heartache for both of us. Col was so busy with tax season that she seemed less anxious than I, but with a couple of weeks to go, she admitted she too was starting to get the jitters.

Meeting Old Chums

"May the road rise up to meet you and may the wind always be at your back!"

So goes an old Irish expression. I had seen it on wall plaques, coffee mugs and other forms of "swag" forever.

And, going over the pond to Ireland, we would have the perpetually prevailing westerly breeze at our back. As we'd be fighting that same wind coming home, the trip back to Chicago was estimated to be an hour or thereabouts longer.

The day arrived before we knew it. We traveled light. Each of us had a carry-on piece that contained essentials.

This included a half dozen single serve airline-sized bottles of Jamie. We figured a couple of cocktails would help us nod off and get some sleep before we arrived in Dublin and we didn't want to pay onboard airline prices.

Oh, now and then I may have dozed off for a few minutes during those seven hours. But whether I watched a movie, read a book or just zoned out, all I could think of was the adventure ahead of us. Certain that I had now shaken off my alter-egos, I could now sit back and drink it all in.

On the other hand, and perhaps the feeling is physiological and harkens back to our days as hunter-gatherers hunkered down in caves, I'm always in protect mode when it comes to Col. I knew I would be paying close attention, not wanting anything to go awry.

We touched down in Dublin and boarded a bus for Dublin City Centre. Angels Kathy Finn, Therese Norris and Bernice Wade were to meet us at the Wynne Hotel.

The bus arrived at Dublin City Centre, leaving us with an hour before we were due at the hotel, so we got a bite to eat at Starbucks—yes, they're everywhere. It was too crowded inside for us and our luggage. We sat on the old stone walk along the River Liffey, watching the crowd.

We did not know why so many people were wearing soccer jerseys and boarding buses. When told there was a major game that afternoon, I thought back to our first and only visit ten years before when, having the luxury of time and without the burden of luggage, we walked the city for half the day.

This trip, we wouldn't get to walk through beautiful St. Stephen's Green, over the Ha' Penny Bridge, or watch an inning or two—if that's what they call them—of cricket as we had before.

The thing I noticed most, just in walking from the bus stand to Starbucks to the river, was that the foot traffic I'd witnessed in 2007 had changed. Dublin now seemed much more international. I overheard voices in different tongues that sounded Eastern European—perhaps Polish or Russian, and others that I couldn't put my finger on.

Ireland has been invaded, since the Vikings in the 8th century to the Brits in the 12th to the Spanish in the 16th to the French in the 18th. Woven throughout those ten centuries were rebellions and internal strife that continues to this day. Hell, the Brits still control a chunk of it.

In the 21st century, those coming to live in Ireland seemed to be doing so not to rape, loot and pillage, but for economic reasons: to live and work because they'll be better off here than in their homelands.

I wondered how the native Irish felt. I would suspect that, just as in the U.S., there are those who want to shut down the influx, feeling that the immigrants are taking away their jobs and changing Ireland for the worse. There are probably many others who welcome the newcomers.

When we arrived, it was standing room only in the small bar area off the hotel lobby. It was packed with people tossing a few down before heading off to their busses and the big game.

The sea of midday drinkers parted on cue, reveling their way out just in time for Kathy, Therese and Bernice to arrive. During the search, Col hadn't gotten to know them as I had.

I had no difficulty recognizing Kathy Finn and she recognized me immediately. An energetic woman, Kathy was the angel who visited the local GRO office and had copies of several birth certs pulled for us, starting with likely Mary Margaret O'Briens all the way through to Molly Shaw.

Therese Norris, who had connected the dots that identified Shanakeen, was on Kathy's heels. She seemed young. Maybe in her twenties. To be a member of ARA one must have a direct connection to adoption in Ireland. Many of its members are adoptees who started out their lives in one of the many Mother and Baby Homes.

Was Therese born in one? I thought they'd closed in the 1990s. If so, she must have been in one of the last "graduating classes" of those hellholes. I made a mental note to inquire.

I had never seen a clear picture of Bernice Wade. Her Facebook pic looks like a cross between an Alice in Wonderland illustration and an LSD-influenced Peter Max portrait. Everything about the woman in multi-colored garb beaming a Cheshire cat grin screamed this was not a soccer fan who'd had one too many and missed her bus.

Commandeering a couple of tall round tops, we huddled a few stools together and ordered. No one let Col and me pay for anything. They said we were guests of Ireland. That's the kind of people these are.

We hadn't even gotten to our ultimate destination, but I felt touched already. All I could do was keep thanking the three of them for their help and support.

There was small talk, but most of the conversation centered around adoption, how draconian laws and attitudes are in Ireland, and how little separation there is between church and state in their country.

What I found odd is that in 2015 same-sex marriage was legalized in Ireland, yet in 2017 abortion was still illegal, and adoptees still had almost no rights whatsoever.

The Adoption and Tracing Bill 2016 was on the table, but it was not overly favorable to adoptees. If passed it would mean that adoptees in Ireland would be able to request their Original Birth Certificate and other information from the adoption files that pertained to them.

This was similar to legislation enacted in Illinois in 2011 that enabled Col to get a copy of her OBC. But the Irish adoptee would also have to sign an agreement to not use the information to try and locate their birth relatives. And it's even more likely in Ireland than the States that the name on the OBC will be bogus.

I don't know about Col, but I know I felt as if I was not completely "in the room". My soul was in Shanakeen. I was anxious to get my body there as well.

Our three angels had errands to run anyway. We parted ways and hung around the river some more, listening to foreigners until it was time to board the bus for Galway City, where Diane Flaherty planned to pick us up for the drive to Shanakeen.

It was a brilliant spring day. The bus cruised over a countryside peppered with cows and sheep, crisscrossed with the usual boundaries of stone walls and gorse hedges. I did manage to close my eyes a bit to recharge my physical batteries during that two hour-plus ride.

And when the bus rolled into the depot in Galway City Centre, there was Diane Flaherty, excited about what was to happen later. It had been decided it would be best for Col and Molly to meet alone at first. At Molly's home. 7:30pm. Ninety-odd minutes later, Diane dropped us off at Villa Clifden.

With a couple of hours to kill after checking in with the sweet and gracious proprietor Irene Callaway, we walked into town and found a small, beyond casual waiterless restaurant with wooden tables named the Pizza Parlor that, according to the menu taped to the window, had other fast, inexpensive food as well. Not wanting to eat that much, we instead headed around the corner to a local grocery store that held everything we like to keep handy when traveling: snacks, apples, wine and beer.

When we returned with our provisions, I realized Villa Clifden doesn't provide a small refrigerator in each room. Some B&Bs do, some don't.

But I found the tile floor of the "loo" was on the cold side.

So I found the best spot—right next to the toilet—and got our beverages chilling. I guessed the tiles to be between 50 and 60 degrees Fahrenheit. Perfect for Col's cabernet.

Because I had bought Guinness, drinkable at well... any temperature below boiling, it all worked out.

About 7:15pm, Diane called Col to let her know she would be downstairs to pick her up in a few minutes. Now Col was visibly nervous. Try as I could, it was impossible to place myself in her shoes.

As if luck had anything to do with it, I wished some on her when she left and then settled in for some Irish television, paired with Irish beer and Irish "trail mix" for dinner. One pint along, I would discover that the open transom window of the bathroom held cans of beverage in the Irish night breeze perfectly, keeping my Guinness even cooler.

I agreed with Diane that alone was the best way for Col and Molly to meet. But, to have been a fly on that wall...

Chapter 13
The Bridge

Putting on Glad Rags

In jet-lagged exhaustion, I struggled to stay awake long enough for Col's return. It was close to midnight.

Col has never smoked, and I had not touched tobacco in over twenty years. I immediately picked up the scent of cigarettes on her. Too excited to inquire, I asked Col to describe the encounter:

She said when they first saw each other, Molly's first reaction was laughter. Molly said that she couldn't help but laugh because Col looks so much like her. Col said she laughed right along with her. There was a bit of mutual hugging and crying, too.

Molly had a dinner of chicken, potatoes, and salad ready for them, but they didn't eat much. Then the two of them sat back and talked like a couple of old friends catching up.

I'll say. Better than half a century of catching up to do.

Other than repeating that she tried to resist John V. McMahon that night, Molly didn't talk much about the past. I had heard that during childbirth, the nuns usually put up a tent-like shroud to eliminate any possibility the bm will ever see her newborn, and that they whisk the infant away as soon as possible. Molly confirmed it.

She knew something was the matter physically with Col at birth because, though she couldn't hear the specifics of their conversation, the doctors were huddled around in discussion and she could tell by the tone that all was not well.

Now and then over the ensuing years, Molly had thought of the child she had given up for adoption, and would always hope that he or she—they don't reveal the gender to the bm, had survived and had a good life.

She couldn't get over the fact that Col grew up less than a mile from her brother Teddie. She would come back to Chicago to visit and always stayed at his home. She really missed Teddie, now little more than three months gone, and would tear up when she spoke of him. Apparently, they were very close and talked on the phone every week.

Before her wedding night in Ireland, she told her fiance Thomas Flaherty of her secret. He replied that this was in the past and had nothing to do with their relationship—that there was no need to ever discuss it again. I found that surprisingly liberal for an Irishman in the early 1960s.

She said it was tough raising seven kids, tending the farm, and taking care of her ailing father while her husband Thomas operated the sheep shearing business.

All these years her greatest concern was how her kids would react if they were to learn of her secret, but now that they had and she realized they were not angry with her, she felt as if a great weight had been lifted off her shoulders.

Diane took a pic of Col and Molly standing shoulder to shoulder that she sent to Col's phone. They were both smiling. Molly had her right arm around Col. Their two faces, side by side, both smiling, said it all. And the resemblance was unmistakably striking.

"Oh, and what a chain-smoker! There was barely a moment she didn't have one going!"

My nose already noticed.

We were both quite tired and slept, though not very well. The next day, Molly wanted to have lunch with us and her five children who were in Ireland: Diane, Marie, Sandra, Patrick, and Jimmie. Molly's favorite restaurant is E.J. King's, on the Clifden town square.

Diane picked us up from Villa Clifden for the short drive. When we arrived, there she was, standing with her offspring in the waiting area near the hostess station.

In person, the resemblance between Molly and Col was uncanny. Now I knew why The Cabbie recognized Col back in 1984. He was seeing Molly Shaw. I walked up, took her hand in greeting, placed the other on her shoulder and said, "Thank you for bringing me this lovely girl."

Looking back on it, that was pretty corny. Even stupid.

Marie, the oldest, is small, slender, and reserved. Sandra is second oldest. She's taller, doesn't appear to get her looks from Molly and is lively and gregarious. Jimmie, the youngest of all, is a tall and broad-shouldered Irishman. I had a hunch he probably looked like his father, Thomas.

Salmon is popular in Ireland, and it was the Lunch Special that day. I determined salmon must be plentiful because there's plenty of it to be had. After all, Ireland is smack dab in the North Atlantic, right?

Perhaps geographically, but before this trip was over, I would learn that like the States, most salmon sold in stores and served in restaurants is farm raised. And if it is wild caught, the menu and price will inform you.

I had the "aquarium salmon". It was fine. I sat next to Sandra and across from Jimmie. Col and Molly sat together. At one point, Sandra looked at me and whispered, "Isn't it something how alike those two look? It's like Colleen's spit right out of her."

You can say that again.

Molly didn't talk much. But, out of the corner of my eye I saw that she always looked happy. Truly happy. Not just pasting on a smile for our benefit happy. I heard later that she had told Diane that she now felt relieved.

And the party continued! After a brief freshening up at Villa Clifden, we met up with everyone but the understandably tired Molly, at Griffin's, a restaurant and bar in Clifden.

This time, Sandra's husband David Collier was there, as was Jimmie's wife Nora. I learned then that Jimmie was originally trained as an automobile mechanic. Well-trained, too. Certified by both Mercedes and Rolls Royce. He was now a service manager at a Citroen dealership in Galway City.

Once again it was hard for us to buy a drink. Every time our glasses got near-empty, a fresh replacement showed up. I found it relaxing that the conversation had nothing to do with the past. It seemed Col's siblings just wanted to welcome her as a new member of the family.

Their big sister.

Homesteads Times Two

The next day Col said she just wanted to rest a bit at Villa Clifden. That morning I walked all around the bay and the town of Clifden.

While in town I secured a small, stick shift Nissan rental car for twenty-four hours. I wasn't going to pay three times as much for automatic. After an initial miscue or two I got used to shifting with my left hand.

There was no set time to meet Col's father's cousin, Elizabeth Crosby. In fact, we hadn't communicated directly with her at all. Peggy McManus had contacted Elizabeth and told her we hoped to be in Oughterard that Tuesday.

We left bright and early. Wound our way along the north coast of Galway Bay and cut right through Galway City, arriving in Oughterard about noon.

Crosby's Tavern was closed. Peggy had mentioned that Elizabeth lived in the home to the right of the tavern. The full ring of keys hanging from the domiciled door was likely her way of not misplacing them.

Knocking gently elicited no response from within. A second, more assertive tapping also produced no reply. I turned the door handle and it opened right up. There was a television or a radio playing. I was reluctant to walk in. After all, this woman did not know us—she might shoot first and ask questions later. I didn't step into the doorway but a half-foot.

"Elizabeth?"

Nothing.

A few doors to the left of Crosby's was a woolen shop. We stepped inside and stated our business. The middle-aged woman behind the counter said it was unusual for "Lizzie" to leave her keys in the door, but there was "no need to be overly concerned". She walked back with us and jangled the dangling keys, following it up with a rap on the door that had thrice the gusto of my lame attempts.

Lizzie Crosby appeared! All smiles and happy to meet us:

"Oh, sometimes I leave the keys in the door. Around here it doesn't matter."

She's small, with short-cropped white hair. Quick-talking, energetic and apparently not missing a beat between the ears.

Lizzie gave us the royal tour of Crosby's. It's a small, single storefront pub. A bar and some tables. We purchased a Crosby's shirt emblazoned with the name and location to bring home with us.

She invited us into her home, set out some tea and "biscuits"— what Yanks call cookies, and filled us in on her story:

All of her relatives had either perished or moved on many years ago, so she was left with the pub and adjacent home. Then, another relative who owned the home on the other side of Crosby's wanted to emigrate to the U.S. and, needing funds to finance the planned relocation, offered to sell his building to her at a very reasonable price. She took him up on the offer.

Lizzie wound up with it all.

Later, when I relayed this Background Information to my friends at the Adoption Rights Alliance, they were tickled pink over the ultimate karmic justice of the adoptee becoming the owner of the family business and surrounding properties.

Lizzie made mention of her cousin John V. McMahon a couple of times. It was apparent she had determined he was Col's birth father. She said John had come back to visit Oughterard "a few times" over the years. She had also met his nephew, Col's cousin— my old school chum Johnny Kafferly, when he came to Ireland.

Lizzie then shared with us that she had never held a great desire to learn more about her own birth parents, and that she was adopted by the Crosbys from the Bon Secours Mother and Baby Home in the town of Tuam, also in County Galway, in 1947, when she was four years old:

"I lived. I was one of the lucky ones."

It was not for dramatic effect that Lizzie considered herself fortunate. I had read of "Tuam", as ARA members refer to the home. During the search I ran across Tuam a lot because it was a local GRO registration point. Typical ignorant Yankee, I'd always pronounced it "Too ahm". Lizzie provided me with the correct pronunciation: "Toom", ironically pronounced the same as "tomb".

Northwest of Oughterard, the home had closed in 1961. But in 2015 a mass grave of babies, children and unwed mothers was unearthed. It was estimated that in its half-century existence, almost nine-hundred children and mothers had perished there and were unceremoniously interred on the grounds.

We engaged in more small talk through our tea and biscuits. Lizzie's kids were off running errands. Before bidding her farewell, we promised to meet them on our next visit.

Our drive back to Clifden worked out. I fueled up the "rice burner"—what we called Asian cars and motorcycles in our youth. The Nissan had averaged over ten kilometres to the litre of petrol—I'll let you Yanks do the conversion, and it got dropped off twenty-three hours and fifteen minutes after I'd picked it up. Dang it. Forty-five minutes to spare before any hourly penalty. We could've safely spent forty-four of them with the delightful Lizzie Crosby.

Wednesday, we boarded a bus for Westport, County Mayo, where in 2007 we'd met Col's Corcoran relatives from her adoptive father Tom Garrity's side. Where, while the Corcorans searched the town and across the ocean for us, we got an education on drinking Jamie from Andrew and Silent John. Westport, where my ineptness at Irish rules of the road had May Corcoran reaching for her rosary, and her brother Tommy paid us back with his frighteningly comical one-handed driving skills.

About an hour and forty-five minute trip, we got there midday. It's a few short blocks from the bus stop to the Castlecourt, which I learned is now one of three hotels. Since 2007, they've built the Westport Plaza and purchased the Westport Coast.

We checked in and asked the receptionist to let Ann know we'd arrived. She bounded into the lobby, looking not one day older than when we'd met her ten years before. It was obvious she was busy. But not too busy to invite us to have a little lunch with her.

Ann's sister Mary and her friend James joined us. Mary and James were all ears. What struck me was how interested Ann was in the emotional aspects of the reunion.

She also wanted to know how we found Molly, and what it was like meeting her seven siblings. We did not reveal any names, but Col mentioned the general area where Molly lived.

After lunch, we met May for tea. Not much had changed, except that she was ten years older and had slowed down a little more physically. I guessed she had to be close to ninety years old by now. Still in very good spirits, she remembered meeting Col in '07—but not me. I was not the least offended. She seemed particularly amused that I take my tea "straight up" with no milk or sugar:

"You're kidding. That must be like drinking poison!"

I didn't think so, but it humored me that this Bridgeport

Yankee at the foot of Croagh Patrick entertained May, Matriarch of the Westport Corcorans.

We also learned that May's brother Tommy had passed away. It was a shame that we would never be treated to his white-knuckle inducing road tours again.

That night, we had street eats, a couple of "Chicken Donner" sandwiches from a stand right by the Carrowbeg River that winds its way through town. They were pretty tasty.

From everything I can tell, "donner" is a pre-seasoned meat; lamb, beef or chicken, on a roll that is shaved from a rotating "spit" that continually cooks the outside edges. In the States, this is how the Greek "gyros" (roughly pronounced "yeero") meat is prepared.

Bellies full, we then walked to the old Town Hall of Westport, which in recent years had been renovated and was being used for live performances and other events.

We arrived half an hour before "curtain up", and got our tickets at the Will Call booth. Seating was assigned and a good-sized crowd was forming, making it probable we wouldn't be able to sit with Louise and her friend Grainne.

I'd never seen good enough pics to recognize Louise Munster on sight, but she said she'd be wearing beige slacks and a black top, and would keep an eye out for us. Not seeing anyone in the lobby who fit that description, we strolled outside the theater, looking around the surrounding sidewalk and non-designated—yet obvious by the stench "smoker's" area.

Two women were standing in the smoke-isphere. One of them was wearing tan slacks and a dark grey printed blouse. I figured I'd found them and walked up all smiles, extending my hand:

"Louise!"

She looked at me as if I were a six-headed being from an alternate universe.

"Oh, I'm sorry. You aren't Louise?"

She struck a street-wise, hip-first stance along with a campy flourish of her cigarette and—just for good measure—added a sideways wink.

"No, but for five quid you can call me anything you like."

We all laughed heartily at her ad-lib. Later, I recognized her face on a poster within the lobby. She was a member of the Westport Improv Troupe. I should've dug into my pocket for some "bob" to continue the dramatic exercise. Maybe next trip.

We went inside and took our seats. I looked up into "the house" and there was the truly black-bloused Louise and Grainne. We waved back and forth and all relaxed to enjoy "The Stolen Child".

It's a well-written play. But it was art imitating life. With all that we had been through—the search, Teddie's passing, the trip here and reunion—we'd been experiencing life that felt like a work of art. An orchestration for our benefit. "The Stolen Child" couldn't and shouldn't have even been expected to hold a candle to our last couple of years.

After the show, we headed across the square to Henehan's Pub. Small and cozy, typical for Ireland. We probably got there about 10:30pm and there were only a couple of locals sitting at the bar.

Louise bought the first round. Much of the conversation was similar to what we'd shared with Kathy Finn, Therese Norris and Bernice Wade in Dublin:

They were both curious about our search, and we were interested in what had prompted each of them to the join the ARA. Grainne was an adoptee, born in the Mother and Baby Home in Bessboro, County Cork.

It was then we learned Louise is not an adoptee. Her husband Noel is the adopted one. And the Munsters are neighbors of Col's Corcoran cousins and know them well.

I'll spare you the small world comment.

Grainne insisted on buying round two and it became too close to closing time for me to offer to spring for our third libation. Wow...

closing at midnight on a Wednesday. I was so used to Chicago, with what we call "two o'clock joints" and "four o'clock joints", open until those hours every morning except Saturday, when they both get to stay open one more hour.

We had closed yet another Irish pub. I was learning that the stereotypical depictions linking the Irish culture and alcohol are a bit exaggerated. Heck, it was starting to look like it's us Yanks who have the bigger problem with binge drinking. In Ireland and other parts of Europe, DUI, "Driving Under the Influence" laws are much tougher, and they enforce them. They know when to close shop for the night, too.

Louise called Noel to come and pick her up and give Grainne a ride home. We could have easily walked back to our room at the Castlecourt, but they insisted we let him give us a lift.

So, after that puddle jump of a drive we were saying goodbye to two more adoption angels. Just as we had with Kathy, Therese and Bernice in Dublin, we hoped to see these two again. I think it's the bond of the common cause that makes me always feel comfortable in the presence of ARA members.

Thursday, we checked out and went down to the main dining room of the Castlecourt for the daily Buffet Breakfast. All the usual stuff and lots of it—including that blood-infused wakeup treat: black and white pudding.

With a meandering bus ride to Clifden ahead of us, we ate very well so we wouldn't get hungry anytime soon.

In short order Ann appeared and insisted on giving us a lift to the bus stop. It was all of a few blocks to the stand, but I think this made her feel good. She is one of the most gracious people I've ever met. In the right business, that's for sure.

Once again, we were bisecting the hills of Ireland on a bus. It was back to Molly in Shanakeen for three more nights before we would head home.

Rock Me Mama

It was midday by the time we arrived and checked back into Villa Clifden. Irene Callaway gave us the same room we'd had the first three nights. She must have noticed my beverage cooling solution and didn't want to toss me the curve ball of a different transom.

Molly's daughter Marie wanted to have lunch with Col, so she stopped by Villa Clifden and picked Col up in the early afternoon. Molly wanted to make us dinner that night. After lunch Col planned to go straight to Shanakeen to hang out with Molly until dinner. Good. I wanted them to have time alone.

I had a quick lunch at the Pizza Parlor, where I had my first experience with an item called "Batter Sausage". It's a banger dipped in pancake batter and deep fried. Sort of like a stateside corn dog minus the corn meal. Not bad.

After resting up a bit at Villa Clifden, I took the mile or so walk to Shanakeen and Molly's house. I had only seen satellite images of the village.

I had a feeling Shanakeen is uphill from Clifden, and it certainly is. It sits atop a hill that seems to be the highest elevation in the area. Molly's small ranch style home has a panoramic view of the always undulating bay to one side and a softly rolling horizon of rocky hills to the other.

As I approached, I noticed a narrow footpath that led around the side of the house. I went up it, and within ten yards came across a well-weathered, unpainted wooden bridge no more than twelve feet long, spanning a rivulet of a ravine.

It looked like a nice spot to reflect and I was running a little early, so I did. Relaxing there, my feet draped over the edge, I noticed others had found this a good spot.

Aged, now indistinguishable initials carved here and there. An old bottle cap below, trapped in the rocks and dead leaves along with other evidence: An empty matchbox. Cigarette butts. The crumpled remnants of a rusty can. A chunk of frayed shoelace.

Is this why Teddie Shaw called Murphy's Tavern "The Bridge"? Had he nicknamed the tavern as a reference to this secluded setting in the hilltop village he was born and grew up in? Murphy's must have been the extension of those roots.

I walked back and entered through the open kitchen door. Molly, Marie and Col were sitting in a small dining room off the kitchen. The sternum-high to ceiling haze of cigarette smoke was layered so thickly it was close to opaque.

This appeared to be Molly's favorite room, where she spent much of her time. She was in an armchair in one corner, next to a small, pot-bellied stove. A small television was conveniently angled toward her.

That meant this was a relaxed situation. She wasn't changing her routine for us. The dining room is where family congregates, Col is now family so that's where we would hang out.

Up to this point, I had not heard Molly say much of anything. I only knew what others had said in describing her. This would probably be the best—perhaps only—opportunity during this trip that I would have to get to know her a little.

On a dark wooden card table in front of her, spread in casino-like fashion was a deck of playing cards. Next to them lay an open pack of cigarettes, lighter and an ashtray that had several butts in it. One live cigarette was reclining at the edge—a long, grey caterpillar of an ash curling its way downward toward the middle.

There was a small bowl half-full of multi-colored "M&M" chocolate candies. On a napkin next to the candy bowl was a half-eaten pastry, the braided and iced type we like to call a "French doughnut".

Molly tore off a small piece and her hand vanished over the far side of her chair. When it returned, the morsel was gone. Needing to see where it went, I inquired where the washroom was to get a better look.

It went to a large, rangy, longhaired pure white cat. She was feeding her feline the doughnut in pieces, but it only enjoyed licking the white icing. Scraps of unfrosted, doughy remains surrounded her pet.

A doorway led to the washroom and the rest of the house. The living room was immaculate and probably only used for special occasions. It was also as white as her sweet-toothed pet. Walls, carpets, furniture, even the religious bric-a-brac on the white shelves.

I got back just in time to see Molly take a short puff from her cigarette and return it to its rightful spot at ashtray's edge, where it slowly smoldered its way in self-immolation, joining the rest of its extinguished friends.

I had been told Molly regretted having to go back to Ireland in 1958. She had a good head for business and wanted to make her way in Chicago, and she made sure to get in those twenty-four continuous months of uninterrupted residency in the U.S., so that she could hopefully return one day and complete the required thirty-six in order to gain citizenship.

But that never happened. Instead, she remained in Ireland, married Thomas Flaherty and raised seven kids, working the farm while her husband worked the family business.

I learned she had to bring water up to the house. That the small stone building that is now Paddy Flaherty Sheep Shearing and Factory Crutching was the dwelling all seven kids grew up in, and it had no indoor plumbing until the 1970s.

This woman had a tough life. I could see it in her stoop, the gait that often needed a cane assist, the twin accordions of rheumatic knuckles that gripped the chair arms, helping to boost herself up so she could join us at the dinner table barely six feet away.

At E.J. King's, her son Jimmie had told me that Molly's joint ailments stemmed from years of working the farm. She is a small woman, and this must have taken a toll on her.

Molly had told Col that she was not in a physical state to be flying and that she regretted not being able to come over for Teddie's funeral. She also said she was not into pharmaceutical drugs and tried to avoid them. She'd had operations and was suffering from rheumatoid arthritis, apparently so severe she often used a morphine patch to numb the pain.

But she was all smiles and behind her glasses there was a childlike twinkle in her blue eyes. I felt she was proud of those years of hard work, and felt the pain she was now in was worth it. She had a lot be proud of. Seven kids who had all made their way, with kids of their own. I was told she did not complain about her pain.

Molly had it rough emotionally, too. When she was young she lost a brother. Then her sister in 1957. Then the unintended pregnancy that brought Col into the world. She had to leave the promised land that she'd emigrated to in order to care for her father.

And now, she diligently visits her husband, keeping vigil for a man she loves very much, but who can no longer enjoy his golden years with her.

Reflecting on all that had happened, and what we had learned, I realized that in a lot of ways Molly was, although twenty-one years old when she gave birth to Col, a "girl", as Marjorie Dooley of the Catholic Home Bureau stated in her 2001 letter.

During that era, a twenty-one year old female, off the farm of rural Ireland only two years, was usually not the same as a twenty-one year old from—say, Chicago. Sure, she'd been in the States for two years, but she came over a girl, a Connemara "colleen".

Marie had helped Molly prepare dinner. Salmon! I didn't mind having it again. It was done to perfection, mildly seasoned and on the brink of sushi-raw in the center. There was salad and potatoes as well. The potatoes were large, whole, peeled and firm. Not overcooked. I was shocked when Molly told me they were boiled. She must've been quite the cook for her seven kids.

It was evident by the M&Ms on her table that Molly has a weakness for sweets, but it was even more noticeable when Marie brought the desserts out of the kitchen.

There was a latticed, iced coffee cake, topped with slivered almonds, that looked and tasted as good as any I'd ever had at the finest bakeries in Chicago. There were dainty cookies composed of butter, sugar, and barely enough flour to hold them intact long enough for consumption. An apple pie with golden currants, too.

I felt I had to be polite so I had a little of each. A tray of fudge then belatedly joined the sugary smorgasbord. I somehow made room for it.

It was all great. I thought the fudge was especially splendid. And Marie said Molly had made all the desserts. From scratch.

Next came the drink she reserved for special occasions. Talisker Ten Scotch. I'd never heard of it. As she doesn't like to have alcohol when she's on her pain meds, Molly only had "a spot".

Ignoring Andrew of Westport's lecture on the correct way to drink whiskey, I asked if I could have mine "on the rocks". Over ice. Marie was more than happy to accommodate but, as ice usually doesn't get used much in Ireland, especially in Molly's house, she had concerns about there being any.

But, deep in the dark underworld of the freezer we found half a bag of cubed ice. Probably a leftover from the last time a Yank paid a visit. It had been so long, the cubes had fused together into one solid, frostbitten football-sized asteroid. I offered to chisel enough off the archeological find to make my cocktail.

Talisker Ten is good. It's got a strong, smoky flavor reminiscent of their beloved turf. It reminded me of our first trip over in 2007, when we met Garrity relatives and the whole house smelled of it.

Peat, not scotch. I wondered if that was one reason Molly liked it, too. Perhaps it reminded her of simpler, happier times—

of burning turf to heat the home.

After dessert, Molly made her way to her favorite chair, fired up a cigarette, set it on the ashtray to fizzle away like incense and one-handedly scooped up the perfectly fanned deck of cards from the table.

She then proceeded, despite crippled knuckles, to deftly shuffle those cards like a "Vegas" dealer, not even utilizing the table to steady them. She started laying out what I recognized as a form of "solitaire" on the card table. I figured this was an after dinner ritual of sorts.

Occasionally she'd stop long enough to keep the current cigarette alive and give her cat, who she called "Casper", more morsels of doughnut.

"The Friendly Ghost". Made sense—as white as everything else in the house.

It was getting late for Molly now. We thanked her for a lovely dinner. I wanted to walk the mile down the hill to Villa Clifden, but Marie insisted on driving us both. She said it's a heavily traveled road at night and that, as there's no shoulder on this two-laner, it'd be dangerous for us because we weren't wearing "high viz"—high visibility outerwear with bright green or orange phosphorescent striping.

I took her up on it. Molly didn't need any more tragedy in her life.

Friday night, we were invited to David and Sandra Flaherty Collier's home for what was being billed a "Next Generation Party". We'd be meeting any of Col's newfound nieces and nephews who were in the area.

We had met Jimmie and Nora's kids earlier in the week, but now we'd meet Marie's son Andrew from Galway City, and David and Sandra and Jimmie and Nora's kids as well. We had no idea what this would be like.

It turned out to be much like every other encounter we'd had.

We were family.

David possesses a rollicking roll of a laugh that he is never reluctant to use. Both he and Sandra had been to culinary school and it showed. At one time she and David owned a restaurant in nearby Annaghdown. There was Stir Fry Chicken with Curry, Lasagna—with hints of cinnamon!—and various cold salads and potatoes.

And oh yeah, beer. Guinness must be "old hat" to these natives. I was the only one having it. Sandra would not let my man-sized, authentic pint of it get empty.

At first, she would ask if I wanted another as she poured. Then, it would get reloaded when I so much as blinked. I was getting buzzed and eventually had to keep my glass with me at all times, even bringing it along to take a pee.

I got to talking to David. When I raved about his mother-in-law's cooking, he turned to me, confidentially chuckling:

"Be very happy that Marie helped with the cooking, Paul. Molly can't cook a meal right to save her life. Had she been in on it, your salmon would've been hard as timber and needing a hack saw. Steamed vegetables? So overdone you need a spoon just to get them to your mouth..."

I interjected, "But David, the cake, the pie, the cookies. And that fudge was truly to die for."

"I said she can't cook. She can bake. She's all about desserts. Breakfast, lunch and dinner is M&Ms and cigarettes. She only eats food when there's company. As for her fudge, she shared her recipe with me. I tried it. Mine just didn't match up to hers. We decided some of her cigarette ashes must fall into the mix and that's the difference.

So, in a way, you're right. It is to die for. Ashes to ashes."

He laughed a little louder.

"And the non-stop smoking? Watch her next time. She never inhales. She just puffs enough to keep 'em goin'. She must go through two packs a day, and the last time she had a checkup they said she'd lungs as pink as a newborn lamb. It's the rest of us who suffer."

He paused, then added a few decibels to his signature guffaw, turning the heads of nearby partiers.

"Did she tell ya' yet why they tossed her out of finishin' school? She was workin' weekends at a dance hall in Edinburgh. The place had a gamblin' den in back, and mum was a cigarette girl and card dealer. She musta' been good at makin' bob for the dance hall."

"One night, the hall got raided by the Garda. By the time they turned everybody loose she'd missed her curfew. Well, when the school found out what she'd been doing for pin money, they threw her out and it was back to Shanakeen for her."

"Whatever ya' do Paul, unless ya' don't mind losin', do not play cards with my mother-in-law. Ya' won't win. It matters not if it's a complete game a' chance, luck o' the draw, anythin'. She'll still beat ya'. I'm just warnin' ya' ahead a' time."

On that final note, he laughed so hard the windows nearly rattled.

Diane then shared some more about Molly, which at first seemed to contradict what Oisin Anderson of Clifden had provided from his anonymous source. Old school, set in her ways. Proud. I saw those in what he'd passed along.

But Diane said her mum is very sensitive and can be emotional, even fragile about personal matters. She also said when they were growing up she was tough on her and her three sisters:

"And don't you dare come home pregnant."

Now they all understood what motivated Molly on that one. She did not want any of her girls to go through what she had.

The highlight of the party came when two generations of Flahertys were weaving in place and singing along to a mix of songs. It moved me in particular when they all seemed to especially love the chorus to a Country and Western tune I had never heard.

Through Guinness-dulled ears all I could decipher was, "Rock me Mama like a wagon wheel..."

Unless in dire condition I'm not sure just how a wagon wheel rocks. But I figured the title was likely "Rock Me Mama".

Close. It's actually "Wagon Wheel", and this Next Generation Party favorite goes back generations:

Originally an untitled track recorded by Bob Dylan in 1973, it had only existed as a "bootleg". Later, I gave the original a listen. The signature line is one of only a few audible phrases from his mumbly Minnesota drone.

According to Dylan, the phrase "rock me Mama" goes way back—to Mississippi Delta bluesman Big Bill Broonzy who, appropriately enough for the many coincidental yet inconsequential interlacings of this book, passed away and was laid to rest in a cemetery on Chicago's South Side in August 1958, two months before Col was born.

It was good to learn royalties earned by those who later filled in the lines, added verses, and gave it the "Wagon Wheel" title were split with Dylan.

Several songs later, stuffed to the brim with wonderful food, drink and emotional overload, we were chauffeured courtesy of Diane, back to Villa Clifden, where we both slept better than any night since we had arrived.

Revelations

Saturday was our last full day in Ireland. In the morning, we found a souvenir shop in Clifden and picked out gifts to bring back to our kids and grandkids.

At Sandra's party, Diane had suggested it would be nice for Col and Molly to have lunch together on Saturday. Alone. I wholeheartedly agreed, so while they were off having lunch, I just walked the town. Took a few pictures.

I stopped in at the Pizza Parlor to bid the operator farewell—until our next visit of course. He said that probably would not happen, as he'd recently opened his own restaurant in County Clare and had a relative managing it for him for a few months.

When I asked why he wasn't running his own place, he said he had a contract with the owner to manage the Pizza Parlor that went until September. He could have broken the contract without financial penalty, but didn't think it fair to burn a bridge with his boss. He informed me he was from Kosovo. Perhaps that was one of the unusual dialects I'd overheard in Dublin. In any event, he was a class act.

I went back to Villa Clifden, pulled a chilled beer from the transom and watched a televised debate regarding a referendum that, if passed, could ultimately repeal Article 8 of the Irish Constitution, which proclaims abortion illegal.

Col returned late afternoon. She and Molly had lunch at E.J. King's again and they had a wonderful, relaxing time. Apparently, neither was very hungry. She had leftover chicken tenders and salad in a "Take Away" carton. Dinner for me.

As it turned out, I would need that blanket of breaded fried bird and greens in my gut to soak up more beer. Col's siblings wanted to meet us at Lowry's Pub in Clifden, where there is always live music. We got there about 9pm and closed another joint. Lowry's reminded me very much of Molloy's in Westport. The music was excellent and it must be illegal to have an empty glass in Ireland.

Sunday we had one last breakfast, compliments of Irene Callaway. We told her we'd be back to snag our bags and settle the bill after saying goodbye to "some friends up the road".

It was a brilliant spring morning. We took our time walking up the hill to Shanakeen. When we arrived Marie was there. Diane was off visiting friends in Galway City.

Molly was still in her robe. A shade of powder blue, it reminded me of that seemingly long-ago meeting—in reality only a few short months before in Chicago, when my choice of a spiritually similar shade so closely matched Diane's at O'Grady's.

Molly seemed quiet and calm that morning. In her usual spot with cards, cigarettes and candy dish in front of her. Casper, so white I couldn't discern if any of today's donut frosting was clinging around the edges of his tiny pink mouth, lounged at her side.

We only had time that morning to have some tea with them. I opted to when-in-Rome and worked a little milk and sugar into mine. Molly had presents for us:

An airline-ready tin of her famous cigarette ash-infused fudge. She also gave us a box of Bewley's Tea. Even though Bewley's is available in some stores in Chicago, I was told Molly would always give Teddie a box to take back with him from Shanakeen. I felt as if Col was now a Chicago replacement for the brother Molly had just lost that January.

She started shuffling:

"Would anyone like to play?"

We adhered to David's Friday night advice and graciously declined.

Marie excused herself to take care of some business on her laptop computer, leaving the three of us alone. Molly started playing solitaire as she spoke:

"Colleen, I'm going to share something with you and Paul that I have never shared with anyone."

Curious Terriers, our ears up-ticked. She kept dealing to herself and continued:

"When I told John McMahon I was pregnant, he said he would marry me. I refused. My heart told me that marriage to him would not work out. I did not want to enter into a marriage that my instincts told me was doomed."

"But I did have to tell Teddie the truth. I knew he would then confront John. If John told Teddie he was willing to marry me, Teddie would have insisted that I go ahead and marry him."

"That was the culture back then. If you got pregnant, you were expected to marry, and in those days the girl didn't have much say in it. I dreaded the outcome. Even prayed for a solution."

Her cigarette fizzled out. Col and I sat, eyes glazed straight ahead in the thousand-yard stare of battle-weary warriors. Molly sparked up another smoke and set it in the ashtray:

"Well... my prayers were answered. John denied it. He said Connor Coneely did it."

"Connie was a very nice man. Like a big brother to me. A protector. But we had no relations beyond that, and never would have. He was married."

"I went off to the other side of the city and lived with a nice Irish family until it came time for you to be born, and then it was back here for me."

"I never saw or spoke to John again. I don't know why he decided to blame someone else. I felt badly for Connie. But I didn't have to marry John, so it worked out for the best."

And that was that. That was all Molly had to say about the past. She lit yet another cigarette, went right back to her game of solitaire and got into some small talk with us. We took her cue, not questioning any further.

My theory?

Realizing he wasn't ready for marriage, John V. McMahon had a change of heart. If he blamed Connie, Teddie would not be sure who to believe. He might think Molly was lying to him, that Connie was guilty and that she had fingered John to protect the married-with-children Connie from the shame of an exposed affair.

Or, Teddie might've thought John was lying and—after beating him half to death—would insist he marry Molly.

Soon, it was time for us to get back down the hill to check out from Villa Clifden. Marie was going to drive us to the bus stop in Galway City that would take us to Dublin International for our flight home.

We were standing in Molly's kitchen and I felt the familiar lump in my throat that told me this wuss of a half-breed Italian American was about to get misty-eyed.

I wanted so much for us to stay a few more days. I didn't care one hoot—well not much of one—about exploring this friendly country. I just wanted to hang out with Molly and Col's siblings more, and get to know that next generation better, too.

We had expected nothing from Molly or any of her relatives, but they had treated us like family, stretching their welcoming arms so akimbo their fingertips spanned the ocean, grazing the azure skies between.

I decided it was best to say goodbye, so that Col and Molly could be alone for a few minutes. Giving Molly a gentle one-two rub on her left shoulder I managed to keep both feet out of mouth's way, whispering in her ear:

"Bye, we'll be back soon".

I walked alone downhill towards Villa Clifden, taking my time and a few pictures. Cows, sheep, dilapidated barns, famine houses, the bay stretching along one horizon.

Looking back over my shoulder, I could see Col and Molly, with Casper beside her—motionless in sphinx-like sentry, together outside her kitchen door. From a few hundred meters away I turned and waved, feeling goosebumps of warmth when Molly's tiny cigarette-clad hand waved, creating a smoke signal farewell in return.

Marie and Col picked me up roadside and we headed down to Villa Clifden. She parked out front. I loaded our bags in the trunk and we waited while Col checked out. It seemed to be taking a little longer than I expected. I figured she and Irene Callaway were chatting a little.

They sure were. We'd not been diligent in reading our reservation. Villa Clifden does not take credit cards! Col promised to post a check to Irene as soon as we returned to Chicago. Irene told her that if it had been anyone else, she would not have allowed this.

We learned later that Irene's grandchildren attend school with Jimmie Flaherty's kids. She likely knew who we were visiting at the top of the hill but didn't know the nature of Col's relationship to Molly.

Marie had us to the bus stop in Galway City in plenty of time. We were seated and it was ready to diesel to Dublin when Diane showed up and boarded long enough to say goodbye one last time.

Rolling easterly over the rounded hills of the Irish countryside towards Dublin, I reflected on what had been a three-year journey for me and a lifelong quest for Col. I now saw the parallels that validated my belief in the power of our unseen consciousness. Surely, with all these relatives so nearby all her life in Chicago, something mystical must have been at play:

From the day she was adopted by the Garritys in early 1959, until 1972 when he moved from the neighborhood with the beginnings of his family, Col's natural father John V. McMahon never lived more than a mile and a half from her. Later, as a young adult in her first apartment, Col would live down the street from her aunt, John's sister Philomena Kafferly.

In the mid-1960s, when Col was a young child and experienced that vision of a couple in her basement window, Teddie Shaw, her natural uncle on her mother's side, was living less than a mile away with his wife Peggy, raising nine children, most of them within five years of Col's age.

In 1984, when The Cabbie recognized Col, two of her siblings from Ireland, freshly arrived immigrants Diane and Catharine Flaherty, were living with Teddie. A few years later, her brother J.T. would arrive and would live with him as well.

In 2000, when The Bookworm had Col paged at Border's Bookstore in Hyde Park, Teddie's wife, their aunt Peggy, had just recently passed.

Most of all, over the years, Col's natural mother, Molly Flaherty, would visit Chicago, and she would always stay at her brother Teddie's.

Slightly less cosmic, physiological but no less affirming, was the fact that when Col was developing in Molly's womb, she was hearing the melodious Celtic brogues of not only her mother, but many of those around her.

The linguist who thought Col was born in Ireland was—in a way—right. Col was on target with those persistent feelings that she belonged "over there". Over there was over here. In Chicago, cradling her the entire time.

All those years, I was also living in similar proximity. Was there a level of my subconscious that knew this was worth pursuing and was driving me, bolstering my passion to solve the mystery?

Did the dart I threw at the map in 2007 that landed on the Bay Mist B&B in Clifden have an unseen "GPS" in its feathers that guided me to that booking? One that in all the B&Bs of Ireland was walking distance to Molly's home in Shanakeen?

Molly Flaherty? My impression of her is a combination of that Lady in Green of our 2007 Ireland trip, lifting her petite glass of Guinness in a roadside pub, and Ed Sheeran's "Galway Girl", fleecing folks at cards.

Later, safely strapped in on the flight home, I used the turbine hums and whoosh of my personal vent as contemplative aids. All I kept seeing front and center on my third-eye screen was Molly, backed by her home on the hill sprinkled with spring greenery, a cotton-candied sky, and her minuscule hand waving to me from the metronome of her pale blue robe.

That singular movement made all else I visualized—the morning breeze and rustling trees, the gentle flutter of the canary yellow gorse blossoms, the low fluid rumble of the bay below, even the curlicue of Molly's blue cigarette smoke, freeze in time.

Epilogue

In early summer 2017, Teddie Shaw's sister-in-law Martha Murphy, Col's neighbor "lady with the dogs", passed away. At the wake, a brilliant green sweater she knitted was displayed. Beautifully designed and intricate, it was better than any I have ever seen in any Irish woolen shop.

Late that same summer, we would learn that Kathleen Hogan Manuel, the Virginia piano teacher who identified John V. McMahon as Col's birth father, was not the veteran "search angel" we had thought she was. Col was her very first case! Kathleen enjoyed helping us so much that she continues to help others with her phenomenal, otherworldly ability to connect the dots. As of this writing, she had solved over two hundred more cases for searching adoptees, refusing any compensation for her efforts.

Also as of this writing, world-renowned genealogist CeCe Moore's Facebook Group DNA Detectives—launched the same week in early 2015 that we confirmed Molly Flaherty as Col's birth mother—had grown to over 145,000 members.

On St. Patrick's Day 2018, we met Col's sister Catharine Flaherty, their cousin Buddy Shaw and his wife Nancy, at Chicago's Irish American Heritage Center. They've updated the men's restrooms and now have adult-height urinals.

On June 2, 2018, at the age of eighty-eight, Dr. Carl Mattioda, who delivered Col in 1958, passed away. It was estimated that in his six-decade career he had "caught" over ten thousand babies, bringing them into the world. In lieu of flowers, it was suggested donations be made to Crittenton Centers, a multi-service children and family welfare organization which was originally conceived as a maternity home for unwed mothers.

Col's cousin on her birth father's side, Lizzie Crosby of Oughterard, who'd said in 2017 that she wasn't curious about learning about her birth parents, has had a change of heart. Lizzie

▲ information can be obtained
▪v.ICGtesting.com
▪ in the USA
V062208250122
26BV00017B/951

has learned that her birth mother had passed. With the help of social workers she is in the process of connecting with her natural siblings.

The DNA spittoon keeps on givin'. Col has been the recipient of numerous inquiries from genetic relatives, usually ranging from 2nd–3rd cousin, who are piecing together their family trees and can not figure out who Colleen Garrity Terrazino is. There have even been a couple of searching adoptees. Between bites of peanut butter sandwich, Ms. Frickert always answers them as best he can, while protecting the anonymity of all.

In October 2018, we would "go over" again, to celebrate Col's sixtieth birthday with Molly on the hill.

Acknowl

Heartfelt thanks to rea
Yovovich for their astute critici
Solutions, editor Mary Leona
deserve kudos for the hard wo
product possible. Special than
Publishing for their thoughtful
encouragements must also be e
Blair and Peggy Miller.